A Circus of Ink

LAUREN PALPHREYMAN

Copyright © 2021 Lauren Palphreyman
All rights reserved

The characters and events portrayed in this book are fictitious. Any similarity to real persons, living or dead, is coincidental and not intended by the author.

No part of this book may be reproduced, or stored in a retrieval system, or transmitted in any form or by any means, electronic, mechanical, photocopying, recording, or otherwise, without express written permission of the publisher.

Cover Design by: Franzi Haase
www.coverdungeon.com

Copy Edit by: Bryony Leah
www.bryonyleah.com

ISBN: 9798726437095

Contact the author:
www.LaurenPalphreyman.com

Part One

Chapter One
Elle

The sky is as black as ink when I hear the footstep behind me.

I'm not supposed to use that word: *ink*. But I do. My father taught it to me before he was taken. He taught me other words too—*library, parchment, pen*—but *ink* is my favourite. I like the way it feels on my tongue.

Ink. Ink. Ink.

I can practically taste it in my mouth—thick, black liquid stories. It tastes like creation. It tastes like possibility. It tastes like *hope*.

But now is not the time to be thinking of forbidden words.

They have found me.

I can smell his body, the scent of man and outdoors, damp like the rain. I stare out through the window a moment longer, my eyes casting over the rows of Draft One skyscrapers and the sky's water puddling on the pavement fifty storeys below.

My heart thrums in my chest like a bird trying to escape its cage. My feet itch to run. But that is what he wants me to do. So instead, I speak.

'I've been expecting you.'

The words come out stronger than I feel them, but I don't want him to know I'm afraid. If I can make him believe I am strong, then to him, *I am* strong. Maybe I can make myself believe it too. My father taught me that as well.

Stories are true when we believe them.

'Then you know why I'm here.' The voice behind me is low and male. There's the gruffness of gravel about it, yet a cutting finality. It tells me there is no space for negotiation. He is a hard, impenetrable shell, just like the rest of his kind.

But no, that is not true. There are cracks in everything. And where there are cracks, stories can grow.

I will not die. Not today.

Slowly, I turn. 'You're here to kill me.'

He stands a few feet away and surveys me with cool indifference.

I think he must be in his early twenties. He is tall and muscular like all the Blotters. And like them too, he has black tattoos curling around his big arms and up his neck. His white vest has turned transparent in the rain, and it clings to his hard chest and torso to reveal more inked symbols.

Gradually, I bring my gaze up to his face, tracing his square jaw and the raindrops that cling to his light stubble. His hair is shaven close to his head, and it is as black as the sky.

He inclines his head. There's no emotion behind the movement—no happiness, no regret, no lust for the kill. Just a nod. Yes. Affirmative. He is here to end my life.

'Run.' His voice is steady and expectant.

'No.'

His brow furrows.

I meet his eyes. They're an iced blue, but there's a black blotch in one of his irises, like it's leaked from his pupil. It makes me think of the moment when ink meets water. An imperfection. A flaw.

There is something beautiful about it. That and the white scar that runs across one of his eyebrows.

Was he created that way? Why?

'No?' His eyes seem to search for something inside of me. 'You're supposed to run. I'm here to kill you.'

'I was hoping to persuade you otherwise.'

'That's not the way it works.'

My gaze travels down his body, moving past his jeans and combat boots to the small puddle of rain he drips onto the threadbare carpet of my bedsit. It's strange how in the big moments, your mind sometimes finds the smallest details to focus on.

'You're ruining my carpet,' I say.

He lifts his feet and appears to study the wet dirt he tracked into my apartment. He looks almost apologetic. Then he blinks, and his features harden once more.

'It's not your carpet. It belongs to the Creators. And you won't have any need for it soon. You're supposed to run. Go on—I'll give you a head start.'

He flicks his hand in dismissal. Then he looks absently around my small, standardised accommodation—at the dim bulb in the centre of the damp ceiling, the tattered mattress on the floor, the metal table, the exposed pipes beneath the sink. And though he doesn't know it, his gaze flits over the impossible door too.

'Go on,' he says. 'Get out of here.'

'No.'

He raises his eyebrows, emphasising the scar permeating one of them. 'I don't think you understand the severity of your predicament, little Twist.'

'I understand perfectly. And don't call me that. I'm Elle.'

'If you understand, then run,'—he moistens his bottom lip— *'little Twist.'* There's a glimmer of amusement in his eyes now. I am a mouse between the paws of a cat; he knows he can kill me, but he can play first.

His amusement buys me time. And time is what I need.

'No.'

'Well, aren't you the stubborn one?' He frowns. 'But I'm going to kill you. Why would you not run?'

'Because you expect me to.'

He is over six foot, too big for my dingy bedsit, and when he shifts from one foot to the other, his confusion is pronounced. 'It's written. You run. You die.' He is sure of this. But his eyes burn with curiosity.

That is unusual for a Blotter: curiosity.

'Where is it written?' I ask. 'Show me.' I take a tentative step forwards, and his biceps clench.

'What are you doing?' He is even more confused now. But intrigued too.

It keeps me alive.

I am supposed to fear him. I am supposed to run away. He is supposed to kill me. Those are the rules. That is how it is obviously supposed to happen.

But I have always found ways to twist the rules.

I take another step towards him. My heart hammers in my chest faster than the rain pounding against the window behind me.

His breathing is heavier now, his chest moving up and down quickly. He's excited, I think. This is new to him. And Blotters do not get surprised. Heat radiates off his body despite the fact he's drenched and it's cold in my bedsit. I'm engulfed in his masculine scent: salt, sweat, and rainwater. There's an odd vulnerability dancing in the cold blue of his irises. He's not afraid—he knows he could kill me in an instant—but he doesn't understand what is happening.

Words hang in the air of my dingy apartment, heavy and unspoken. They're new. They crackle between us. Untold stories twist like smoke. I feel them curling around our bodies, pulling us together. Now we have met, our tales are entwined. They will be now until they end.

How else could it be?

He touches my face, and my breathing hitches. His thick eyebrows knit together as if he doesn't understand what he's just done. His fingers are rough, and his arm is strong, but he is gentle.

He studies me, and I steady my nerves. My skin burns as his gaze drops to my collarbone. Then he looks at the black vest top, the drab factory overalls I'm wearing with the sleeves tied around my waist, and the combat boots I got from the black market.

I study him too. Ink covers almost every inch of him except for his face—tattoos depicting his past and the scenes that are written into his future.

I have never seen a Blotter up close. I have avoided them in the five years since my father smuggled me out of the Final City before he was killed. He fascinates me. We are new to each other, and despite the fact I should run, and he should have killed me already, he continues to stare. His thumb presses against my cheek near my lips.

It is then, standing so close to him, that I see the small mark on his chest through his wet top. It's small, barely a smudge, but something draws me to it. *What is that?* I lift my hand, and very lightly, I touch it.

His muscles harden beneath my fingers, and his eyes narrow. I tense.

I feel like I have just put my hand on one of the mutated wolves that on occasion stray into the outer Drafts or stuck my fingers into the flames that roar in the trash cans under the bridges.

He is dangerous. He is a weapon controlled by the Creators. He is a monster wearing the skin of a man. He is a killer.

What am I doing? Why am I not pulling away?

His heartbeat pounds against my palm.

And then his fingers are up in my white-blonde hair, and his expression hardens. His cheeks flush, and his breath lands hot on my skin.

'What the fuck are you doing?' he hisses.

I grapple at his fingers, and his grip tightens. 'Where is it written?' I try to keep my voice calm, but panic begins to rise from my gut. 'Where is it written that I die? Show me.'

What if I was wrong? What if I can't talk my way out of this one?

'Where is it written?'

Behind the anger, I can still see the intrigue in his face. His entire life is mapped out for him in ink on his skin. But this wasn't written. He didn't expect this interaction. In that confusion, there is hope. If I can push him hard enough.

He pulls my hair, baring my throat, and I bite back a cry.

'Show me!' I yell.

A roar tears from his throat as he releases me. I stumble back into the table and grip the edge to steady myself.

'Why are you frustrating me?' He yanks down top of his white vest, exposing his chest. *'Here, see? Are you happy now!'*

Above his heart, amongst the other black lines and symbols, is a black circle. Within it is a twisted line, broken in the centre. Ice spreads across my chest. It marks my death. I can feel it. As can he.

We are bound by ink. He is supposed to kill me.

To the side of it is the tattoo I put my hand on seconds before. It's something I recognise. Something that means something to me. It's a dandelion seed, floating there in the narrow space between the images.

It reminds me of something my father used to say to me.

Stories grow like dandelions in the cracks in the pavement.

I have the same tattoo on my ankle, though ink is forbidden to people like me. It is a message of hope, of love, of rebellion. Why would a Blotter have the same tattoo?

He drops his arm to his sides. The fear and anger are wiped from his face. Only his ragged breathing and a slight twitch in his jaw betray any hint of emotion.

'If you won't run, I'll have to do it here.' He moistens his lips. 'It's only a slight deviation. It will be permitted.'

'Are you sure?'

'Yes.'

The black images that mark him a monster become more pronounced as he tenses his biceps, preparing himself for the kill. I push myself backwards into the desk.

'You don't have to do this.'

'I do. It is written.'

'I won't die today.'

His expression darkens. 'Sorry, little Twist, but you will.'

My eyes dart towards the door he does not know about—the door that isn't supposed to be there. The door I don't fully understand. The door I think I *created*.

I need more time. 'I'm going to run now.'

His hard edges soften somewhat. He's relieved that things are finally going the way he expected them to go.

'Go ahead.' He steps to the side, clearing the way towards the only exit in my bedsit. The same exit that is built into every bedsit in the Draft. 'But I know where you'll go. It is written.'

'Is it?' I flash him a smile.

I think I detect a hint of regret on his face. But that doesn't make sense. Blotters don't regret.

'Yes.'

His eyebrows knit together as I dart in the opposite direction he expected, towards the cupboard at the end of my mattress. I throw open the impossible door. Then I jerk my head over my shoulder and catch his widened, ink-blotched eyes.

'I'll see you soon,' I say.

I disappear inside.

Chapter Two
Jay

The girl disappears into the cupboard.

It makes no sense. I stand rooted to the threadbare carpet. Then I laugh. It surprises me—like the girl, like the situation. It's been a long time since I've laughed. It's been a long time since I've been surprised.

'Did you seriously just go and hide in a cupboard, little Twist?'

I should pull her out and get this over with. She's a Twist. She's dangerous. But her Ending isn't written until midnight, so I have a bit of time. Killing her now would be a deviation. That's why I walk across her bedsit instead of doing what needs to be done. Why else would I be looking around?

It would be a sin for me to be curious about the girl with wild white hair and bright amber eyes who dared to touch a Blotter and hide in a cupboard instead of running away.

There's a blot of ink in the corner of the table by the window. I touch it. It's cool and glossy on my fingertip. Forbidden. I push my thumb against it, watching as the thick liquid flattens then smudges over my skin. I bring it to my nose and smell its metallic tang.

'I can see why they sent me after you. Can you *write?* Have you been *writing*, little Twist?' I talk quietly. The Creators have eyes everywhere, and I'm bound to them by the ink in my veins. Even I have to be careful with the forbidden words. 'What have you been writing? Where is it?'

I stare at the cupboard. 'Why don't you come out and show me?'

Anticipation buzzes beneath my skin, and that is a new feeling. I could drag her out. I could make her show me. I could push her against that wall, press my body against her to hold her in place, and feel her struggle. I could slip my hand into her hair and force her to look up at me. I could feel her breath quicken as it hits my skin.

I could make her tell me where she hid her ink and her words. I've no doubt of that.

But I don't do any of those things.

I want her to come out by herself. I want her to surprise me again.

A pang of disappointment mingles with the frustration building in my chest when she doesn't.

'Fine. Have it your way.'

I change course on my way to the cupboard. Not yet. I'll let her think she's safe for a moment longer. It's not time yet anyway.

I head over to the small mattress on the floor instead. The sheets are crumpled. This is expected at least. Most Twists I've Ended have been messy. I pull back the covers. My pulse quickens when her scent hits me—soap and sweat and a weird note of honey.

An image of her comes to me unbidden: her body tangled in the sheets. I rub my face. Fuck. Blotters don't imagine things. Especially about Twists they have to End. That's fucked up even for me.

I push back the mattress and recoil when I see the book beneath it. My heartbeat steadies when I recognize the symbol on the crimson leather-bound cover. It's the Sacred Stylus. This is a *Book of Truth*. It's the only book that isn't sacrilege. But only the Tellers are allowed to read from it.

Why would a Twist have this? Where would she get it from? Can she even read it?

There's a piece of parchment in between its pages. I slip it out.

I've seen parchment before during black market raids, and once in a room in the Citadel. I've poured fuel on parchment and watched it burn as books and paintings and ink. But I've never properly studied it. It's dry and scratchy against my fingers. I lift it to my nose, and it releases the musty scent of memories. Then I flatten it out on the mattress.

It looks like a map, though they are forbidden too. There's a line that could be the river, and there are 'X's marked around a scribble in the centre. If it was a map, that would be where the old power plant stands.

I don't like this. This is dangerous.

'What have you been up to, little Twist?'

I should put it back. I'm not supposed to snoop around. Go in, End the Twist, get out. That's what was written by the Creators. That's what I'm supposed to do.

And yet, without knowing why, I fold it up and slip it into my pocket.

I take a deep breath, then I look up at the cupboard. I think of her small hand on my chest and the way she looked up at me with eyes as sharp as the stars that shine over the Final City.

Endings don't bother me. They are written, and we all must serve our purpose. Everything that begins must end, and I have no say in the plans of the Creators. Even if I did, who am I to question the gods who created this world?

But this time, it feels different. There's a small part of me that doesn't want to deliver this girl's Ending.

I blow out hot air and shake my head. The decision has already been made. The curious girl will die. It is written. She is already dead.

I crack my neck as I prepare myself. 'Okay, time's up. Let's get on with it.' I throw open the cupboard doors. *Fuck!'*

I can't move. I can't think. I step back and put my hands on my head.

'Oh, *fuck!'*

How is this possible?

There's no bottom to the cupboard. Instead, a long ladder leads into darkness. The faint scent of shit indicates the Draft One sewers lie below. I've lost her.

This is impossible. We're on the fiftieth floor of the tower block, and I know every inch of it. I know every inch of every tower block within this Draft. They're all the same. If the Creators had put this here, I'd know about it.

'Little Twist?' I say. If she's not dealt with by midnight, I'm well and truly fucked. I swallow hard. 'Um . . . Elle?'

My voice echoes back to me.

'Fuck!'

I clasp my hands behind my head and look around the room. For the first time in my life, I don't know what to do. This isn't written.

How could I have fucked this up so badly? She was supposed to run, yes. But not through a fucking trapdoor in the cupboard! I slam my hand against the wall, and the plaster cracks. Then I close my eyes and steady my breathing.

Okay, Jay, pull it together.

I think of the teasing smile she flashed me. 'See you soon,' she said.

She expects me to find her.

Do I follow her down the trapdoor into the unknown, or do I head to the place I expected her to run to? Something weighs heavily on my chest. I don't make decisions. This is new. This is wrong. This is dangerous.

Like her.

Water drips below. The ladder creaks against the narrow confines of the hole. I touch it. It's cold. Sturdy.

This shouldn't exist.

Where does this lead? Is she down there?

My throat feels tight, and I suck in a breath as I move closer. Then I shake my head and flex my fingers.

This isn't written. This can't be right. This can't be expected of me.

I touch her death warrant tattooed on my chest. I remember her hand in the same place, my heart beating against it. No one has ever touched me like that before. No one has ever surprised me before.

There's something dangerous about her. I don't think she's an ordinary Twist.

For a moment, I let myself wonder. I recall the feeling of her hair through my fingers, the challenge dancing about those bright amber eyes. I think of her face close to mine, her breath tickling my skin. I think about sliding my leg between her thighs to hold her against the wall, then tasting her throat then her lips.

I exhale. This is wrong. It does no good to dwell on things that cannot be.

I close my eyes, and my pulse starts to calm down. I know where she'll go, though the path in my mind seems less certain than usual.

I shut the impossible cupboard door and stride out of the small bedsit.

'See you soon, little Twist.'

Chapter Three
Elle

Stories have teeth. And they're hungry. Some stories starve before they have a chance to grow. But some stories are so big and powerful and ancient that people feed them without even realising it. The Creators' story is like that.

I see it all around me as I hurry through the Draft, the rucksack I left hiding behind the impossible door on my back. There are hints of it in the constant rain that soaks my overalls and the bleak rows of black, crumbling skyscrapers. In the distance, smoke signals the factories and the power plants that never shut. They take people's dreams and never give them quite enough to live on in return. I pass billboards with black-and-white images of the Creators on them, reminders of who is letting us live here. And neon Sacred Styluses flicker in the darkness, marking some buildings as Houses of Truth where the Tellers can spread their gospel.

There are hints of the Creators' story too in the spattering of bullets that crunch underfoot as I cross a square, and in the blood that runs into the drains. Even in the tattooed men I have to hide from as they head into a tavern.

Reminders not to sin, not to deviate from the story that has been written, not to get curious. They remind us that we belong to the Creators, and if we step out of line, we will be Cut from the story altogether.

Like I am supposed to be Cut.

I glance over my shoulder, wondering how close *my* Blotter is to catching up with me. I wonder if he followed me down the ladder into the sewers or if he took a more conventional route. I quicken my pace.

It takes me about twenty minutes to reach the black market. It's housed in the old power plant, a series of looming shadows beside the river. It shut down when an earthquake struck just before I arrived in the Draft, and I have heard whispers it's a sign the foretold Ending of the Creators' story is upon us.

The slightly brighter lights from the Draft Two skyscrapers blink across the river as I hurry towards the doors, the smell of river weed hanging in the air.

Does the Blotter know I'll come here? Is it written? Am I a part of the Creators' story? Or is this a story of my own? Either way, it is the obvious place for me to go right now, and I'm not trying to escape him. Not yet.

I think he is different, and different is dangerous.

I am dangerous too.

The main hall of the power plant is lit by candles and roaring fires in metal bins. People trickle through the wooden carts and tables selling forbidden items: ink, tattoo needles, weapons, food, pieces of parchment. Low voices echo around the room.

There's a tavern at the end where I intend to wait for the Blotter, but I make a detour when I spot my book dealer—a dark-haired girl around my age, nineteen—behind a table covered with battered tomes.

'I've got an old one for you today,' she says, her breath misting in front of her face. She hands me one of the leather-bound books the Tellers read from. 'Any good?'

It's called The Book of Truth, a tool used to spread the Creators' story, and I flick through the scratchy pages, unable to stop myself from inhaling its musty scent. How can something so dangerous smell so sweet? I shake my head when I get to the end. This isn't the version I'm looking for. My disappointment is reflected on her face as she slips it back into her satchel.

When I walk into the tavern, it's quiet. There are only a few people drinking at the metal tables in the dank space. It's quiet enough that I can hear water dripping from a leak in the roof.

I grab the arm of a young girl as she scampers past. 'Where is everyone?'

She looks up at me with wide, frightened eyes. 'A hurricane is coming.'

I smile, satisfied. My story is spreading. Then I crouch in front of her.

She's scrawny and dirty, her blonde hair tangled in knots and her clothes swamping her body. Her parents have probably been Cut and she's been left to fend for herself.

'You remind me of someone,' I say.

'Who?'

My smile widens. 'Once, there was a girl just like you,' I tell her. '*She had hair as white as the tiled streets in the Final City. And she was brave, like you. Part of her was afraid of the Blotters, but do you know, it was the Blotters who should have been afraid of her.*'

'Why?'

'Because the girl had a dragon,' I say, 'and one day, the Blotters came for her. And do you know what happened next?'

She shakes her head, and her eyes brim with curiosity. I like that about children. They are so often curious, even when it is dangerous to be so. Even though soon, if she survives and is taken into one of the workhouses, they will drill it into her that to wonder, to question, to imagine, is to sin. And those lights will die from her eyes.

I grin. 'The dragon ate them.' Swinging my rucksack in front of me, I hand her a couple of nutrition bars. 'Head to the Edge of the World. There's a place for you there.' I give her a little push. 'Hurry. There's a hurricane coming.'

At the bar, I hand a couple of bronze coins with Creator Michael's face to the owner, and he pours me two beakers of weak beer in return.

'Don't stay long,' he says. 'I'm clearing out soon. They've kept pretty quiet about it, but the Creators are sending a hurricane at midnight. I've heard the Ending is approaching, and you know Draft One will be the first to go.'

'Thanks,' I say.

I carry the drinks over to a table and take a seat, throwing down my rucksack. I slip out of the arms of my too-big overalls and wring them out on the floor, then I let flames from the metal bin behind me cast warmth onto my skin.

I keep my eyes trained on the door as I wait for him. I wait for the hurricane too. They will both be here for me soon.

Some stories have teeth, you see. But some stories are like dandelions. You plant them, and if they take, they grow roots and flower and spread on their own. My father told me that.

I used to try it when I was a child. I wasn't allowed out of my living quarters, so I'd give the seeds to the nannies and maids and cooks. I'd tell them about dusty hallways filled with butterflies, and birds singing in the dark, and bees nesting in the rafters.

And sometimes they'd take root and I'd hear the fluttering of wings through my keyhole, or a bird would perch by the bars of my window, or the sweetest amber honey would dribble down my walls.

My father was angry when he found out what I had been doing. Because stories are forbidden. Because stories are dangerous. Because stories are hungry. He was afraid the Creators would find out about me—about what I could do. He was afraid their story would swallow me whole.

Well, now they have found me.

And now they have sent one of their monsters to kill me.

But he had curiosity in his eyes. He let me touch him. His rough hands were gentle as they brushed against my cheek. And he had a dandelion seed tattooed on his chest. Why would he have that inked amongst all the murder?

It makes no sense.

I think he might be different than the others. I think I might be able to persuade him not to kill me. I think I might be able to get him to deviate from the Creators' story. I think he might even be useful.

And if not, well. . .I have been planting a story of my own.

Chapter Four
Jay

The girl has to be here. She has to be. If she's not, I'm fucked.

And yet for the first time since I was a boy, I'm not certain of it. Usually, I'm certain of everything. My life is mapped out for me. I'm bound to the Creators' story by the ink that runs in my veins. Yet right now, I'm not sure what is going to happen next. I don't like the feeling. My chest is tight, my shoulders are knotted up, and my stomach turns.

I don't know what the fuck is going on.

I don't know how she did what she did. I don't understand why she wasn't afraid of me, or why, when she touched me, I didn't feel like a Blotter. I felt like a man.

Are the Creators testing me? Have I not proven my loyalty to them? Was that Cut I made in the Final City not enough? Have the past five years in this shitty Draft been for nothing?

And now I'm thinking blasphemous thoughts and questioning the Creators. That's what this Twist is doing to me. I need to get my shit together and regain control of myself. I need to end this.

At least people start to pack away their forbidden shit as I walk through their stalls. At least they're acting like they should be. They have the sense to be afraid even though I'm not here for them right now.

The girl should be afraid of me too.

It pisses me off that she isn't. That's why my skin buzzes and my heartbeat gets faster as I approach the tavern. Yeah. Pissed off. Not *excited*.

I exhale when I reach doorway to the tavern, because she's there like she's supposed to be. But then I see there's a beaker in her hands like she's waiting for me, like she knew I'd come. Something else about the place doesn't feel right, but her eyes lock onto mine, and I can't look away. Even though my clothes are wet, I'm hot. Why the fuck is she looking at me like that?

I approach the table. 'What the fuck are you doing?'

I shouldn't be asking questions. Questions come from curiosity, and fuck, doesn't that particular question imply I'm curious about her? The corner of her lip lifts as if she knows it.

'I was waiting.' There's that little smile again, like she knows a private joke. She nods at the beaker on the other side of the table. 'I was hoping you'd join me for a drink.'

'I'm here to deliver your Ending,' I say.

'Okay. But drink with me first.' Her hair is wet and tangled, and heat from the flames gives her face a flushed glow. It stirs something primal within me.

I'm not allowed to want her. I should just get the job over with before I do something stupid.

'I can tell you about the impossible door if you'd like.'

There's something so self-assured about her—her straight posture, her unwavering gaze. No one has ever looked at me like that before. It's as if she thinks she's calling the shots here, which is fucking ridiculous.

And I don't know why I do it. Fuck, I know I'm not supposed to. But I sit down and pick up the beer.

'One drink,' I say. I reckon that's okay. That still fits with the Creators' story. It is written that she dies today, and it is written that she'd come here. I still have ten minutes before this day is over. 'And then we have to get on with it.'

'It's almost midnight,' she says.

The metal beaker is halfway to my lips. 'Yeah.'

'One drink is all I need.'

And then I get it. It makes sense again. She's a Twist. She thinks she can stall me until tomorrow. But she can't. The realisation makes my chest heavy.

'If that's what you think, little Twist.'

The beer is shit, weak, watery stuff, nothing like the stuff they have in the Final City, but it eases some of the tightness in my chest. The Twist watches me over the rim of her beaker.

'How do you know I didn't poison it?' she says.

'I'm a Blotter. I know when I'll die. And it isn't now.'

'How can you be sure?'

'I'm not sure. I'm certain.'

'You're not certain about me.'

I don't like that she's right. In fact, I fucking hate it.

I lean closer, and I can smell her. Most people smell acrid. Fear smells like that. Not her. She smells sweet, like soap and sweat and honey. Why would she smell like honey? Why isn't she afraid?

'I'm more certain than you think.' I take a deliberate sip of the beer. 'I knew where you'd be. I knew you would come here. And I know what you're doing now.'

'Do you?'

As my gaze moves down her body, she shifts, and the corner of my lip twitches.

I like that she feels uncomfortable. I'm regaining control.

'I found your little map,' I continue.

She raises her eyebrows, surprised. They're slightly too big for her face and darker than her hair, but it makes her more beautiful somehow.

And fuck, did I just think a Twist was beautiful? What the fuck is wrong with me?

'You're not supposed to have parchment. Or ink.' I lean back and brush my hands over my head. 'The map. What were the marks on it?'

'I thought Blotters weren't supposed to question things.'

'You'd be wise to exercise a little more caution when speaking to a Blotter.'

'What are you going to do about it? Kill me?' She smiles.

'Careful.'

Something in my face must finally scare her because the humour disappears from her eyes. 'It's where I planted the seeds.'

She's making no sense. Nothing she says makes sense. Nothing she does makes sense. She's trying to piss me off.

'It's not smart to provoke me.'

'You seem to think I'm going to die tonight, so what harm could it do?'

'I don't *think;* I know. It's written.'

She studies me, her gaze lingering on every part of my body visible above the table. 'Was it written that you'd have a drink with me?'

I narrow my eyes. 'Shut it.'

'I know why you sat down,' she says.

Resting my elbows on the table, I lean forwards. 'And why is that?'

'You're curious.'

'Careful, little Twist.'

'That's an unusual trait for a Blotter.' Her warm breath tickles my face as she leans forwards too. She's close enough that I could taste her if I wanted to. 'You're different than the others. I can see it in your eyes.'

Different is bad. Different is dangerous.

'You're wrong.'

'You want to know where the secret door came from, don't you?'

A muscle in my jaw twitches. 'I know where it came from. The Creators. Like everything else.'

'You don't believe that. Not really.'

I can't do this. It's not right. I'm not supposed to be doing this. It's a test. It has to be. I push away the thought of her hand on my chest.

'Enough.' I down the rest of the beer and stand up. 'Get up.'

For the first time, I see fear flash across her face. 'You don't have to do this.'

'I do. It is written. Get up.'

'No.'

Why is she making this more difficult than it needs to be? I grab her arm and pull her to her feet. I know what I have to do. I have no choice. A snap of the neck, and it'll be over.

She's a Twist. She's dangerous. She's—

She knees me in the balls then punches me in the jaw. And it's not even the pain of it that makes me cry out—I've experienced torture much worse than a little Twist trying to hit me—it's the surprise.

What are you doing?

I grab her arms again and pull her into me. She struggles, but she can't win this. She must know that. I slide my hand in her hair and tilt her head back.

And then we both freeze.

There are voices outside, accompanied by heavy, rhythmic footsteps. More Blotters are coming. For the same girl? Why?

I should get rid of her now. Before they get here. Before they see me holding her with my fingers threaded in her hair, not really trying to do what has to be done.

She dies. It is written. There is no other way.

'There's a hurricane coming,' she says.

I thought I couldn't be more surprised, but I am. The Creators create the weather. Why would she say that?

'What the fuck do you mean? No, there isn't.'

Yes, there is.

Her fingers dig into my biceps, and there's something urgent in her eyes, like she needs me to understand something. 'Why do you think it's so empty in here?'

I realise why something felt wrong when I walked in. We're completely alone. But there's a perfectly logical explanation for that.

'It's because I'm here.'

'No. It's because they know there's a hurricane coming.'

'It's impossible. I'm a Blotter. I'd know.'

'Not if the Creators didn't send it.'

My throat constricts. 'What the fuck are you talking about?'

She doesn't tell me, because five men enter the room. They're typical Draft One Blotters—not as big as me, sloppier, more relaxed in the way they hold themselves. They're covered in the same ink as I am though. And they're just as deadly.

One of them, a guy I've seen a couple of times in one of the taverns by the factory, looks us up and down. His eyes are bright with lust for the kill even though Blotters are not supposed to enjoy what they do.

'What's going on here then?' he says, hand on his gun.

Even if I had to answer to some shitty Draft One Blotter, I couldn't. Because I have no fucking clue what's going on.

'What time is it?' asks the Twist.

I meet her eyes, frowning. 'Midnight.'

'*A hurricane is coming.*'

The high windows of the power plant shatter inwards, and the Blotters by the door are thrown into the walls. The girl's hair whips my face, and I taste rain and the river. We cling onto each other as we stand in the eye of the storm.

Adrenaline pumps through my body as I grab her arms and shake her. '*How did you know this?*'

There is triumph in the Twist's eyes when she pulls away from me and runs. As she reaches the door, a chair flies at her head, and she's hurled into the wall. Shielding my face from the glass, beer barrels, and tables that are being swept up by the wind, I push towards her.

She's unconscious, but the Blotter who spoke stirs, ink leaking from the corner of his mouth.

I could leave. If I leave the girl, she'll die. It wouldn't be exactly how it was written, but her Ending would still be delivered. A deviation. But a minor one.

It would mean I don't have to do it myself. And for some weird fucking reason, I don't want to do it myself.

She looks so peaceful amongst the chaos, her flushed face relaxed, her chest moving softly up and down.

I shake my head and walk out of the door.

Then I stop. I think of her hand on my chest. She should have run away from me. She should have been afraid. That hot, unwelcome feeling stirs inside me again.

Fuck's sake.

I stride back in and scoop her up off the floor. Holding her warm body against my chest, I carry her through the hurricane, away from the Blotters.

As I walk through the power plant, her tattoo burns. I grunt, gritting my teeth to withstand the pain.

It's starting already.

Why the fuck am I doing this?

She looks so peaceful. So fragile in my arms.

I shake my head. 'You're going to be the death of me, little Twist.'

Chapter Five
Elle

The thought comes to me slowly, like a drop of ink spreading on dry parchment: *It worked.*

The next thoughts are quicker and as sharp as quills.

I'm not dead.

The Blotters came for me.

The tattooed killer was there.

I'm hurt. I don't know where I am.

Danger.

I open my eyes.

The room is dim. A bulb buzzes in the ceiling. Springs dig into my back. I sit upright and wince. My head throbs.

Then I jerk back, pressing myself against the wall and clenching the sheets in my fists. My heartbeat hammers in my chest.

The Blotter is sitting on a metal chair at the end of the mattress. His legs are spread, and his corded forearms rest on his knees. There's anger in his cool eyes. My rucksack sits at his feet.

I control my breathing and try to calm my pulse. Because I'm not dead.

I'm supposed to be dead. He is a Blotter, and he is supposed to kill me. It's written in ink on his skin. But he hasn't done it. That means he doesn't want to. It doesn't mean he won't, but still, there is a crack in his convictions, a chance for me to survive this.

Where there are cracks, stories can grow. That is what my father used to say.

I hold his cold gaze, noting again the strange blot-like imperfection in his left iris. The silence hangs heavily between us.

Finally, he looks at the threadbare carpet and rubs his face. He exhales heavily, a low, masculine sound. Then his gaze travels slowly over my body.

'You're awake.' His voice is gruff.

The bedsit we're in is similar to mine: grey carpet, mattress on the floor, and a dingy kitchenette. It has no windows though, and it feels even smaller. Behind him, black mould darkens the wall, and the air is heavy in my lungs. I think we might be underground.

'Where are we?' I ask.

He waits a beat as though deciding whether to answer. 'Draft One.'

'You live here?'

'Yeah.'

'You live in shitholes like the rest of us then. I always wondered.'

'Are you trying to piss me off?'

I shift on the lumpy mattress. Am I?

There is something different about this Blotter. He is curious, and he has a dandelion seed tattooed on his skin. He was supposed to kill me, but he brought me here.

Yet he works for the people who killed my father. He is a relentless, ink-blooded killer. He does whatever he is supposed to do without question, or emotion, or thought. He is a soldier for the Creators. A monster. A weapon.

He stands for everything I hate.

And I'm cornered. I'm trapped in his room, sitting on his mattress. I can smell him on the sheets, masculine and consuming. And I find that I want to torment him. I want see how far I can push him. I want to prod him and unleash the beast disguised as a man.

'I'm not sure,' I say.

'You'd better get sure.'

'You weren't supposed to bring me here.'

All the muscles in his jaw tighten. *'Don't you think I know that?'*

His vest is wet, and I can see distorted black shapes inked onto his chest as it rises and falls quickly. A desire to touch them overwhelms me. I want to take off his top. I want to study the symbols on his skin. I want to understand. I want to feel his heart pounding beneath my hand.

But that would be as dangerous as touching a lion, so I stay where I am.

When I meet his gaze again, the look in his eyes is different. The anger is still there, but there's something primal mixed within it too. It stirs something hot inside me.

'Careful, little Twist,' he says quietly.

I swallow. 'You don't want to kill me.'

He leans back in his chair. 'That doesn't mean I won't.'

'What do you want? Why have you brought me here?'

His expression turns to stone, and he runs a hand over his mouth. I don't think he knows why he did it. 'I have questions. You're going to answer them.'

'I thought Blotters didn't ask questions.'

His eyebrow raises slightly, emphasising the white scar across it. I wonder who gave him the scar. Who could hurt a Blotter?

'Yeah, well, you've pretty much fucked all that up for me, haven't you? So how about you shut your smart-arse mouth and keep your thoughts to yourself unless I ask for them? It'll end better for you if you do. Okay?'

'Fine.'

He sighs. 'Good.'

I shrug. 'I like it that you're curious.'

'I'm this fucking close.' His finger and thumb are a short distance apart. 'Do you have any kind of comprehension of what is going on here? Do you know the shit I'm in right now? And do you know how much I could resolve by finishing this, by doing what I was supposed to do from the start?'

I don't say anything. Truth be told, I don't know what is going to happen to him. I don't know if this has ever happened before—a Blotter not committing a murder that was written on his skin. There are black shapes all over his arms, all over his body. If they represent the people he's already killed, there are a lot of them.

The fear creeps back, but I won't show him. 'Am I supposed to feel sorry for you?'

'No. You're supposed to shut the fuck up so I can ask you some questions.'

'And then?'

'We'll see.'

He is volatile. He has not had to make decisions before. This is unnatural for him. He's like one of the springs in his mattress: coiled up for now, but as soon as whatever maintains his interest is gone, he's going to unwind.

He doesn't want to kill me.

But that doesn't mean he won't.

'Fine,' I say. 'What do you want to know?'

'The hurricane—' He bends over double on his chair, slamming a hand on his chest. *'Ah, fuck!'*

I clench his bed sheets. My mind buzzes through different scenarios. I could run. I could leave him here. He is dangerous, and I can escape him. Whatever is happening to him right now is an opportunity; a way for me to get out.

But he is an opportunity too. He's different than the others. He brought me here when he wasn't supposed to. This interaction wasn't written. And so, something keeps me here with my back pushed against the wall.

He was supposed to kill me, but he was gentle. He saved my life. We are both living outside of the One True Story now. We have a new story. Our own story.

I approach with the wariness I would exhibit if encountering an injured animal and shift between his legs. I put my finger under his chin and tilt his head up. His face is flushed.

'You're hurt,' I say.

I push him back into the seat and prise his hand away from his heart. I pull down the top of his damp vest, exposing inked skin and hard muscle covered in a light sheen of sweat.

'Don't,' he says through gritted teeth.

He flinches when I touch him and grabs my wrist. His eyes don't move from mine, and within them, there's something like wonder mixed with the pain.

'What's wrong?' I ask.

His lips harden.

'Tell me,' I say.

Gradually, his heartbeat steadies beneath my fingers. I touch a black shape that marks my death warrant: a twist within a circle. I glance at the tattoo of the dandelion seed.

'Stop.' He yanks my hand away then releases my wrist.

I should move away from him. But I don't.

'What hurt you?' I ask.

'Doesn't matter.'

'You put your hand on the tattoo of me.'

'Drop it, little Twist.'

'Is it something to do with—?'

'Don't push it.'

Both his arms hang by his sides, leaving his body exposed. I want to pull down his vest again. I want to see properly.

As if sensing what I'm thinking, he shakes his head slowly. 'Don't even think about it.' There's a finality to his tone, but I think I catch the corner of his lip twitch. 'I can see why the Creators wrote your End. You're frustrating. Even for a Twist.'

He leans back, putting space between us. When he runs his hands over his head, he exposes his armpits and the tattoos that curl up towards them—including the Sacred Stylus that's branded on his forearm. He opens his mouth as if he's going to say something, but then he sighs and drops his arms back to his thighs.

I know what he wants to know. But I wait for him to ask.

Maybe to torment him further; to watch the inner turmoil as he fights to contain the questions Blotters are forbidden to ask. Or maybe because if he proves he is curious, it proves that I'm right about him.

'Look, just tell me, how the fuck did you know about that hurricane? How could you possibly have known when the Blotters didn't?'

'You really want to know?'

He leans closer, and his hands almost brush against my thighs. I can smell him, hot and primal and distracting. 'Yes.'

I bite my lip, and my pulse quickens as I consider telling him something that could change *everything*.

'Well?' he says.

'I didn't *know* about the hurricane. I created it.'

Chapter Six
Jay

'You what?'

The curious girl stands between my legs, and her chest rises and falls distractingly close to my face. Her wet hair clings to her unblemished shoulders, and I itch to touch her. It's fucked up. I was supposed to kill her. Instead, I saved her. And now, rather than finishing the job and giving myself a fighting chance, I'm looking up into those big amber eyes and wondering what she tastes like.

I crack one of my knuckles and bring my fist to my mouth.

I can't wonder. Blotters don't wonder. Blotters can't be curious. This is bad enough as it is.

'I created the hurricane,' she says again.

I shake my head. 'Yeah. I thought that's what you said.'

'You don't believe me.'

There's a cut across her forehead, and the blood is starting to congeal. I stand up. It brings our bodies even closer, and for some reason, she doesn't back away. Her breath hitches though.

'What are you doing?' she says.

'You're bleeding. It needs to be cleaned. Sit down.'

She just stands there, and I swear to the Creators, if she refuses, I'm going to lose my shit. I run my hand over my mouth.

'Sit. The fuck. Down.'

The corner of her lip briefly quirks. It adds fuel to the fire that's already burning inside of me. Why won't she do as she's told? I'm trying to fucking help her!

I reach for her arm, but she sidesteps me and sits on the chair. I sigh as I stride over to the sink. I grab my one chipped ceramic bowl from the draining board and put it beneath the tap. The pipes scream, and it takes a couple of minutes for the rusty water to trickle out.

I don't know why I'm doing this. I just need a minute away from her, I think. I'm struggling to contain this frustration and fury and this weird animalistic urge that's come over me. I need to get a hold of it. I need to think.

Does she really think she created a hurricane? Or is this just part of her game to antagonize me?

'Was the pain in your chest because of me?' she says.

'Be quiet.'

'I think it was. I think it was something to do with the tattoo of my death.'

I stare at the water as it fills the bowl and try not to lose my cool.

'You're frustrated,' she says.

'No shit.'

'I think I understand. I think I get why you would be.'

I grab my cleaning rag, rinse it, and then drop it in the bowl. I cross the room. 'Yeah? I'm frustrated because you're frustrating.'

I kneel down and spread her legs so I can shift my body between them. She tenses, but her eyes remain fixed on mine. My hands linger on her inner thighs for a moment too long before I pull them away and reach for the rag.

'No,' she says. 'You're frustrated because you're a Blotter.' She glances at the tattoos curling up my neck as I wring out the rag in the bowl. 'Your life is mapped out for you, isn't it? You always know what is going to happen next. But you didn't kill me like you were supposed to. You've diverted from the One True Story. You don't know what's coming anymore.'

Her gaze is searching. It's as if she's trying to see through the depths of ink and darkness inside me. She shouldn't do that. She won't like what she finds.

'That must be scary,' she says.

I lift the wet rag to her forehead, bringing my face close to hers. 'Blotters don't get scared.'

'Everyone gets scared.'

'Are you?' I dab the wound, and she winces. Good. I hope it stings.

'Do you want me to be?'

'Yeah.' I pull away, rinsing the cloth in the bowl. I watch the blood dancing in the water for a second. 'Yeah, I do. Because you should be scared.'

'Because I'm supposed to be dead?'

'Because you're with me.'

'Is it true Blotters know when their Endings are written?' Her warm breath tickles my face as she speaks. 'They know when they're going to die?'

I shouldn't be talking to her about stuff like this. I shouldn't be cleaning a wound on her head. None of this is the way it should be.

'Yeah,' I say.

'That must be hard. Knowing when you're going to die.'

'It's not. It's written. That's the way it is.' I rub a smudge of dried blood off her cheek with my thumb. 'You're supposed to be dead right now, little Twist.'

Her eyes narrow. 'I'm not though.'

I drop the rag back in the bowl. 'Yet.'

She leans forwards. I could count all the brown and burnt orange hues in those curious amber eyes. I could bite her bottom lip and see if she tastes as good as she smells.

'I'm not afraid of you,' she says.

She should be. It would be so easy to kill her; to end this.

My heart hammers against my chest. It would also be so easy to scoop her up in my arms, to hold her, to have her legs to tighten around my torso. I want to kiss her neck. I want to hear her unravel.

Fuck.

I have to get away from her. I knock the bowl as I move back onto the edge of the mattress, and the bloody water sloshes over the sides onto the carpet. I rub my face with both hands and then drop them to my thighs. A ghost of a smile plays about her pale lips.

'Is this amusing to you?' I ask. *'Do you think this is fucking funny?'*

This is fucked up. She shouldn't be here. I shouldn't be thinking things like this. She should be dead.

Her back straightens, and the humour drains from her face. 'No. Why did you bring me here?'

'I don't know.'

'Are you going to let me leave?'

'No.'

A heavy silence hangs in the air. This is all wrong.

'What happens next?' she says.

'I don't know.'

I always know. But right now, I have no fucking clue. My mouth is dry, and my throat tightens. There's a dull burn beneath my skin, and I supress the urge to rub the tattoo above my heart.

I could make it all better, maybe, if I just did what I was written to do. But would the Creators forgive me now? Have I taken this too far already?

I said Blotters don't get scared. They don't.
So what does that make me now?
I'm fucking terrified.

Chapter Seven
Elle

I grip the edge of the metal chair and watch the Blotter warily.

His jaw is clenched, and his hands are in fists. There's a thin layer of sweat on his body and it makes his tattoos shine in the dim light. He says he isn't scared. He is. He must be.

'Not knowing isn't a bad thing.' I talk to him as if I'm coaxing a wild animal, and his eyes narrow.

'You don't fucking get it. You don't understand anything.' He looks at the exposed pipes beneath the metal sink but seems to be focusing on something faraway.

I open my mouth—

'Shut it. I'm thinking.'

I cross my arms. 'A Blotter thinking. I thought I'd never see the day.'

His head snaps up, and a vein throbs in his thick neck. My heartbeat races. I've pushed him too far. Adrenaline floods my system, and I prepare to run.

Then he surprises me.

He laughs.

It's a low, throaty sound that seems to come from somewhere deep inside. He looks almost innocent. It's as if the darkness has lifted. No amount of laughter could undo the ink that marks his skin and soul, but still, it is a nice sound. Unexpected.

There are cracks in everything.

After a moment, it makes me laugh too.

He pinches his bottom lip before dropping his arms to his sides. 'You really do have a death wish, little Twist. Why are you trying so fucking hard to antagonise me?'

'Maybe for the same reason you brought me here.'

'And what reason is that?'

'Curiosity.'

The smile falls from his lips. 'Curiosity is a sin. And I'm a Blotter. Do you understand?'

He stares at me, and his breathing is heavy. It's as if he's containing a storm in his chest. His face flushes, and his whole body is taut. He puts his head in his hands.

'Fuck. I can't do this. I can't do this . . .'

I catch the words *'Creators,'* and *'repent,'* and *'forgiveness.'* He's starting to think if he killed me it might make everything okay. I don't have time for him to decide it won't. More Blotters will come. They'll be here for both of us soon.

I glance at the door. He's not going to let me leave. He will overpower me if I try. He is bigger than me, stronger. He was created that way. A physical fight won't end well for me.

My strength does not lie in muscle.

Nonsense tumbles from his lips as his hunched shoulders rise and fall. I have to do something. I have to provoke him into making a decision, one way or another, before it's too late.

He has a storm inside him. But I created the hurricane.

I grip the bottom of my chair and hope I am right about him.

'Hey,' I say softly. 'Look at me.'

His eyes are bloodshot when he does. With all my force, I kick him in the chest.

He grunts as he falls back onto the mattress. I knock over the chair in my haste to get to the exit of his bedsit. My heart pounds because I know it isn't a good idea to turn my back on a predator.

His hand slams against the door by my face as I pull it open, and it clicks shut.

The Blotter's scent floods me: masculine sweat and salt. His breaths are hot and angry on the back of my neck.

'You're not going anywhere.'

'I'm not staying here while you decide whether or not you're going to kill me.'

'Turn around. *Now.*'

I flatten my back against the door. His body cages me, traps me.

'Do you really think I'm going to let you walk out of here?' he says.

'Do you really think you can make me stay?'

His lips twist into a smile that doesn't reach his eyes. 'I can make you do whatever I want, little Twist.'

I swallow. His hand is by my face, and I can see the Sacred Stylus tattooed on his forearm. It reminds me of what he is. A soldier for the Creators. A killer.

What if I was wrong about him?

I struggle to keep my breathing steady. 'I know what you're trying to do.'

'Yeah? And what's that then?'

'You're trying to scare me. Because you're afraid.'

'Blotters don't fear anything.'

'Blotters don't deviate from the path that was written for them. But you did.'

His hand curls into a fist against the door. 'Careful, little Twist.'

'No. You're not going to hurt me. You would have done so already.'

'You don't know that.'

'You want me to do as you say. You think if I do, you will gain the control you lost when you deviated from the path that was written for you.'

His jaw twitches, and I know I'm right. *'Shut it.'*

I grab the front of his vest, and his hand snaps to my throat. I breathe in sharply, but he doesn't squeeze like a part of him wants to—he just leaves it there, the top his thumb pressing the underside of my chin.

'I cannot be controlled. Tell me why you brought me here.'

He brings his face closer to mine. 'I don't know.'

'Yes, you do. You're afraid. You're afraid because you didn't follow the story the Creators wrote for you. But their story doesn't matter, because I have a story too. Tell me why you brought me here.'

His skin is damp with sweat, and I smell the slightly acrid note of fear on it. 'You'd be wise not to provoke me, little Twist. I've killed people far more dangerous than you. And you're naïve if you think you're safe with me.'

'No. You're naïve. You've lived your whole life serving the Creators, thinking there's a point to everything you've done, every life you've taken.'

He slides his hand from my neck into my hair. 'Shut it.'

'But you've wondered,' I say. 'I see it in your eyes.' I grab his wrist as his grip tightens.

'Blotters. Don't. Wonder.'

'But you do. Tell me why you brought me here.'

'No.'

I need him to say it. I need him to admit it to himself so we can move forwards. 'Tell me.'

'No!'

I pull on his vest, and he slides his thigh between my legs, holding me against the door. The air feels too hot. *'Tell me!'*

He cries out in exasperation. *'What the fuck do you want me to say, Elle? I did it because I wanted to.'*

'And . . . ?'

'Because . . . because I don't want to kill you.' He sighs and then rests his forehead against mine. 'I'm not going to kill you.'

I touch his heart. The dandelion seed is inked just above it. 'Why?'

His breathing begins to steady, but his eyes burn with intensity. *'Because I'm curious.'*

Chapter Eight
Elle

He stares down at me.

He confessed his curiosity—a trait so blasphemous, so unusual for his kind. I should be relieved. I should be pushing him away and deciding what happens next. But I'm caged within his body, and I'm curious too.

I'm curious about his body and his tattoos. I want to trace them with my fingertips. I want to know if they brand his ridged torso and follow the hard V of his hips.

I wonder what his skin would taste like. Would he taste like salt and the rain? If I sunk my teeth into his flesh, would he make a sound? Would the ink that connects him to the Creators bleed from his veins?

His eyes drop to my lips, and I hate that a man I've just met is provoking such an ache within me. I hate that I'm thinking these things about a monster.

A flash of amusement crosses his face. It's as if he knows he's regained some control over the situation. 'What are you going to do now, little Twist?'

I close my eyes and try to calm my speeding pulse. What is wrong with me?

'The Blotters from the market, they'll come for me. Won't they?'

He steps back, and his arms drops to his sides. He exhales. 'Yeah.'

'We need to leave before they get here.'

He raises his eyebrows. 'We?'

'Yes, *we*. I presume they'll be after you now as well.'

He walks across the bedsit, picks up the metal chair, and turns it to face me. He sits down and rests one arm over the back. 'I can handle a few Blotters.'

'And then what?'

His expression hardens. 'I told you. I don't fucking know.'

I lean back against the door, fixing my gaze on a damp spot on the ceiling.

'What's wrong?' he says.

'You. You're frustrating.'

'*I'm* frustrating?'

'Yes.'

He leans forwards. 'I admitted I'm curious,' he says. 'I'm curious about you, little Twist. I'm curious about what you taste like. I'm curious about how it would feel to take you against that wall. I'm curious about what you would sound like when I made you scream. But I'm *not* curious about going on some crazy little Twist adventure while you carry out whatever terrorist schemes you have planned.' He glances down at my rucksack sitting by his feet. 'What exactly *are* you up to?'

'I thought you weren't curious about my *little Twist* adventure.'

His brow furrows. 'I'm not. I—'

'I created the impossible door. I created the hurricane. And I'm heading through the Drafts to reach the Final City. That's all you need to know for now.'

He laughs, but there's an edge to it. 'You'll never make it to the Final City.'

'I will.' Silence stretches between us, and I exhale. 'You can't stay here. They'll come for you too. You broke the rules. You twisted from the Creator's story.'

'I told you, I can handle—'

The sound of male voices in the corridor causes us both to look at the door. My insides twist. It's too late. They're here. There are no windows to escape through, no impossible door, no hurricanes—just me, the Blotter, and a group of men who mean to kill me.

'*Shit!*' My outburst provokes a genuine smile from the Blotter. 'Is something funny?'

'Yeah. You. I like you scared, little Twist.'

He's on his feet and striding towards me by the time I remember my rucksack. 'There's a knife—'

He grabs my arm and drags me across the room, picking up my rucksack as he passes it. 'Get in the cupboard.' He flings the doors open. 'Inside. Now.'

I push against him. If I'm going to die, I will not die hiding. That's not how my story Ends. He lifts me up, though, like I'm one of the dolls they have in the Inner Drafts and deposits me ungracefully inside. I stumble through his hooded tops and vests and hit my head against the wall.

'I'll deal with it,' he says.

'Are you insane? You'll get killed. And then they'll kill me. I'm not dying in a cupboard—'

The Blotters pound on the door, and he points at me. '*Shut it. And*'—he glances warily at the wooden bottom of the cupboard—'*you'd better still be in here when I'm done.*'

He slams the door shut. I push, but there's a thud as he grabs something and slides it across the handles of the cupboard. Panic surges through my body. I do not want to be trapped in a dark space that smells like him and damp clothes.

There's a crash as the door bursts open.

'Where is he?' says one of the Blotters.

Breathing quickly, I push my eye against the crack between the doors, trying to catch a glimpse of what's going. Gunfire fills the air, and I throw myself back.

He's going to die. The curious Blotter who was supposed to kill me will die. And I don't want him to. I don't want to die either.

I throw my hands over my ears until a deadly silence fills the cupboard.

My chest is heavy. My throat constricts, and I swallow, straightening as footsteps approach the door. I cannot let my emotions get the better of me. I have to survive. The element of surprise is all I have on my side. Blotters don't get surprised. It might be enough.

I leap forwards as the doors are flung open.

A strong arm hooks around my waist, and I'm yanked into a hard body. My hair whips my eyes and gets caught in my mouth. I cry out, jamming my elbow into his ribs. He curses. And I still.

The walls are black, my earlier question answered: Blotters *do* bleed ink. The scent of it is heavy in the air, metallic and acrid. There are five bodies on the floor. Men with broken necks and gunshot wounds.

But my Blotter is not one of them.

His heart beats fast against my back. When my breathing steadies, he releases me. I turn and look up at him.

There's something animalistic about him right now. His pupils are big and wild, his skin is flushed, and his top is drenched in black Blotter blood. His breathing is ragged and uneven.

He looks every bit the monster he's supposed to be. He could have killed me a thousand times already. He really has been holding back with me.

'Are you hurt?' I ask, and my voice is quiet.

'No.' He takes a step back and rubs his face, smearing ink across his cheek. 'No, I'm not.'

We stare at each other, both unsure of what happens next. Unsure of what to say.

'Come with me,' I say.

'You won't make it to the Final City.'

'You can't stay here.'

'You don't get it, little Twist. I can't leave.'

'I do get it.' I take a tentative step towards him, and he flinches, his eyes still wild. 'This is familiar, and you don't know what to do now you're not following the Creators' story anymore. You're not ready to make your own yet. But that's okay, because until you are, you can be a part of mine.'

I lightly touch his forearm, and he tenses.

'But you have to decide now, because I have to go.' I glance at the tattoos that mark him as a monster, and the blood on his vest that proves it. 'And if you're coming with me, you need to change into something that covers up your ink. You'll draw the wrong sort of attention where we're heading.'

He drags his teeth across his plump bottom lip. And I can't wait for him any longer. I grab my rucksack and step over one of the corpses. I look over my shoulder as I reach the door.

'Well? Are you coming?'

He looks like one of the statues of the Creators they erected in the courtyards of the Citadel. Still. Metal. Unbreakable. Then he exhales and averts his gaze to the ceiling, shaking his head.

I try to hide my disappointment. I try to hide that I wanted him to come.

'You won't make it to the Final City, little Twist,' he says.

'Yes. I will.'

He closes his eyes, the corners crinkling. He looks like he's in pain again, and I wonder if it's the tattoo of me that's causing it.

'Not alone, you won't.' He touches his mouth. 'You know where you're heading next?'

I grip the pocket of my trousers and will myself not to do or say anything in the next few seconds that might scare him away. 'Yes.'

He opens the cupboard doors. He peels off his bloody vest and drops it on the floor to reveal his muscular back. It has as many tattoos on it as his chest. I've barely had a chance to look at them before he pulls on another top and throws a large black hoodie over it. He zips it up as he crosses the room.

'You're going to be the death of me, little Twist,' he says, pulling the hood over his buzzcut.

The corner of my mouth twitches. 'Do you mean to tell me you're coming on my "crazy little Twist adventure" after all?'

He lets out a low sigh. 'Don't get smart with me. Come on.' He puts his hand on the small of my back and gently pushes me out into the corridor. 'Let's get on with it before I change my mind.'

Chapter Nine
Jay

This is fucking insane.

The curious girl strides down the corridor away from my bedsit, her white-blonde hair wild and tangled down her back. I traipse behind her, head down, scuffed knuckles stuffed in my pockets, following like one of those ridiculous puppy dogs they have in the Inner Drafts.

What the fuck is wrong with me? My chest is heavy, and my mouth is dry. I can barely breathe. I shouldn't be doing this. Nothing tonight is going the way it should be, and from the irritating purpose in the Twist's step, I have a feeling it's going to get a whole lot worse.

I'm almost glad I got to kill those Blotters. At least it allowed me to work out some of the frustration that's been building up inside of me since I first laid eyes on her. I would rather have worked it out some other way. But it was better than nothing.

I head up the concrete steps to street level. The wind sprays raindrops into my face, and the air smells like wet concrete and leaking drains.

'Where are we going, little Twist?'

'The Edge.'

Lightning forks across the sky, lighting up Creator Michael's face on a billboard over the road. Is it a sign? A warning? Does he know what I've done? What I'm about to do? I rub the Sacred Stylus tattooed on my forearm, my throat constricting. Course he fucking does. He's my patron. He knows everything.

'You want to go to the Edge of the World?' I ask.

'Yes. Which way is it?'

I shake my head. 'This is a bad idea. Wherever you think you're taking us, it won't work.'

'There's a place we can go.'

'A black market?'

'Of sorts. Look, I know you're scared—'

'Blotters don't get scared—'

'—but more Blotters will come for us. I don't have time to explain everything. You need to trust me. I'm not going to die today. I'll ditch you if I have to.'

She sounds as frustrated as I feel. I let out a low breath in an attempt to get some kind of release. It doesn't work. The weight on my chest is getting heavier. But Creator Michael's eyes bore into me from over the road, and I need to get the fuck away from that billboard, so I gesture left, and she starts walking.

'You realise I'm a Blotter and I'm supposed to kill you,' I say. 'Tracking you is in my blood. You don't seriously think you could ditch me.'

'I did it before.'

'You're oddly confident for someone who just witnessed me kill five soldiers.'

'And you're oddly curious for a Blotter.'

I stuff my hands into the pockets of my hoodie to stop me from grabbing her. She really does have a death wish.

'I told you.' I struggle to keep my voice even. 'I'm just curious about you. That's all.'

And when I told her how curious I was, how I wanted to taste her, how I wanted to make her scream, she didn't even blink. She wants me though. She can barely take her eyes off me. She keeps touching me. She tried to peel off my top when my tattoo was burning. And when I pinned her to the door, she wanted to bite me.

'You're curious about me too, aren't you, little Twist? You know, if it's my body you're curious about, you're welcome to it. I can show you. Any part you like. I don't mind.'

She stops at the end of the alley. A flickering light strains through the cracks of a boarded-up window behind her so her face is in shadow.

'How many people have you killed?'

I press my lips together, my good humour disappearing.

She puts her head down as she walks away. 'That's what I thought.'

I grab her arm. 'If I'm that disgusting to you then I may as well just go.'

She tries to pull away, but I tighten my grip. When her eyes hit mine, she looks furious. Good. I'm glad she's angry. I want her to tell me to leave. I want everything to make sense again.

As we stare at each other, her breathing slows. 'No. I want you to come. But what do you expect me to feel? You stand for everything I hate.'

'You don't think it's the same for me?'

'You hate me for existing. I hate what you've done. It's different.'

I pull her closer and lower my voice. 'I've defied the gods by not doing what was written, so how about you give me a fucking break?'

'Fine.'

There's a different kind of tension when we start to walk again. I grit my teeth so hard my head hurts. I saved her life. I helped her. I'm still trying to, for all the good it'll do me. I should just go.

Yet I'm tailing her like some kind of fucking guard dog.

I refuse to look at her for a couple of hours as we navigate the Draft One labyrinth of black, crumbling skyscrapers, metal, and scaffolding. But when I finally do, she's shivering. Good. I'm glad she's suffering.

I sigh. 'Take my hoodie,' I say.

She raises her eyebrows, surprised. Because monsters like me obviously can't do anything nice. 'You need to keep your ink hidden. If they see you're a Blotter, it'll cause problems. Thank you though.'

She speaks to me in the same condescending way you'd talk to a child when they've done something right, like she's teaching me to do the same again next time. I can't tell if I'm pissed off or amused. Either way, she should know that won't work on me. That wasn't the way I was trained.

The urban landscape around us gets increasingly decrepit as we journey on, and about half an hour later, we reach a long road where most of the skyscrapers have been demolished. There's a wall of white mist at the end of it, tendrils creeping forwards. I could have sworn the Edge was farther back than this. I snatch the Twist's wrist to stop her walking straight into it.

'Are you insane?' I ask her. 'Where are you going?'

'Come on.' The corner of her lip lifts as if she's enjoying that I'm way out of my depth here.

'Elle, it's the Edge of the World. You'll fall off, and then you'll be gone.'

'So the stories say.' Her smile spreads. 'But have you ever seen for yourself?'

'Course not.'

'Exactly. Blotters avoid it. It makes it a good place for people like me.' She puts her hand on my chest. 'Look, it's okay. Trust me. There's nothing to fear.'

She turns away and walks into the thick wall of mist. It swallows her.

'Fuck.'

The Edge of the World is the edge of the Creators' creation. Beyond it is pure nothingness. Passing over it deletes you from existence. Everyone knows that.

I run a hand over my mouth. *'Fuck.'*

Am I really going to do this?

I take a deep breath that tastes like mist and rain.

Then I follow the curious girl over the Edge of the World.

Chapter Ten
Elle

The Creators' weather cannot reach here, so other than the thick mist, it's silent and dry, the rain contained within Draft One.

I could keep moving. I know where I'm going. But I should wait for the Blotter. This will be new to him. Different. Like a wild animal, he becomes agitated when he's afraid. That won't do him any good here.

I rub my arms, fighting the gooseflesh.

I know he doesn't want to come here, but there's no doubt in my mind he will. I hear him before I see him, heavy footsteps and agitated breathing. Ghostly tendrils grab his hunched shoulders and trail behind his long legs. His head, concealed by his hood, jerks left and right as he attempts to survey his surroundings.

'What the fuck?' he says.

I supress a shiver and then smile. 'You've seen nothing yet.'

'Nothing is all I can fucking see . . .' His big hands are stuffed into his pockets, and his arms are tense as he falls into step slightly behind me. 'Where are we?'

We both halt when we hear a click.

'Hands in the air if you want to keep your brains in your heads,' a woman speaks, about ten metres or so ahead. She's barely visible through the mist.

The Blotter releases an agitated breath. 'Great plan, little Twist.'

Several more clicks permeate the mist around us. '*Now.*'

The Blotter slowly complies, but I feel him working out how many people surround us, no doubt planning a sequel to the scene in his bedsit.

'Raven,' I say quickly, before he has a chance to act. 'I'd almost forgotten how hospitable you were to visitors.'

'Elle? Is that you?' The mist ebbs and flows as she comes into view.

I've only been gone for a few weeks, but she looks as if she's aged a few years in my absence. There are ink-like smudges beneath her eyes, and a new scar perforates the dark skin across her cheek. She's thinner too, and her scuffed leather jacket hangs from her athletic frame. I take note of the heavy-duty firearm across her chest—the type the Blotters have access to. It must have been hard to get a hold of.

She's looking at me as if she can't figure out whether to shoot me or hug me. 'What the fuck? We thought you were dead.'

'I'm supposed to be.'

'Yeah, well, you just might be when Sylvia finds out you're alive. Seriously, Elle, where the fuck have you been?'

'You remember what we talked about before I left? About me planting some seeds outside of the Circus?'

'I remember Sylvia explicitly telling you *not* to try it.'

'Well, I did it.'

Raven stares at me, eyes narrowed. Then she shakes her head. 'You're such a little shit, Elle.' Her long braids flick over her shoulder as she looks around. 'All right, people, stand down. And can someone go break the news to Sylvia that Elle's back, because for the love of the Creators, I don't want to be the one to do it.'

The dark figures surrounding us move back into the mist. The Blotter watches them with narrowed eyes, his breathing audible.

Raven jerks her head in his direction. 'Who's the new guy?'

I can't tell her the whole truth. Not when she's holding a gun. Blotters aren't welcome here, and for good reason too. We've been hiding here, amongst mist and stories, from the Creators' ink-blooded killers for years.

But I can tell her part of the truth. 'He's going to help us.'

His eyes bore into the side of my skull, and I feel the irritation bristling off him. He may be reluctant to help, but he is here. That is helpful in itself. He is exactly what our story needs.

Raven steps in front of him and looks him up and down. 'Where are you from?' When he doesn't reply, she prods him in the chest with the gun. 'Hey. Don't look at her—look at me. I'm speaking. Take your hood down.'

Slowly, he complies, revealing his murderous expression, and my heart beats a little faster. I believe he is important to our cause, but he needs to be acclimatised first. He's not ready yet. He's a bomb that hasn't been neutralised. And if he can kill five armed Blotters without a weapon, I'm pretty sure he can kill Raven. He's looking at her as if he wants to.

'You're hiding something,' she says. Her eyes narrow on the inked symbols curling around his wrist. 'Pull up your sleeve.'

When he doesn't, she prods him with her gun again, and he closes the space between them, towering over her. *Do that again, and you'll wish you hadn't,*' he says.

'Raven,' I say, 'let's talk in private.'

She can't know that he's a Blotter. Not while she's holding a gun. And if he pulls up his sleeve and bares the extent of his tattoos, she will know.

Raven holds his gaze, glowering. 'You vouch for him?' she says.

'Yes.'

'If he causes any trouble, Sylv will have you both banished.'

'I know.'

She lowers her gun and walks away. 'Fine. But you know the routine. He needs initiating like everyone else. No exceptions, even for you. And something tells me he hasn't got it in him.'

The Blotter and I look at one another. I've only just met him, but I feel as if I can read him. Not the tattoos that tell his story in ink, but his face, his expression, his body. I can read the slight shake of his head and the hard line of his jaw. I know he thinks this is a bad idea. I know he wants to leave.

I hope he can read me too.

I want him to know that this will be okay. We will be safe here. So long as he can hold it together.

I raise my eyebrows and gesture at Raven. He breathes out sharply through his nose, then he follows me.

The corner of Raven's lip quirks up as I fall into step beside her. 'So, you did it then?'

I grin. 'Yeah. I created a hurricane.'

'Are you sure it was you?'

I try to push down the rise of anger. The whole reason I slipped away three weeks ago without telling anyone was to avoid this sort of thing. Even after everything I've done, I'm still met with scepticism when I try something new.

'Yes.'

'It's just they're saying the Ending of the One True Story is coming, Elle. There have been earthquakes and fires and storms all over the Draft. And the Edge is getting closer to camp.'

'It was me.'

She shrugs. 'Well, I'm glad you're back anyway.'

The mist parts as we approach a twisted black iron gate. The Blotter eyes the two guards on either side warily as he brushes up beside me.

'Where the fuck are we?' he says.

A CIRCUS OF INK

White-and-red lights blink along the tops of big metal shipping containers and small white trailers. They illuminate the flowers and dragons and pirate ships graffitied onto the walls. There are about twenty in total, and they're arranged to create pathways to the vast black-and-red high-top tent in the centre—the Circus.

People ebb in and out of its entrance flap, laughing and chatting and carrying planks of wood, buckets of paint, and weapons. The mist coils around their ankles, making it seem as if they're walking through clouds. A group of kids scream and giggle around them, playing tag, while a woman yells at them to eat their breakfast.

I smile. 'Home.'

Raven leads us through the settlement, and people eye us in curiosity. It's not only because I'm back; the Blotter draws just as much attention. He's huge, and even with his ink hidden he looks like a killer. It's the set of his jaw and his unsmiling mouth, and the death stare he gives anyone who looks in his direction.

'This place has grown since I was last here,' I say. 'Our story is spreading.'

'Yeah. Sylvia was worried it would fizzle out after you left, but we've kept it going. We tell the odd story about the Edge of the World when we visit the black markets for supplies. And we keep it fed in the usual way every night.' Raven shakes her head, a grin broadening on her face and creating dimples in her cheeks. 'Fuck, people are going to be excited to see you again, Elle.'

She stops outside a shipping container on the edge of the campsite. There are clouds painted onto the sides, and standing beneath them, three pink stick figures that look as if they've been drawn by a child.

'This one is empty for now, but Sylv wants it for Maggie when she gets back. She got wind of some Darlings in trouble in Draft Two.'

I was hoping Maggie would be here now. I told her about the special version of the Book of Truth that I've been looking for before I left, and she said she'd help me if she could.

Raven gestures at the door, and I slide it up.

'Scarlett and Johnny went out to get supplies last week and never came back. Their little kid went after them. Gone too. Only six years old.' Her hands tighten on her gun. 'Blotters. I swear, the next Blotter I see is going to lose his brains.'

If her words affect the Blotter, he doesn't show it. He strides inside the container after me, our footsteps echoing as they hit the metal floor. A buzzing lightbulb hanging in the centre of the ceiling casts a dim glow onto the metal walls, and a couple of sleeping bags are bundled in the corner.

Raven immediately turns on the Blotter. 'So, who are you?'

He dominates the space, and the top of his head almost brushes the ceiling. He crosses his arms and opens his mouth to say something. I'm sure he will say the wrong thing. I don't think Blotters can lie.

'He's a Twist,' I say carefully.

He won't like being called that, but technically, it's true. He did something that was not written.

His gaze meets mine, and he answers me instead of Raven. 'I'm Jay,' he says, his voice gruff as gravel.

I smile. In all the drama, I never even asked him his name. It suits him.

'Jay,' I say softly.

'You have tattoos,' says Raven. 'That's unusual.'

Jay nods at her collarbone, where a dusting of stars tickle her dark skin. 'So do you.'

'Where are you from, Jay?'

'The Final City,' he says, looking at me again. I didn't know that either. He touches his mouth. 'Originally.'

'I thought you were too well-built to be from around here.' Raven bites her lip. 'He's a Twist?'

'Yes,' I say.

Her eyes narrow, and I'm sure she knows there's something more to all this. But I think she may be willing to play this story out.

'Okay,' she says with a shrug. 'If Elle says you're good, you're good. You've been travelling all night?'

I nod.

'Rest. Get some food. Show him the works. Then come to the main tent tomorrow evening. I'll send word around that we're initiating a new Darling.' She looks over her shoulder as she jumps to the ground. 'Maybe you could tell a story too, Elle. It's been a while.' She gives me a half-smile. 'It's good to see you.'

As she walks away, I pull down the metal door, and it clangs shut. When I turn, the Blotter arches a thick eyebrow.

'Are you going to tell me what's going on? Who are these people?'

'They call themselves the Darlings.'

His lips harden. 'They're people who should have been Cut.'

'Yes.'

'You're telling me we're in a terrorist camp?'

'*You* might call it that.'

'What are they doing here?'

'It's a long story.'

'What are *we* doing here?'

'It's part of my plan.'

He rubs the back of his head, looking around the metal shipping container. 'Fuck. You're a real pain in my arse, little Twist.'

I cross the space between us and put a palm on his chest even though I know I shouldn't touch him. His eyes drop to my hand, his face unreadable.

'Your name is Jay,' I say.

'Yeah.'

'Jay.' I drag my teeth on my bottom lip. I like the way his name feels. 'Is what you said true? About the Final City?'

'All Blotters start off there.' If it's possible, he seems to tense even more. 'But yeah. I was there for most of my life.'

'Are you okay?'

'I'm not the person you should be worrying about.' His forehead creases. 'I could kill every person in this place if I wanted to. You don't seem to realise that.'

I glance at his biceps, straining against the sodden fabric of his top. 'There are things in this world that are stronger than muscle. You'll learn that here.'

'Yeah?' He folds his arms. 'And where are we, exactly?'

'We're at the Circus at the Edge of the World.' I look at him in curiosity. 'Have you heard of a Circus before?'

'Course I fucking haven't.'

'I didn't think so.' My lip twitches. 'You're going to hate it.'

Chapter Eleven
Jay

This whole night has been ridiculous. But everything has happened so quickly my mind hasn't had a chance to catch up.

Now, we're alone, and the only sound is the water dripping off our clothes and hitting the metal floor between us. I can't even hear rain drumming against the shipping container. There's no weather here. It makes no sense.

I never feel uncomfortable or awkward. No Blotter does. We always know what is coming. We always know what we're supposed to do next.

Right now, I have no fucking clue.

All I know is that I'm in the middle of a terrorist camp with a Twist I was meant to kill, and none of my tattoos are telling me what to do anymore.

Is this what normal people feel like all the time? As if they're struggling for breath, not knowing which way is up or down? I've only felt like that once before, when I was drowning. But I was prepared for it. I knew my head would eventually breach the surface. I knew I was doing what had to be done. I'm not prepared for this though.

I want to drag the Twist down into the depths with me. But I also want to keep her afloat. I want to kill her like I'm supposed to. But I want to protect her too. I want her to want me, and I want her to be afraid.

I want a release, somehow. I want to stop feeling like this.

'You going to tell me what a Circus is?' I ask, because it's all I can think of saying.

'Soon.' The Twist's eyes bore into mine, and if she knew what was good for her, she wouldn't be looking at me in that way. She wouldn't be standing so close. She wouldn't be antagonising me. If she knew the things I wanted to do to her, she would be running away.

'Take off your clothes,' she says.

I laugh, surprising myself. It's not the release I wanted, but it eases some of the pressure on my chest. I should be pissed off she thinks she can tell me what to do. But it's so strange and weird and unexpected that I'm tempted to do it, just to see what she does next.

I drag my teeth over my bottom lip. 'I suppose I did say I'd show you any part of me you wanted to see.'

She arches an eyebrow as I unzip my hoodie. 'Your clothes are wet,' she says. 'We need to get dry.'

She doesn't look away though. When my top hits the floor, she frowns and tentatively puts her hand just above my heart, her shoulders tense as if she's not sure how I'll react. She smells like honey. Why does she smell like that? There are no bees and no flowers outside the Final City. Nothing about her makes sense. It makes me curious, and I hate that she's making me sin. But I can't stop.

She traces one of my tattoos, and my breathing deepens.

'What are you doing?' I say, my voice low.

'What does this mean? The dandelion seed?'

'I don't know.'

'I thought *Blotters* knew everything.'

I grab her wrist. 'I told you before, we don't.'

'I don't understand.'

'Some things are clear from the start; some of the smaller details reveal themselves when they need to.'

'What was I?'

I slide my hand over hers, pressing her palm into my chest. 'Everything about you is unexpected, little Twist.'

'But you knew you had to kill me?'

'Yeah.'

My heartbeat pounds against her fingers. This is wrong. A Blotter being here, amongst terrorists and rebels. A Blotter talking about the sacred marks on his skin. A Blotter letting a Twist touch him. Everything about this is wrong.

'I don't understand,' she says.

'You're not supposed to.'

She looks unimpressed, and for some weird reason, I don't want her to look at me like that.

I exhale. 'Most times when I deliver an Ending, the person runs. Even though they know their time is up. It's instinct.' I slide her hand over her death warrant. 'That's what this is like. Instinct.'

'But you didn't kill me.'

'No.'

Her eyes meet mine. 'How does it feel?'

'Wrong. But . . .' I touch her cheek, my thumb grazing her lip, not sure how to explain it. Then I drop my hand. *What am I doing?* 'I don't know, little Twist.'

She bites her lip as she studies the markings on my skin. 'How did the Creators know where I was going to be? *I* didn't even know I was going to be there.'

'They're gods. They created the world. And they bound us all to the One True Story. They know everything. They can *do* anything.'

'They cannot kill me.'

I tense. Because they can. I've seen their power. I've felt it. It runs in my veins.

'They can, little Twist.'

'I do not believe it.'

'It's the truth.'

'I do not believe it is all inevitable.'

'It is.'

'No.'

Her chin is sharp as she tilts her head back to meet my gaze. It provokes something hot inside me. Irritation. Anger. Frustration. Why can't she get this into her head?

'Yes,' I say deliberately.

'You didn't kill me,' she says.

'I fucked up.'

She narrows her eyes. 'Is that really what you think?'

We stand like this for a long, uncomfortable moment. Then she shakes her head and bends down to undo the laces of her boots. When she kicks them off, they clang angrily onto the metal floor. She peels off her sodden socks.

'Just . . . take your clothes off,' she says.

Some of the tension in my stomach unknots. It's as if I've finally managed to piss her off. And it's about time. I've been frustrated all fucking night, while she's been taking this all in her stride.

'Fine,' I say. I take off my boots. Then I unbutton my jeans and step out of them. I should probably cover myself up. This is getting dangerous. But I want her to look at me. I want to see what she'll do.

She's trying not to look, but then her eyes hit mine and her cheeks flush. Her gaze drops, and her lips part. She takes a deep breath.

Her hand twitches by her side, and she balls it into a fist as if to stop herself from reaching out. Or maybe she wants to punch me. I'd take either at this point.

I tense, forcing myself to stay where I am.

'Get under the covers.' She's trying to sound commanding, but her voice quivers.

My lip twitches despite the building frustration. She wants me. It's fucking obvious. It's the only reason I do it, the metal floor cold on the soles of my feet as I get inside the grey sleeping bag.

After what she's put me through tonight, I want her frustrated. I want her to feel a fraction of the storm that's been building up inside me since I didn't do what was written. The fact I'm about ready to explode is a small price to pay.

I sit down, stretching out my legs and leaning against the wall. When I turn my attention back to her, she's shed the factory overalls I'm convinced never belonged to her, and she's peeling the black vest over her head.

Something like the instinct that drives me to do what is written hits me, and I have to fight it to stop myself from crossing the room. My jaw clenches. Her pants are cotton and black, and they are all that stand between me and what I really want right now. Does she not realise that?

I'm scrunching the sleeping bag in my fist, and I force myself to look at the floor. There's a black shape on the inside of her left ankle.

'You have a tattoo.' My voice sounds too rough, and I clear my throat.

'Not as many as you.' She grabs a white vest from her rucksack and pulls it on. Grabbing our clothes, she walks to the door of the container and slides it up, letting in grey light, the sound of people talking, and the mist.

I lean forwards. 'Where are you going?'

She looks over her shoulder at me. 'I'm going to hang these up to dry. You'll need them for the performance.'

I frown. 'Performance? What do you—?'

A couple of minutes later, she hurries back inside. She's shivering as she pulls the door back down.

'Elle, what the fuck do you mean, *performance?*'

'We're at a Circus,' she says as though that explains it. She grabs the other sleeping bag, bringing with her the scent of outside and sweat and that weird note of honey. There's not even a hint of fear coming off her. I can't remember a time when someone hasn't smelled like fear when they were around me.

I want to touch her. I want to grab her legs and hold her in front of me. I want to look at her forbidden tattoo and see what the curious girl would have inked on her own skin.

But I also want to know what the fuck she's talking about. That's why I don't do it. It's nothing to do with the fact she's shivering. It's nothing to do with the fact I don't want to make her smell like fear. I'm a Blotter. Blotters don't care.

I force my hands to my sides as she climbs inside the sleeping bag and pulls it up to her waist before sitting against the wall beside me.

I turn my head to her, rubbing the back of my neck. 'You going to tell me what the fuck that means? What is this place?'

A half-smile plays on her lips. 'Do you want to hear a story?' she says.

Chapter Twelve
Elle

Jay's eyes bore into mine, and again, my attention flickers to the black smudge in his left iris. It is beautiful. An imperfection. A flaw. Just like me, and the Twists, and the Darlings. Why would the Creators create something imperfect? It gives me hope. Because perhaps they didn't mean to do it.

There are cracks in everything.

He swallows, his brow furrowing. 'A story?'

He is a Blotter. Blotters do not tell stories. They do not listen to stories. There is only one story that they know, and it belongs to the Creators. It is the story told by the Tellers in the Houses of Truth. The story written on their skin. The story they are duty-bound to enforce.

His shoulder is almost touching mine, and he's like a furnace. His heat washes over me, comforting somehow in the chilled air. It's because I'm cold that I want to get closer. That is the only explanation. My gaze drops to the V of his hips where he's pulled the sleeping bag, barely concealing himself.

When I meet his eyes again, there's a trace of amusement alongside his blatant conflict at my question. It's as if he knows what I'm thinking about doing. I wonder what would happen if I slipped my hand into his covers. I wonder if he would make a sound when I touched him. I wonder if he would stop me.

I shouldn't be thinking about things like that. I need to remember what he is. Someone like him killed my father. He is my enemy.

He rubs his mouth, then he inclines his head slightly. 'Go on then. Tell me a story, little Twist.'

My heart beats fast, and I will it to slow down as I lean against the wall. I don't usually feel this way about men. I don't usually think about touching them. I don't usually wonder what sounds they would make if I made them fall apart. My story has never been one about love or lust or longing.

My story is one of vengeance.

I cannot get distracted. Especially not by him.

'Once, there was a man,' I say, *'and the man had a secret.*

'He lived in the Final City. And he was a powerful man, as men in the Final City are. Before the stories of him disappeared completely, some said he was a cruel man. Maybe the secret changed him. Or maybe he was never cruel to begin with. Maybe that was just a story.

'But he thought things could be different than what they are. And he knew that when his secret was discovered, danger would follow.

'And so he began to plant a story.

'He spread it to the helpless: the Darlings, the Twists, the Secondaries who seemed doomed. He spoke of a place at the very Edge of the World, hidden by mist, barren of food, but so far from the Creators' perfect city that they would not look for them there. He told them the Darlings had formed a settlement.

'And some believed his story. Some travelled to find it.

'The first people to travel to the Edge of the World did not all make it. Some were killed, some died of starvation, or wounds, or infection. And when those who did not die got there, they were disappointed.

'For there was no settlement.'

'So, he lied?' The Blotter rubs the back of his neck. 'Great story, little Twist.'

'Not a lie. A story. And stories are true when we believe them.'

'Right.'

I arch an eyebrow. 'Do you want to hear the rest of the story or not?'

He sighs. 'Fine.'

'There was no settlement when the first travellers arrived,' I continue. 'But there was mist. And it was untouched by the Creators. And so unwavering was their belief there would be something here for them that there became something here. They built it for themselves. The next part of the story starts with a girl,' I say. 'She lived in the Final City. And she was in danger.

'And so she was smuggled out of the city. She was taken by a group of Secondaries who had just had their Final City citizenship revoked. They needed to flee from the Blotters before they were killed. And they had heard a story—a story about a settlement of Darlings at the Edge of the World.

'They didn't want to take her with them. She had a connection to something they feared. But that connection created an easier passage through the Drafts. And so they took her along.

'The journey was bleak, and at times, they felt they would never make it to the end of the world. To help ease the suffering and to stop their descent into certain hopelessness, the girl told stories on the way—because that is what someone had once done for her. She knew, you see, that words could be powerful. Why else would stories have been forbidden?

'She told stories of hope, and change. Of dragons, and hurricanes. Of ink, and parchment. And of a group of people who would one day rise to fight against the darkness; a group of people who would bring back the light.

'They were not used to stories. And the stories started to grow within them, like seeds, and from them flowered hope. They saw the power of words, and they saw why they had been forbidden by the Creators. For a story in the wrong hands is a dangerous thing indeed.

'Before long, they started to believe. They started to believe things could be different.

'When they reached the end of the world, the settlers did not want the stories to stop. They wanted to learn how to tell them themselves. They wanted to be the wind that spread the dandelion seeds so they could grow in the cracks between the pavements.

'And so, while they fought and scavenged and built on their settlement, the girl created a place where they could tell their stories.

'The girl created the Circus.'

Jay's brow furrows. He looks uncertain. When I put my hand down on the floor, my little finger almost brushes against his, and he looks at it for a moment.

'Is that true?' says Jay.

'It's a story.'

'Yeah. But is it true?'

I smile. 'There's one last part to the story. And it's the most important part. The girl and the Darlings told many stories in their Circus. And they started to notice little dandelion seeds floating through the tent. Soon, those seeds joined together in a big swirling mass of light. Every night, as they told their stories, it got bigger, stronger, more powerful. It fed off their stories, you see. And after a while, they realised what they had done.

'They had grown their own story. A story that could rival the One True Story. A story that could change the world.'

Jay's breathing is audible, and his shoulders are stiff. He shakes his head, unable to look at me. 'You shouldn't be saying things like that.'

'Why not?'

'You know why.'

'I'm not afraid of the Creators.'

'You should be.'

He sucks his bottom lip and then looks at me. 'The girl . . . the girl in the story . . . Is she you?'

'It's a story.'

'You said stories are true when we believe them.'

'What do you believe, Jay?'

The rise and fall of his chest deepen, and his breath tickles my face. Something passes between us, unspoken words, untold stories, and something deep and old and somehow familiar. He touches my face, just for a moment, as if he feels it too, before he frowns and rubs the back of his head.

'Fuck. I don't know. What you're saying is impossible.' He stares at the wall for a few minutes. 'Wait a minute . . . what did you mean earlier when you were talking about a performance?'

'Everyone here is part of the Circus,' I say carefully. 'To join their community, they need to know you can be trusted. They need to know you believe in what they believe—that you can help them with what they're trying to achieve.'

'What do you mean, Elle?' he says, his voice dangerously quiet.

I think he knows exactly what I mean. That familiarity, that pull in his eyes disappears and is replaced by something wild and dangerous. A muscle twitches in his jaw, and he looks as if he is ready to murder someone. Maybe me. But I don't put distance between us, even though that is the sensible thing to do. Because I created the hurricane. And a part of me—the frustrated part of me that hates what he is, that hates what he's done—still wants to provoke him. Still wants to see what he will do.

'They initiate all the Darlings in the Circus tent,' I say. 'Jay . . . they want you to tell them a story.'

Chapter Thirteen
Jay

'No.' I turn away from the Twist and rub my face. The air around me is too heavy. I can't breathe properly. What the fuck am I doing here?

'I know it seems—'

'I'm not fucking doing it.' There's pressure on my chest, and my throat constricts. The ink in my veins burns—it's been burning since I didn't do what I was supposed to do. None of this is right. I can't do this. I can't fucking do this. 'I need to go.'

She grabs my wrist before I can stand. 'Jay—'

'*What?*'

'You can't go.'

'Course I can.'

She nods at the covers, and the corner of her lip quirks. 'Not without your clothes.'

'Do you think I give a shit?'

'You should. If anyone is watching our shipping container, which I presume they are, they'll see in an instant that you're a Blotter. And that won't end well for either of us.'

I pull away, and her hand falls to her lap. *'Why are you trying to piss me off so much?'*

'Because—' She bites her lip and looks away, sighing. 'Because I don't want you to leave. Because I think you're important.'

'I'm not important. Get that out of your head right now.'

'Yes. You are.' She turns back to me. 'Because you're different. And different is good.'

I hate that fucking look in her eyes. Like she thinks I'm more than what I am. Like she thinks I can help her.

'Do you know how many people I've killed, little Twist? Do you?' My voice comes out cold.

She grits her teeth. 'I can guess.'

'Doubtful. Do you want me to tell you? Do you want me to give you a number?' I lean closer, and she stiffens. 'Do you want me to tell you how I did it? How I took their lives? How I spilt their blood?'

'Stop it.'

'Do you want to know how they sounded when they died? How they screamed? How they begged for mercy?' Pain flickers across her face. *Good.* I lower my voice. *'Do you want to know how young some of them were? Do you want to know how defenceless?'*

Her chest rises and falls quickly as if she's trying to keep something inside. Her cheeks flush with anger.

'Do you want to know how little I felt when I did it?'

She turns away from me, her jaw set. 'I know what you're trying to do.'

'Yeah? And what's that?'

'I know what you are. I know what you've done,' she says, ice in her tone. 'I know that you stand for everything I hate.'

'Do you?' I grab her chin and force her to look at me. She grips my wrist, and I catch the glimmer of panic crossing her face. Is she finally understanding? 'You don't know the half of it.'

'Get your hands off me.'

My lips twist into a smile. And I'm done. Whatever weird thing has been going on tonight, I'm done with it. If anyone stops me outside, I'll kill them. Because that's what I am. A killer.

I release her. 'We're finished, little Twist.'

'I'm not.'

I laugh. It's a horrible, cold sound that should make her recoil. She doesn't. She should be afraid. She isn't. She's agitated though. Breathing fast. Conflicted, I think. Because she may not fear me like she should, but she knows I'm her enemy. She knows I'm a killer.

'I know what you are. I know what you've done. I know that you stand for everything I hate.' She swallows hard. 'But I know you didn't kill me when it was written.'

'That means nothing.'

'I know you carried me, unconscious, to your home instead of leaving me to die.' Her voice is louder. 'I know you killed five Blotters when it would have been easier to hand me to them. I know you followed me to the Edge of the World, through the mist, even though you thought it would make you disappear. I know you're afraid. I know you're trying to make me hate you because you think that makes it easier. I know I *should* hate you.' She bites her lip as she glances at the dandelion seed on my chest. 'But I'm not going to let myself hate you. Because you're different.'

'I'm not different.'

And that fucking curious, wondrous look is in her eyes again. I glance away, palms still flat on the ground beside me. Air escapes through my teeth.

'You're important, Jay. I don't know why, but you are.'

'I can't stay.'

'You can.'

'You don't get it, little Twist,' I say. 'I'm a Blotter. I can't make up stories.'

Tentatively, she reaches for my thigh, and my skin hums at her touch. It pisses me off. She shouldn't be having this effect on me. It's weak, and weird, and full of sin.

'You don't need to make up a story,' she says. 'You *are* the story.'

'What are you talking about?'

Her inability to turn the fuck away from me like she should makes my skin itch. Frustration rises inside. I want to grab her, sink my fingers into her flesh. I want to rip off her top and put my hands on her. I want her to moan with pleasure as I push her onto the floor and hold her body down with mine. I want to feel her heat around me.

I want a release—no, I fucking *need* it. A release from the rage, and the conflict, and the irritation. She knows what I'm thinking. I can see it in the raw curiosity of her gaze, and the way her chest is lightly flushed. Yet still, she doesn't turn away from me.

'What do you want from me, little Twist?' I lower my tone. 'Do you want to fuck me? Is that what this is all about?'

Her eyes widen, and a sudden vulnerability flashes across her expression. It lasts half a second. But it fills me with relief and terror in equal measure. Because for the first time since I met her—for the first time since I've been drowning in all this shit—it occurs to me she was supposed to die tonight, and I am a killer, and maybe she's feeling out of her depth too.

'I want you to stay,' she says.

We stare at each other. Then I exhale, and my whole body deflates. I lie on my back, crossing my arms behind my head. She sighs, her shoulders relaxing. Out of the corner of my eye, I catch the half-smile toying on her lips.

'Don't make a big fucking thing out of it,' I say. 'I still might leave once our clothes are dry.'

She lies down beside me, and for a moment, I think she's going to touch me. I want her to. I don't want her to at the same time. I don't know what I want. Not since I messed everything up so badly. Nothing makes sense anymore.

'I don't think you'll leave,' she says.

I close my eyes and try to slow down my racing pulse. 'Shut it.'

I don't tell her what I'm thinking. Because the thought terrifies me.

I betrayed the Creators. I saved her life. I followed her to the Edge of the World.

I don't think I'll leave either.

I think I'm going to see this through to the end.

Chapter Fourteen
Elle

Do Blotters dream?

I lay on my side watching him.

His heat washes over me along with the masculine scent of dried sweat and rain. His breathing is steady, and his bare chest moves softly up and down.

I should sleep too. I need to rest. But I don't think I can. So instead, I prop myself up on my elbow and study him.

He is tense even in sleep. His lightly stubbled jaw is set in a hard line, and every now and then, his arms tighten behind his head. Is that a dream stirring him, or just a reflex? I can't imagine the Creators would allow one of their creatures to dream. Dreams are stories that cannot be controlled. Dreams belong only to the dreamer.

If he could dream, what would he dream about? Death and darkness? The murders he has committed? Perhaps robbing him of his dreams is a mercy.

My eyes trace the black patterns that brand his hips, his chest, the undersides of his arms. Some are thick black lines joining together like a roadmap across his body. Others are small and disjointed—a flame curling around his belly button, a dot on his neck, a ring around his arm.

A dandelion seed.

I shift closer, twisting my body over his. His arm twitches, and I still, holding my breath until he softens once more. Why would he have this tattoo? Why would we both have this tattoo? It doesn't make sense.

My father always said stories grow like dandelions in the cracks in the pavement. This seed is a symbol of hope and change. It is defiance of the Creators. And yet, alongside the deadly path they have written for him, there it is.

I reach for it.

Jay grabs my wrist. 'What are you doing, little Twist?'

'I want to touch it,' I say as he opens his eyes.

His lip twitches. 'Touch what?'

'The dandelion seed.'

His forehead creases. 'Why?'

'It reminds me of something someone used to say to me.'

He looks at me studiously. Then he moves his arm back behind his head, leaving my hand hovering above his chest. My heartbeat quickens. I'm not sure if it's an invitation or if he's just playing with me. He killed five trained Blotters with ease earlier, he grabbed my hand even though I was sure he was sleeping. His reflexes are fast.

Tentatively, I touch the dandelion seed. When he makes no move to stop me, I trace it with my fingertip. His breathing deepens.

'How do they do it?' I ask. 'How do they map out your life?'

'I don't know, little Twist. I'm a Blotter. I don't know the mechanics, do I?'

I slide my fingers down to the circle with the twisted line above his heart—the tattoo that told him that I must die. His pulse thuds beneath it.

'Were you born this way? With the tattoos? With ink in your veins?'

He sucks his bottom lip. 'No.'

'How did it happen?'

His expression darkens. 'There's a Ceremony.'

'What happens?'

He shakes his head.

'Does it hurt?'

He swallows. 'It's an honour.'

'But does it hurt?'

He averts his eyes from mine, body tensing. 'Yeah.'

I have always seen Blotters as mindless monsters. Puppets of the Creators. It never occurred to me the Creators hurt them too.

Cautiously, I move my fingers down one of the black lines. His breathing quickens as I trace it over the hard ridges of his torso. Then I slide my palm back up to the dandelion seed.

'You said it reminded you of something someone said,' he says. 'The seed.'

His eyes are heavy-lidded when I meet them. 'My father.'

'Why?'

'He said stories grow like dandelions.'

'So, crazy runs in the family then?'

My lip quirks. 'I guess.'

'Is he . . .?'

'Dead?'

Jay inclines his head, and I sigh. 'Yes.'

'What happened?'

'Blotters.'

He chews his bottom lip, his face darkening. 'Oh.'

The air seems to get heavy around us. It's filled with things that do not need to be said. We are supposed to be enemies. He stands for everything I hate. I was supposed to die at his hands.

Someone like him killed my father.

'Everything happens for a reason,' he says finally—as if he expects me to find some comfort in that.

My insides turn to ice. 'Everything happens for the *Creators'* reason.'

'I just mean . . .' He shakes his head. 'The Creators may seem cruel at times. But they have their reasons, and the reasons are for the good of everyone. For the good of the One True Story. That's just the way it is.'

I frown. Why can't he see? 'Just because something is the way it is doesn't mean it's right.'

'You're being naïve.'

I'm naïve?'

'Yeah.'

I flatten my hand on his chest and I'm overcome with an insatiable urge to hurt him. To dig my fingernails into his flesh, to bite him, to make him bleed. Before I even realise I've moved, my hand is lingering at the base of his neck.

'What? You're going to choke me now, little Twist? You're going to choke me because I don't agree with you?'

My fingers twitch. He doesn't move. He doesn't flinch. He just lies there, looking up at me with cool blue eyes.

I know I couldn't. He is too strong.

And somewhere deep within me, I know I wouldn't choke him even if I could. I told him I wouldn't let myself hate him. It isn't his fault he thinks this way. Yet still, frustration buzzes beneath my skin like an angry swarm of bees, and I want it out of me. I want a release.

So I tighten my fingers.

Before I can even process what is happening, he flips me onto my back. His body moves on top of mine, holding me in place. His covers shift, and I'm suddenly very aware that he is naked, his strong, bare legs pinning mine down through my sleeping bag.

His face is inches from mine. One of his hands is flat on the floor beside my head, the other curled gently around my neck.

'I'm not naïve,' I say.

I feel his breath on my face. 'You *are* naïve, little Twist. Or you would be afraid of me. But you're not, are you?'

My heart beats hard against my ribs, betraying me. I will it to slow. I will myself to calm down.

'You know what I am. You know I'm a killer. And yet you're naïve enough to think you're safe around me. You're naïve enough to think you can fix me.'

'I don't think I can fix you.'

'No? Well, there's only one other reason you're keeping me around then. Do you want to know what I reckon, little Twist?' The hard weight of his body shifts on top of me. 'I reckon you're keeping me around because you want to fuck me. You want to know what it would be like to be with a Blotter. You know it would be different to anything you've experienced before. And once that curiosity has been satisfied—and believe me, you would be satisfied—you'll be less bothered about keeping me around. And then you can do whatever crazy shit you have planned, and I can be left the fuck alone. So I'm going to make it easy for you. Ask me. Ask me to fuck you. And I'll do it, right here, right now. You get what you want, I get what I want, and this whole ridiculous night can be brought to an end.' His rough thumb trails down my neck. 'Ask me, little Twist. You just have to ask.'

My breath catches in my throat. No one has ever spoken to me like that before. My insides clench. I can feel my pulse throbbing through my core.

And I hate it. I hate this feeling that makes no sense to me. I hate that my body is responding to his touch, his rough words, his hardness pressing against my thigh, when I'm so angry with him. I hate that I want to sink my teeth into his bottom lip, and tighten my legs around his waist, and feel him hard inside me.

That animal look is in his eyes again—only this time, it's focused solely on me. As if he wants to devour me.

'The little Twist speechless?' he says softly. 'I never thought it was possible.'

I hate that I want him. I hate that I want him to ease this ache growing inside of me.

But I refuse to say it. I refuse to let him know. Because he's wrong about me. That is not all I want him for. As much as he wants me to prove to him that's all he's worth, as much as I want to succumb to his offer, I won't.

And not just because he is a Blotter.

Our stories are linked now. I won't let it end here.

I shake my head, my breathing fast.

He stares at me for a moment longer. Then he exhales and rolls off me.

I turn my back on him. My heart hammers against my chest, and I'm hot. I don't want him to know. I don't want him to see.

I am not vulnerable. I am not afraid. I do not want him.

Stories are true when we believe them.

Gradually, my pulse steadies.

'I don't think I can fix you,' I say quietly after a while, unsure if he's even still awake but feeling it needs to be said.

'No shit.' He sounds frustrated.

'I don't think I can fix you,' I say, 'because I don't think you're broken.'

He lets out a bitter laugh. 'No?'

'No,' I say. 'I think the world is broken.'

'And you're going to fix it?'

'Yes.'

He laughs again, but this time, the bitterness is gone.

'Crazy little Twist,' he says quietly. 'You know, my offer still stands. If you decide you can't wait, feel free to wake me up. I'm happy to oblige.' His voice roughens. 'But otherwise, go the fuck to sleep and don't disturb me again.'

I look over my shoulder and catch the ghost of a smile on his lips, though his eyes are now closed. Soon, the sound of his steady breathing fills the shipping container again. And again, I wonder if he's dreaming.

I lie like this for a long time, listening to the sounds of the Darlings moving around the settlement outside—laughter and chatter and the roll of barrels of food and drink. My mind buzzes, but I need to get at least a few hours' sleep.

Soon, we'll have to go to the Circus, and I think the Blotter will be difficult. I need to prepare him. I need him to stay calm so I can get the Darlings on my side.

I need them for my plan.

Because the world is broken.

And I'm going to fix it.

Chapter Fifteen
Jay

I slam my hand onto my chest. My body's on fire. *Fuck*. I breathe through my teeth, sucking in the musty air, until the pain subsides. The tattoo still burns, but it's a dull throb now. Manageable.

I sigh, trying to get rid of some of the tension. It doesn't work. I'm sweating, and I feel like shit. There are noises outside: clanging metal, voices, footsteps. It aggravates my headache. Today is going to be a bad fucking day.

I kick off the sleeping bag and sit up, rubbing my face with both hands.

'Go get my clothes, little Twist,' I say loud enough to wake her. 'I need a piss.'

Nothing. I glance over my shoulder. Her covers are in a ball on the floor behind me.

What the fuck? Where is she? Has she left me?

The weight that's been building on my chest since I didn't do what was written gets heavier. None of this is right. I don't belong here. I need to go. Yeah, I'm naked, and they'll see that I'm a Blotter. But if anyone has an issue with that, I'll kill them. That's what I do.

Blotters don't wait around for little Twists. Blotters don't take orders from little Twists. They don't sleep beside them, or think about kissing them, or roll on top of them and offer to fuck them.

Blood pounds through my body as I imagine what I would have done next; how I would have explored every inch of her with my hands, and my tongue. How I would have taken my time with her. How I would have made her writhe beneath me. I would have made her beg for it.

I want to agitate her. I want to frustrate her as much as she's frustrating me.

I want to make her cry out with pleasure.

And now I'm sinning again by imagining things. Heat floods my body, and I don't know if it's shame or if I'm turned on.

All I know is that I'm still here, waiting for her instead of leaving. All my life, I've done what the ink has told me; now it seems as if my cock is calling the shots.

You fucking moron, Jay.

Footsteps approach, and the door slides up. Elle ducks under, turning to pull it back down again. She's dressed now, in jeans and a battered leather jacket that's too big for her. Her hair has dried weird, and it's all tangled and wild down her back.

Something stills inside of me at the sight of her. She didn't leave.

'Where the fuck have you been?' I ask.

She's got my clothes under her arm and is carrying a metal flask, so the answer to my question is pretty fucking obvious. And the look she gives me shows she thinks I'm an idiot. What was I expecting? That if I gave her a hard time, she'd climb on top of me and take me up on my offer?

'Jay. You're up.' Her gaze drops.

'Hey, my eyes are up here, little Twist.'

'I . . . uh . . . coffee.' Her cheeks are pink, and there's a ghost of a smile on her lips. 'I got us coffee. And food. I thought you might be hungry.'

'And you didn't think about telling me?'

'I thought about it. But then I remembered I wasn't supposed to disturb you unless I wanted you to fuck me, so . . .'

I bring my forearms back to my knees and raise an eyebrow. 'Funny. You going to give me my clothes or what?'

She smells like rain and leather when she walks over. And honey. A memory surprises me, flashing unbidden behind my eyes. I never think about the past. It is written, unchangeable, just like the future. But I see myself as a boy, sneaking into the larder in the Citadel Barracks and sticking my finger into that pot of honey—so rare and expensive, even within the Final City.

I shouldn't have eaten the honey. I shouldn't be thinking about tasting her.

I take the clothes, and our fingers brush. Then I get up. She's no longer smiling. I think she's going to touch me, but then she turns to her rucksack. I pull on my clothes.

The Twist takes a weirdly long time to wrap a lathered bar of soap into a rag before putting it into her rucksack. I feel awkward again, like I did when we arrived here. I don't know what to do, what to say. Does she feel like that too? Doubtful. I'm guessing the little Twist always knows what to say. And yet the air in here feels charged and heavy.

'You seem tense,' she says finally.

'I *am* tense.'

'It's going to be okay, you know?' She meets my eye.

'I'm not telling a story.'

'I told you, you don't need to worry,' she says. 'You *are* the story.'

I shake my head. 'I'm going for a piss.'

I head over to the door and slide it up. It bangs against the roof, and a couple of nearby Darlings carrying a metal keg turn their heads. I narrow my eyes at them, and they hurry towards the red-and-black tent in the centre of the camp.

'Jay?'

'What?'

'Be discreet, will you?' The corner of her lip quirks. 'I know how you like to expose yourself, but no one wants to watch you weeing. There are kids out there.'

I grab the roof, stretching. 'Hey, you were the one who told me to take my clothes off, little Twist.'

She laughs as I step into the mist and veer away from the big tent. It's early evening, but the air still carries the same drab grey light as it did when we arrived. Red-and-white lights blink around the trailers at the same irritating speed as a group of kids who are chasing each other through the pathways between them. They're laughing like there's nothing to worry about, nothing to fear.

I shake my head.

After I've finished pissing against the back of the shipping container, the Twist comes to join me outside, carrying the flask.

'We have a couple of hours to spare,' she says. 'Do you want to see the Circus? I can show you the story we've been growing.'

'No. Absolutely not.'

'Edge of the World it is then.'

'No. I don't want to go there either.'

'Well, where *do* you want to go then?'

I fold my arms. There's a girl nearby sharpening knives in the doorway of a trailer. Ahead, a couple of Darlings come into view, pulling a cart filled with firearms through the misty pathway to the tents. A group of kids scamper around making a nuisance of themselves, and a teenager paints on the side of a shipping container.

I want to get away from all *this*.

Elle touches my arm. 'Come on.'

I rub the back of my neck. Then I follow her away from the camp, pulling my hood over my head and stuffing my hands into my pockets. The mist that's moving past our ankles speeds up as we get farther away from the Circus.

Ten minutes later, I halt, overcome with the same sense of vertigo I get when I'm on the top floors of the tallest skyscrapers. Just ahead, the mist cascades off the edge of something, like a waterfall.

'*What the fuck . . . ?*'

'This is the Edge,' she says as she moves cautiously forwards.

'I don't think that's a good idea, little Twist.'

She doesn't listen to me.

'Elle.' I snatch her wrist. '*What are you doing? Don't stick your hand into that.*' I shake my head. 'Fuck's sake. You're like a child!'

'What? It's fine. Look.'

Before I can stop her, she plunges her other hand into the nothingness. As she does, her eyes widen and her lips part. I wrench her back, pulling her into my body.

She tilts her head to grin up at me. 'Just kidding.'

She wiggles her fingers, and the mist curls around them. I have an urge to shove her over the edge. But although that would solve a lot of my problems, I drop my arms to my sides.

'Great to see you're in such a good fucking mood this evening.'

She smiles as she sits down and dangles her feet over the edge like an actual maniac. 'I am in a good mood. I've missed this place.'

She pats the ground beside her, and even though I think this is a bad idea and I kind of want to vomit, I sit down.

She untwists the cup off the top of her flask and pours black liquid into it. She passes it to me. It's weak and watery, but it still has that smoky bitter coffee taste.

'I've not had coffee since I was in the Final City,' I say without thinking.

'Sylvia—she's kind of the leader here—says she can't function without it. She gets it from one of the black markets.' She takes a sip directly from the flask. 'It's not as good as the stuff they drink in the Final City, but it's something.' I feel her eyes boring into the side of my head. 'The One True Story says the best Blotters are stationed there.'

'Yeah.'

'So, you are one of the *best?*' She says it in a careful way, as if it's occurring to her that being one of the best Blotters might not be a good thing.

I exhale. 'You know what I am, little Twist.'

She bites her bottom lip. 'If the best Blotters are in the Final City, it stands to reason that the worst would be stationed in Draft One. How did you end up here?'

'How am I supposed to know? It was written that I'd come here. So I came.' I stare into the nothingness.

Elle lets the silence hang between us as if she's expecting me to fill it. And for some weird reason, I want to live up to her expectations. Even though I don't like talking about this stuff.

'I always thought . . . I thought I was being punished. Or tested. Or something. But now . . .'

'What?'

'I think I'm here for you. To kill you.'

She nods. 'I should be flattered they sent one of their best, I suppose.'

'You should be afraid.'

'Are you?'

'Blotters aren't scared of anything.'

'Except for telling stories.'

I give her a hard look. 'Except for defying the gods.'

'The Creators aren't gods. They're just men.'

'No, they're not,' I say. 'They created the world we live in. They created the land and the seas. They erected the first skyscrapers from the dirt and put the coal in the mines to give us the light. They create the weather that feeds the crops in the farmlands and give us earthquakes to rid us of evil. They created *us* and set us on our path to stop us from falling to temptation like the First Twist. They're *gods*. Do you have any idea—?' I shake my head. 'Are you trying to piss me off again?'

'No.' Her gaze is steady when it meets mine. 'But they're not the only ones who can create.'

She shouldn't be saying things like this. 'Why do you have the Book of Truth in your bedsit if you have such blasphemous thoughts?'

She shrugs. 'I'm looking for something.'

'What?'

'A story. And they're not blasphemous thoughts. They're true. You saw the hurricane.'

'Hmm.'

'I think you're scared. But you're safe with me.'

I laugh, and it eases the tension. The funniest thing is, she actually believes what she's saying. I lean back on my hands, shaking my head.

'Crazy, little Twist.'

A smile tickles her lips. 'You'll see soon enough.'

Chapter Sixteen
Elle

We share some stale bread and sit in silence for a while with our legs dangling over the Edge of the World.

Raven was right before: the Edge is closer to the settlement than it was when I left. I wonder what that means. Are the Creators planning to get rid of the Outer Drafts in one big Cut, letting us fall away into oblivion? Or are the whispers true? Is the Ending of the One True Story upon us?

I have read many versions of the Creators' story, and all say that what begins must someday end. But if the world ends, what happens to the Creators? Why would they allow the Ending to happen? Is there a purpose to it, or is it a flaw in their design?

I choose to believe they are flawed and their story is not as stable as they think. Like my father used to say, there are cracks in everything, and that is where the dandelions grow. Jay is tense beside me, his expression dark. I wish I could make him see that he is in the right place, that there is hope.

'Do you want to talk about it?' I ask.

He shakes his head.

'Do you want to hear a story?'

He drags his teeth over his bottom lip. 'Okay.'

I stare into the billowing mist ahead.

'Once, there was a man,' I say. 'He was a clockmaker, and he was so in tune with the mechanics of time that he made himself immortal. He had lived on this earth for a thousand years or more, and he believed he had gained much wisdom—because how could a man live for so long and not absorb the wisdom of time?

'But there was a price to his immortality that he had not realised. As he aged, the world became more and more grey, until finally, it was drained of colour altogether . . .'

Jay shifts beside me, leaning back on his palms.

'So gradual was the transformation that soon, all had forgotten there had once been colour at all.

'Until one fateful night, during a wild and deadly hurricane, the boundaries of time were temporarily shifted, and the man met a woman who lived half a clock-tick behind the world he knew. He glimpsed a darker place than he ever imagined could exist, but within it, he saw beauty too. And for a moment, he was sure he saw a flash of colour within the depths of her eyes.

'He pleaded with her to come with him. He pleaded with her to obey the rules of time—to live within the realms of clockwork like him and everyone else he knew.

'But either she could not or she would not. And instead of following him, she left him a gift.

'It was a seed.'

Jay glances at me, and I think I catch an eye-roll. He seems too big and monstrous to roll his eyes like a teenager, and it makes me smile.

'He cast it aside in anger and forgot all about it,' I continue.

'Until one day, he looked out of his window and saw a dandelion, bright yellow amongst the slates of grey. He had not seen colour in a thousand years or more, and so filled with joy was he that he wanted to show the world what they had forgotten.

'But it was just one dandelion. And soon, it withered, taking the one burst of colour away. When he told people of it, no one believed him. Despite his years of wisdom, his words did not fit with what they knew, and they feared this. So they punished him.

'On the day that the clockmaker died, something peculiar happened to the withered dandelion. It became a different kind of clock, a dandelion clock, sprouting seeds that were carried in the wind. And though he was gone and the world was still grey, the seeds began to spread. Soon after, dandelions started to grow—bursts of colour in the cracks between the pavement.

'Every now and again, someone would stumble upon one, and those who saw them began to remember what they had forgotten. They began to wonder about a world filled with colour. And as they wondered, the seeds continued to spread, until one day, the cities were filled with them—great fields of vivid yellow that swayed amongst the skyscrapers.

'And though the clockmaker and the woman who lived half a clock-tick behind were gone, their legacy lived on. The world was no longer grey.'

I smile. 'All because of that one small seed and the dandelions that grew in the cracks in the pavement.'

Jay shakes his head, but there's a softness behind his eyes. 'You really like your dandelions, don't you?'

'I suppose I do.'

He runs a hand over his mouth. 'When we were in the black market, you said you'd been planting some seeds. Dandelion seeds?'

'Yes.'

'You make my head hurt.'

I laugh. 'You'll see. It'll help when we go to the Circus.'

His thigh hardens against mine, and the softness disappears from his face. 'I told you, I'm not doing that.'

'It's not as bad as you think.'

'I can't tell stories, little Twist.'

'You can.'

'You still don't get it,' he says. 'I can't make shit up like you. I can't talk about dandelions and clockmakers and Circuses at the Edge of the World. It's not who I am. I kill, I track, I destroy—that is my purpose. I strengthen the One True Story. I don't tell my own.'

I take his cup and pour him another coffee. 'Okay.'

It's cold now. We've been here a while, and we need to get to the Circus soon. If he doesn't tell a story, he'll be kicked out of camp. But he's important to our cause—I feel it with every part of my being—and that's why I don't want him to go. It has nothing to do with his chiselled jawline and big muscles and the ludicrous offer he made me last night.

He takes a sip, the cup dainty in his hand.

'You said you hadn't had coffee since you were in the Final City,' I say.

'Yeah. So?'

'Where were you when you drank it?'

'What does it matter?'

'I'm just curious.'

He exhales. 'In the Citadel Barracks.'

'Did you drink it alone?'

'No.'

'Well? Who were you with?'

His expression darkens. 'One of the cooks.'

'So, the last time you were in the Final City, you drank coffee with one of the cooks from the barracks,' I say. 'There. A story.'

He turns his head slowly and gives me a withering look. 'That's not a story. It's something that happened. It's true.'

'The best stories have a seed of truth at their core. The Creators have been burning books for hundreds of years, and yet still, we hear whispered stories of witches who used words to cast dark magic and threaten the gods.'

'Witches don't exist.'

'Maybe. Maybe not. But the truth at the heart of those stories isn't the fact witches existed. It's the idea that there were people who fought against the Creators. It's the idea that people *want* to fight them still.' I sigh. 'You don't have to make anything up, Jay. You don't have to be something you're not. Stories aren't about making stuff up—not deep down anyway. They're about telling your truth.' He turns away, but I reach for his cheek, pulling his face back towards me. 'For all this time, you've been a part of someone else's story, but that doesn't mean you don't have your own. Your story belongs to you, Jay.'

'You don't get it—'

'When you get on that stage, just tell them who you are,' I say. 'Tell them something about yourself. Tell them *your* story.'

'I'm a Blotter, little Twist.'

'Yes,' I say. 'You're a Blotter. And you're here, at the Circus at the Edge of the World. It's an excellent story.'

'What? So I'm supposed to go up there and say, "Hi, everyone, I'm Jay, I'm a Blotter. I've probably killed some of your friends and family. It's nice to meet you."'

'Well, I probably wouldn't open with that,' I say. 'But that's the general idea.'

He rubs his face and groans. 'This is so fucked up.'

'If you don't do it, we'll have to leave, and that will be worse. Come on.' I get up. 'We should go.'

'These Darlings have a lot of guns. You realise they're going to shoot me if they find out I'm a Blotter, right?'

'It's a risk we have to take.'

He laughs, and it warms something inside of me. I have only seen him laugh a few times, but I like it. It lightens his whole face. There's something innocent and boyish about it, and it makes me wonder what he would be like if he hadn't gone through that ceremony that turned his blood into ink. It makes me wonder what he would be like if he hadn't been forced to be a monster.

'Yeah, *you're* taking a real fucking risk, little Twist,' he says.

I smile. 'They won't hurt you. I won't let them.'

'Great. I've got myself the world's smallest, most annoying bodyguard.' Slowly, he pulls his legs from the Edge of the World and comes to stand beside me. His amusement dies. 'But it's them you should be worried about. If anyone tries anything with me, I'll kill them. Understand?'

I ignore the lick of doubt in my stomach. 'No one is going to get hurt.'

He shakes his head and mutters, *'Naïve,'* under his breath as we walk away from the Edge and head back through the graffitied makeshift homes. He tenses as we get closer to the red-and-black tent in the centre of camp, his lips hardening. *'This is so fucked up.'*

'It'll be okay.'

I duck through the entrance into a backstage area, breathing in the familiar scent of memories and wet paint. Jay's eyes dart around the small space when he follows me inside, taking in the racks of old clothes, the open paint tins, the candle flickering on the table, and the flap that leads into the auditorium.

We're not in there long before Lucy—a teenager from Draft Three with straight dirty blonde hair and a long oval face—comes in. 'Elle! I'm so glad you're back. Sylvia was worried you weren't going to show. Are you—?' Her eyes widen as they take in the sheer size of Jay and the scowl on his face. She shuffles from one foot to another, fiddling with the pockets of her beige trousers. 'Well, we're . . . er . . . ready for you in there whenever you are.'

Jay stares at the rippling red-and-black material as she disappears into the auditorium. There's a vein throbbing in his neck.

'I could leave,' he says.

'You could stay.'

We look at one another. Then he breathes out sharply through his nose.

'If anyone gets hurt out there, it's on you, little Twist.'

'No one is getting hurt. You can do this.'

He runs a hand over his mouth, shakes his head, and then strides into the auditorium. I don't know if I'm relieved or worried. Heartbeat thumping in my ears, I peer through the crack and watch as he walks into the bright spotlight.

If he looks up, he may see the source of it, the tangible ball of energy, writhing beneath the roof of the tent. The story I am creating. But he doesn't. He scans the forty or so faces on the tiered benches, his hands plunged into the pockets of his jeans. His shoulders are hunched, and I see his biceps straining against the sleeves of his hoodie.

I take a deep breath, and I hope—not for the first time—that I am right about him.

'Come on, Jay,' I whisper.

He rubs the back of his neck.

Then he opens his mouth.

Chapter Seventeen
Jay

My mouth is dry. I open it. No sound comes out.

Bright light shines in my eyes. Through it, I can just about make out the crowd. I can smell them too. Warm bodies and damp clothes. They're watching. Waiting. And the wait feels like a tangible, heavy thing. It's suffocating.

There's buzzing above my head. What *is* that? It sounds like bees. I look up, and the spotlight burns my eyes.

This isn't going to end well.

I should have just killed the Twist. *This is what you get, Jay. You followed your cock to the end of the world, and now you have to tell a story in a Circus tent to a bunch of terrorists.*

I feel her eyes on me, boring into the back of my head. I glance over my shoulder, and she has that irritating look on her face again. She believes I'm going to actually do this. Am I?

I don't know anymore. I don't know what comes next. I'm at a fork in a road. I don't know what lies in either direction, so how am I supposed to pick?

Someone coughs, bringing my attention back to the benches. I'm sweating. It's too fucking hot. I open my mouth to speak again. And I close it. It's not that the words are stuck; it's that they're not there at all. I can't do this.

I can't tell stories in Circuses. I'm a Blotter. I'm bound by ink to the world and the gods and the One True Story. I serve the Creators. I do what is written. Why can't she see that?

She has no idea how the world really works. She's infuriating. So why do I want so badly to fall on my knees in front of her, to explore every inch of her with my tongue?

And why now, standing here in this ridiculous fucking situation, do I want so badly to live up to that wonder in her eyes?

I can't do it. The moment they find out what I am, shit is going to go down. She's naïve to think otherwise.

An insect lands on the back of my neck, and I swat it. There's shuffling on the benches. I scan the crowd and spot a couple of guns. The closest is in a holster on Raven's belt. She's leaning forwards on her knees, hands dangling between her legs in a show of relaxation. But her eyes are trained on me. She doesn't trust me.

When this all goes to shit, I'm going for her first.

I rub my mouth. I'm actually going to do this, aren't I?

'I'm Jay.'

The crowd stills.

And I can't fucking do it. I can't tell them a story. Of course I can't. This isn't me. But the Twist said I was the story. I know it's a terrible idea, but I slowly unzip my hoodie. Taking a deep breath, I pull it off and drop it to the floor.

I show them my story. And they see it.

They see my tattoos. They see the life that's mapped out in ink on my skin. They see my connection to the Creators—the gods that have forsaken them. And they see what I am. A Blotter. A killer. An enemy.

Movement erupts around me, but I'm across the floor with my arm around Raven's neck before she can raise the gun. I drag her into the spotlight.

'Guns down, or I kill her.'

There's a bang as someone tries to land a shot on me from the benches. I shove the barrel of Raven's gun into her chin, and this time, everyone stills.

'I said, *guns down,*' I say.

'*You arsehole,*' says Raven. '*I knew there was something off about you,* Blotter. *What was Elle*—?'

'*Shut it.*'

This is a fucking mess. I don't know what to do. I'm surrounded. I could take Raven's gun and use her as a shield as they rain the bullets down on me. But I'm just standing here like an idiot, as if I'm waiting for something. As if I'm waiting for her.

The back of my neck prickles, and the scent of leather and honey washes over me.

'Jay, it's okay. Let her go.'

My throat tightens. She was the one who got us into this stupid mess, and she's talking to me as though I'm out of control. I'm not. If I were, half of this Circus would already be dead. And if I let Raven go, I'm going to be the one who gets shot.

'Not a good idea, little Twist.'

She stands in front of me, and there's a silent plea in her eyes. 'Please, Jay. Let her go.'

I exhale. Then I shove Raven forwards.

Immediately, four women jump down from the benches and surround me. Raven raises her gun.

'On your knees, Blotter.'

Elle nods, and I don't get it. I don't understand why she's so calm. Can she not see the situation we're in right now?

'It's okay, Jay,' she says again. And that's when it hits me. She planned this. Of course she did. She brought me here. She twisted the truth with her words. She tricked me, and she led me into a trap because she knew it was the only way she could overpower me.

A CIRCUS OF INK

Everything is faraway. I'm underwater. The Circus blurs around me. My pulse drums in my ears and blocks out whatever shit Raven is saying. I'm hot. I'm cold. Blotters kill because they have to—there's no emotion in it. But right now, rage surges through my body, and it's unfamiliar, but it makes sense.

I meet Elle's eye. She sees the expression on my face.

'Jay, no!'

I lunge at her. There's a bang, and my arm drops to my side. I smell ink and metal and gunpowder. I'm vaguely aware of pain in my shoulder, but the room is still swimming.

I can't believe she did this to me.

Movement catches my eye from the benches and snaps me back. There's a woman with a raised pistol, and I realise my blood is spilling down my arm. Raven kicks me from behind, and I fall onto my knees. She shoves the barrel of her gun into the back of my neck as I start to get up. I still.

'Easy there, sweetheart.' The woman who shot me makes her way down the benches.

She's tall and slender, and she's dressed in a long red tailcoat. Her sleek black hair hangs in a low ponytail beneath a black top hat. She walks with a limp and has a cane in one hand that clicks against the floor with each step.

Her lips curl into a smile that doesn't quite meet her dark eyes.

'I know your kind,' she says. 'I know you think you're not going to die right now because that's not how your Ending was written, was it, honey? But here's the thing: the rules don't apply out here. Do they?'

The Darlings stamp their feet in agreement. This is a fucking nightmare. I can't control my breathing, and it's not because I'm afraid or because I've been shot. It's because of her. Because she surprised me again. Because she betrayed me.

I swear to the Creators, once I've gotten out of this, she's going to pay for it.

'Sylvia,' says the Twist.

'Welcome home, love,' says the woman in the hat. 'You and I need to have a chat once we've dealt with this. Things have changed around here since you left. I can't imagine what you were thinking, bringing a Blotter here.'

She puts her cane beneath my chin, so I have to meet her eyes.

'And I can't imagine why you would have come here, sweetheart. Do you know we lost three members of our family recently? Scarlett, Johnny, and dear little Jade. She was six years old.'

Something changes in the air. A whisper passes through the crowd.

'Sylvia,' says Elle, 'You need to—'

Sylvia raises her hand, and two Darlings grab Elle's arms. Her eyes lock onto mine. She looks as if she's trying to tell me something. Whose side is she on? I have no fucking clue what's going on.

Sylvia traces a tattoo on my shoulder with her cane, and I'm forced to focus on her again. 'I wonder how many you've killed, Blotter.' She pushes the bullet wound, and I hiss through my teeth as more ink spills down my arm.

'Do that again, and there'll be one more,' I say.

'Are there any more of your kind on the way, sweetheart?' asks Sylvia.

I stare at her. If she thinks I'm going to answer her questions right now, she's as insane as the Twist.

'I'll take that as a no.' Sylvia looks at Raven over my shoulder.

'Stop,' says Elle.

I get ready to move.

'*I said stop.*' Elle's voice is quiet, yet somehow it fills the room. Sylvia's expression changes as she looks at Elle properly for the first time. 'Or h*ave you forgotten?*' Her eyes are blazing. '*Have you* *forgotten the story of the heart thief and the woman who chased her to the edge of the earth, only to find her heart belonged with the thief all along?'*

The two women holding Elle's arms glance at each other over her head. Then, tentatively, they release her. Elle steps forwards.

'Or perhaps you have forgotten the couple who lived in darkness until their baby opened her eyes and cast light from her irises more powerful than a thousand suns.'

The woman to my left moves back. A man shifts in the crowd.

'Do you not remember the girl who blew the dandelion clock so her sister could follow the trail of flowers that grew in the pavement?'

The women grabbing my arms glance at Elle, then Sylvia, then they release me.

'Or have you forgotten about the woman who was bound to the world, until she fell in love with a star? How she followed the map in the constellations to a place where the sky met the earth.'

'Fuck's sake,' mutters Raven. She moves the gun from my neck, and I exhale as she steps back.

'Or perhaps you have forgotten the group of travellers on the night of the storm where the winds howled like wolves and lightning forked the sky.' Her voice lowers, and the fabric of the tent begins to flap. *'When mechanical men with compasses for hearts vowed to track them to the ends of the earth.'*

Rain patters against the roof. A crack booms across the sky. And a chill creeps down my spine. Because there's no weather here. This place exists outside the realm of the Creators.

'How they were afraid, because the only way they could be safe would be to stray from the paths they had walked their whole lives.'

A cold wind howls around the tent.

'But they did it anyway. Because they had heard that somewhere off the trodden path was a place where they could be safe.'

Light flashes outside, and Elle turns away from Sylvia to face the crowd.

'And perhaps you have forgotten the girl. The girl with stories that raged through her veins like fire. The girl they smuggled with them to the edge of the earth.' Her voice is raised above the sounds of the storm. *'The girl who created the Circus.'*

Rain pounds against the roof like metal bullets.

'Perhaps you have forgotten who you are, who you were. Perhaps you have forgotten how your stories started. But I have not. You all lived the story that was written for you until that one moment you did not.

'And I have a new story for you.'

Thunder rolls across the sky, and the hairs on the back of my neck stand on end.

'It's about a man with his life mapped out in ink on his skin, who was bound to the Creators, who was supposed to kill a Twist. But instead, he carried her through a wild and deadly hurricane and came with her to the Circus at the Edge of the World.'

She points at me. *'This is not our way. This is not our story. We are here because we are different from them. And different is good. '*

Her chest rises and falls hard, and my heart pounds.

'This man is different too.'

The impossible storm rages outside the tent. I don't know if it's the lightning or something inside of her that makes her eyes blaze like stars. I no longer notice anyone else. I no longer feel the pain in my shoulder. I just see her. Wild. Beautiful.

Terrifying.

She steps towards me and extends a hand. My fingers curl around hers.

There is a crash of thunder as I stand up.

And then an eerie silence falls over the tent.

'Tell them your story, Jay.'

I swallow hard. My mouth is dry. My chest tightens. The words that are sticking in my throat are wrong. And I need to shut up. I need to get the fuck out of here. But I don't. I can't.

Because of her.

'I'm Jay.' My voice is quiet, but the Circus listens. 'It's true. I'm a Blotter. The Creators' ink runs in my veins.' I suck in a deep breath. 'But I didn't do what was written. I followed a Twist to the Edge of the World.'

And then I say the thing I've been thinking since I met her—the thing that is wrong. The thing that will be the end of me.

'And I'm different.'

Part Two

Chapter Eighteen
Elle

I duck under the fabric.

The auditorium is empty, but the spotlight still beams onto the centre of the stage. Dust and dandelion seeds dance through it, glittering like the snowflakes in the Citadel's winter gardens. Jay sits on the front bench, half-hidden by shadow, and stares at it.

I smile, because not everyone can see the source of the light and he clearly can. It's a pulsating ball of energy that hovers beneath the roof of the high-top. The story. Our story. The one we have been growing here at the Circus, untouched by the Creators. It's brighter than it was earlier, bigger, more excited. Because stories are hungry—even ours.

Perhaps my stories fed it. But I think it was Jay. A Blotter defying the Creators and coming to the Circus at the Edge of the World. It is a good story. He will be useful to our cause. I feel it.

I cannot tell what he is thinking though. His head is angled upwards, displaying the hard line of his jaw and a streak of ink on his cheek. His legs are spread, his bad arm dangling between them. He's ripped off the sleeve of his hoodie and tied it around the bullet wound. His good hand grips the bench beside him.

Perhaps the heavy rise and fall of his chest means his thoughts are consumed by the Circus and the stories and his revelation to the crowd. Perhaps he's confused by what he's looking at. Perhaps he's just angry he got shot. I can't imagine Blotters are often harmed.

I'm not sure if he's aware of my presence as I watch him, although a part of me thinks he must be. He is a Blotter. His reflexes are fast—he killed five men with ease, and he had Raven in his grip before she even had chance to raise her gun.

'What the fuck is that?' he says as I approach. His chest is damp with sweat and blood, and his scent immediately washes over me, a primal masculine smell mixed with the metallic tang of ink and blood.

'What can you see?' I place the chipped bowl, full of water, and the medical kit I took from Anita's infirmary on the bench beside him.

He frowns. 'What do you mean, what can I see? The same as you. Loads of bees.'

My smile widens, and I look up at it. It looks different to everyone. Raven sees a collection of stars that light up the dark; Sylvia sees flames that threaten to spread; Maggie sees yarns of thread that can be weaved. To me, it looks like a collection of dancing dandelion seeds. I have never known someone to see bees before. But it makes sense. Bees spread pollen from one flower to the next. Bees allow new flowers to grow.

As I try to see what Jay sees, the dandelion seeds morph into bees, caged by the ball of pulsing white energy. There's a hum in the air, a slight vibration from the movement of their wings.

'What you can see is the heart of a story,' I say. 'The Story of the Circus. Stories are tangible things, you see. They are powered by other stories, and imagination, and, most importantly, by belief. The Creators have a story—the One True Story. It's bigger and older and stronger, and it stretches over the whole world. But it's the same at its heart.'

He sighs, and there's a look of resignation on his face as if I've finally worn him down. 'You shouldn't say things like that.'

'It's true.'

He meets my eyes for the first time. 'I thought you said no one was going to get hurt, little Twist.'

'I thought you were going to remain calm and not attack anyone.'

He runs his good hand over his mouth. 'Really?'

Blotters are cold and emotionless, but Jay has been anything but calm since our stories collided. I didn't think he would remain calm.

I sigh. 'No.'

He shakes his head and looks at the ground between our legs. 'You set me up then.'

I put my hand on his cheek and bring his gaze back to mine. 'I didn't set you up, Jay.'

His eyelids are heavy. There's a smudge of blood on his bottom lip, and I have an urge to wipe it off with my thumb. When he raises an eyebrow, I notice again the small white scar that runs across it—proof that someone else hurt him once.

'Okay, look, maybe I thought you might be a bit difficult,' I say.

'Yeah, I'm the one who's difficult.'

'But I didn't think it would go as far as it did.'

'I got shot!'

'At least you weren't killed.'

'Your stupid terrorist friends are the ones who could have been killed.'

'Yes. They looked like they were in a lot of trouble while you were on your knees with a gun to the back of your neck.'

I wait for the burst of anger I'm sure will come. Instead, I catch a flash of amusement in his eyes.

'You're really infuriating, you know that?'

I look pointedly at his shoulder. 'Does it hurt?'

'Yeah.'

My lip twitches. 'Good.'

He shakes his head. 'I could have killed them.'

'Maybe. Maybe not. Actions have consequences out here, Jay. You don't automatically get a happy ending written for you. You're not coasting on the Creators' story anymore. You attack someone, you're probably going to get shot. That's just the way it is.'

This time, the darkness comes. He clenches his jaw, and his hand, slick with blood, grips the bench tighter beside him. 'You think I ever had a happy ending written for me, little Twist? You think I'm expecting *this* to end well for me?' He looks at the ground between his scuffed boots. 'You know fuck all about me.'

'Tell me then.'

'I have a few pretty big questions for you before I tell you anything,' he mumbles.

'Go on then.' When he doesn't say anything, I grab the rag from the bowl. 'I'm going to clean your wound and bandage it up.'

'The bullet's still in there.'

'I know. But it's not doing you any harm.'

'Get it out.'

'Jay—'

His cool blue eyes narrow. 'Get it out.'

'It doesn't need removing.'

'It does.'

'Why?'

'Can't you just, for once, do as I fucking tell you?'

Annoyance flames in my chest. 'No. I'm not here to serve you or do as you tell me. You're here in my Circus. Now, stop acting like a child. Removing a bullet as deep as this can do more damage than good.'

'Fine, I'll do it myself then.'

I push him back down onto the bench as he starts to get up. 'Sit down.'

That wildness flashes behind his eyes. He's like an animal in a trap. His face is flushed, and heat blazes off him even though the air in the tent is cool. 'I don't want it in my body.'

'Why?'

'Because . . . it shouldn't be there. It's not part of me. It's not . . . right.' His voice cracks.

'Okay, okay,' I say, and some of the tension in his shoulder relaxes beneath my palm. 'Fine.'

'Okay. Good.'

I stare at him for a moment longer, wondering why it bothers him so much. Could it be something to do with the Ceremony? He said his blood wasn't always ink. I want to know, but it doesn't seem like a good idea to ask him right now. Not when he's so on edge.

I drop the rag back into the bowl, and some of the water sloshes over the side. Then I open the leather medical pack, pulling out the roll of gauze and a small bottle of alcohol.

'Finally,' he says. 'Something that can improve my bad mood.'

'It's to sterilise the wound.'

'You got me shot, little Twist. You're seriously going to try and stop me from having a drink?'

That feeling of wanting to see how far I can push him still buzzes beneath my skin even now. I think part of it is the conflict inside of me. Someone like him took away my father. He called me naïve. He pinned me to the floor with his naked body. He told me he would fuck me if I asked him to.

'You got yourself shot.'

But he is in pain. His face may be impassive, but the hard line of his jaw and the slightly acrid note to his sweat gives it away. He'll be in even more pain if I take the bullet out.

I pass him the bottle. 'Don't drink it all.'

He uncorks it with his thumb and takes a swig. As he moves it away from his full lips, he exhales, closing his eyes for a moment. Then he passes it back to me.

'I'm going to take your top off,' I say, and the corner of his lip twitches.

'You want me naked again, little Twist?'

'Be quiet. Can you lift your arm?'

His face reddens as he raises it, and a vein throbs in his neck. I grab his fist and push it back down then slide a pair of scissors from the pack.

'I've got it.'

The rise and fall of his chest accelerate slightly as I position myself between his legs. Reflexively, it seems, he slips his good hand beneath my jacket and grips my hip. My skin hums beneath his thumb, and it distracts me. It feels right, somehow, for his hand to be there. Firm and familiar and enticing, all at the same time.

Can it be possible for two people who barely know one another, who are supposed to be enemies, to fit together like two pieces of a puzzle?

'What?' he says.

'Nothing.' I drop my gaze to his shoulder and peel the damp cotton away from his skin. I look at the thick black tracts that cover the tattoos on his arms. 'Your blood—'

'I'm a Blotter, little Twist. I have ink in my veins. You know that.'

I take the blade and carefully cut down the side of his top. He breathes in deeply. I rest my hand on his shoulder, and reluctantly, it seems, he releases his grip on my waist, raising his arm for me so I can pull his vest completely off his body. Something hot rises inside when I catch the look in his eyes. I drop the scraps of his top to the floor beside us.

'I know. But you said there was a Ceremony. You weren't created this way.'

'No.' He swallows. 'I was born. Just like you.'

I reach for the small bottle of alcohol and tip the liquid over his wound. He inhales sharply, the corners of his eyes creasing. His chest rises and falls harder as it runs down his arm and washes with his blood.

'How old were you when they mapped out your story?' I ask.

'What does it matter?'

'Talk to me.'

He sighs. 'Five.'

I grab the rag and start to rub away the blood. 'How do they do it?'

'How am I supposed to know?'

'But you were at the Ceremony.'

'I don't like talking about this stuff.'

'I know. But it could be important.' I slide the tweezers out of the leather pack and then hold his shoulder, feeling the knotted muscles beneath his skin. 'And as I'm doing something for you . . .'

'You got me shot.'

'Jay . . .'

He shakes his head, looking at his feet. 'There are pools of ink beneath the Citadel. It's hot. Boiling. You go in. The Creators are there. Whispering. Creating your story. One of them, your patron, takes charge of it. And it . . . it just happens.'

'It sounds painful.'

He raises an eyebrow. 'It's boiling ink, little Twist. Of course it's painful.'

I raise the tweezers. 'Are you ready?'

He nods. He holds firmly onto my hip, his thumb pressing into my stomach. I stick the tweezers into the bullet hole, and he grunts, a low, primal sound. The edge taps the bullet, and as I dig deeper, hot ink spills down his arm—and down mine. It's not easy to keep a hold on it.

A CIRCUS OF INK

His grip is painful now, and his face is red. We're both breathing quickly. Finally, I catch it. As I pull, he groans, a masculine crescendo that vibrates inside of me. The bullet slips from the tweezers and lands with a click on the floor before rolling away.

He's breathing hard, his head lowered, staring at the space between our legs. '*Fuck.*'

Blood cascades down his arm, and I knew this was a bad idea. I grab the alcohol and douse him in it. His face is covered in a thin sheen of sweat, and he groans again. I push the rag into his shoulder. Like ink on parchment, the hot liquid spreads on the damp cloth.

Slowly, his breathing steadies.

'You've done that before,' he says after a moment has passed.

'There was a girl once,' I say. '*She travelled in—*'

'No. Not a girl. You.'

I sigh. 'Yes. When I escaped the Final City, Sylvia got shot in the leg with a poisonous bullet before we made it to the train.'

His expression darkens. 'Where did the storm come from before?'

I put my finger beneath his chin and tilt his gaze upwards. 'I think you know.'

'The storm. The hurricane. The door. You can't have created them, Elle. Only Creators can do that kind of thing.'

'I don't think that's what you believe.'

He looks beyond me, at the dandelion seeds and the light and the bees. 'You can't tell me that *thing* is a story. It makes no sense.'

'It *is* a story.'

'It's impossible.'

'Everything is impossible. Until that one moment it is not.'

'*Fuck.*' He bends his neck, the top of his head close to my chest, and I have an urge to pull him closer. 'The girl in the story who travelled across the Drafts and created the Circus . . . she's you.'

'Yes.'

'How? How is this possible?'

'Stories are true when we believe them.'

He shakes his head. 'No. Prove it. Right now. If you can create something, show me.'

'It doesn't work that way. Words and stories only have the meaning we give to them, Jay. You can't believe it without proof, but I can't prove it without belief.'

His chest moves up and down hard, glistening in the glare from the spotlight and the story.

'The dandelion seeds, the map of the Draft. . .You said you were planting seeds.' He swallows hard. 'You said dandelions grow like stories in the cracks between the pavement.'

'Yes.'

'You were planting a story. A story about a hurricane.'

I incline my head.

'*How?*' When he looks back up again, his thumb slips farther up beneath my vest. 'Stories are true when we believe them. You told people there was going to be a hurricane, and they believed you? So it became real?'

'Yes.'

He grips me tighter. *'Fuck, Elle. What the fuck?'* Then he shakes his head. 'No. That can't be true. The storm—that happened here. You didn't "plant any seeds."'

'It's easier here,' I say. 'We're outside of the Creators' story. We have our own story—you can see it yourself right now—and people believe in it. I can draw on its power. Like a . . . battery, I guess.' I drag my teeth across my bottom lip. 'But it's harder the farther away from it I am, and it's harder in the Drafts because people believe in the One True Story, not mine.'

Jay blows out hot air, his chest moving beneath my fingers. 'Fuck. This is some seriously fucked-up shit, Elle.'

I grab the gauze and lift his arm to wind the white, stretchy material around his shoulder. When I'm done, he looks up at me again. 'What are you up to, little Twist?'

'I'm going to create a new story to overpower the One True Story. I'm going to start a revolution. I'm going to overthrow the Creators.'

He closes his eyes. 'I thought so. What are we doing here?'

'I need some help from the Darlings to plant the seeds.'

He blows out hot air again. Then he nods. 'Okay.'

'Okay?'

'Okay. You created the impossible door. You created the hurricane. You created the Circus. You created the storm.' He shifts back on the bench, dropping his hand from my waist, and leans against the row behind him. 'You said stories are true if we believe them. I believe you. Show me.'

Chapter Nineteen
Jay

This is insane. I'm trying to stay cool. I'm trying to keep my shit together. But words and thoughts run through my head at the same rate my heart hammers against my chest. It's fucking deafening.

I must have lost a lot of blood, because it seems I've just told her I believe her.

I don't even know if that's true. Or whether I just want it all to stop—the questions, the wonder, the curiosity.

I was supposed to kill her.

Her death is written into the One True Story. It's marked on my skin in the same ink that's smeared on the oversized leather jacket she wears. It's all over her hands too. She brushes her hair out of her face and smudges it onto her cheek. A Blotter's blood on a Twist? Has that ever happened before? How did it come to this? Both of us at a Circus at the end of the world—me with a bullet hole in my arm; her telling stories, and talking about dandelion seeds and creation. And blasphemy.

None of it makes any sense. It doesn't make sense that she can create. And yet with all I've seen, I'm not sure it makes sense that she can't either.

I created the hurricane.

Run.

No.

Maybe I do believe her. I rub my mouth and look up at the Twist, one hand gripping the splintered wooden bench by my knees. She's still standing between my legs, close enough that I could grab her if I wanted to. I do want to. But not now. Not when I don't know what the fuck is going on. Not when I don't know what I'm dealing with here.

I knew she was dangerous from the moment I met her. I knew she wasn't an ordinary Twist.

But she can't create. Only the Creators can do that. And even if, somehow, someone else could, she's a woman. Women can't be Creators. It is written. That has always been the way. It's impossible for her to do what she says she can.

But I saw the storm. I saw the hurricane. I saw the impossible door.

Everything is impossible. Until that one moment it is not.

My head is a mess, and her close proximity isn't helping. She's radiating heat, and I can smell her: salt, rain, and leather. And honey. Always that weird scent of honey. The spotlight blazes behind her, and there are bees buzzing inside of it. She said *that* was a story.

What the fuck?

I need to get it together. I need to calm down.

I need to know.

'Show me,' I say.

She steps back and holds out her hand. I stare at it for a moment. Then I take it. Her grip is firm, and her skin is cool. I let her pull me forwards, swaying a little. I've never lost this much blood before. Not since I was a child.

She stops in the centre of the beam of light, turning to look up at me. My chest rises and falls at an accelerated rate. Because I don't know what she's going to do.

Before her, I always knew what was coming. But not now, as her breath tickles my naked chest and her hand rests in mine. It excites me. My heart pounds. I need to get it together.

'Well? Go on then.' I want to sound tough, but the words come out uncertain.

'Close your eyes.'

'What?'

'Just do it.'

I sigh, and then I do as I'm told. It's weird because I don't do what Twists tell me; I'm the one who tells them what to do. She slips her hand out of mine, and then her fingertips trace one of the tattoos on my chest. The corner of my lip twitches. She can't keep her hands off me.

'What are you doing?'

'Shush.'

She rests her hand on the tattoo that told me she would die. Her breathing hitches when she feels how fast my heart is pounding. She knows how excited I am right now. I wonder how that makes her feel. Afraid? Curious? Excited?

Not long ago, a storm raged and ripped through the Circus tent. It should have cleared the air. But something is coming. I want to look at her. I want to do a lot of things to her—even if the bullet wound throbs and my arm hangs heavily by my side.

But I also want to see what she will do.

I want her to surprise me.

'There once was a man,' she says, 'and he had a clock instead of a heart, just like everyone else in his world.'

'Another story.'

A CIRCUS OF INK

'Close your eyes . . . It beat to the pulse of Time. He could hear it always, a deafening pulse that rumbled through the land, through his body, and through his heart.'

Th-thump, th-thump. Th-thump, th-thump. She taps my chest in time with her words.

'So loud was the pulse that he could not hear past it. He could not think. He could not imagine anything beyond it.'

Th-thump Th-thump. Th-thump Th-thump. Again, she taps my chest. It stokes a heat inside of me.

'The man, however, had a secret. He kept the key to his clockwork heart on a chain around his neck. Every night, at the stroke of midnight, he took his key and wound up the clock in his chest to make sure it continued to beat along with the pulse of Time.

'Because his clockwork heart was faulty, you see. It was not like the others. Without maintenance, it beat a moment too fast—'

Th-thump. Th-Thump. Her taps quicken.

'—or a moment too slow.'

Th—thump. Th—thump.

'This troubled him greatly.' She lets silence hang between us, so all I can hear is my own heartbeat. *'He thought he was broken.'*

What did she say before? That I wasn't broken. I open my eyes.

'What are you doing?'

'One day,' she says, 'at the stroke of midnight when he was supposed to wind up his clockwork heart, he collided into someone instead . . .

'A woman. She was not bound to Time like him—she was bound to no one. She was Chaos. And while a clock beat in his chest, a hurricane raged in hers.'

Her eyes meet mine, and something feels dangerous. Because even though I do not have a clock for a heart, and she does not have a hurricane in her chest, I think she's talking about us. And it's all wrong. This is not part of the story that was written by the

124

Creators. A part of me wants to stop it. But a bigger part of me wants her to keep going.

'Close your eyes,' she says.

'No.'

'I want to show you.'

'How can I see with my eyes closed?'

'You've had your eyes closed your entire life, Jay.'

I don't know if I'm feeling light-headed from being shot or if it's because she's so close to me. But I do it. I submit to her again. I'm fucking pathetic. I told her I could make her do anything I wanted, and yet here I am doing everything she asks of me.

'And so,' she continues, 'at that stroke of midnight when he collided with the girl, he didn't use the key to wind up the clock in his chest. And something changed.'

I didn't kill Elle at midnight and something changed. I am certain now she is making something up about me, about us, and I don't know what it means. I don't know what comes next. I should make her stop.

But I want to know what happens.

'The pulse of Time he had heard for all of his life grew a little quieter. There were longer gaps between the seconds. Cracks. And through them, he heard something he had not heard before.'

'What?'

Music.

'It was quiet at first. An elongated note carried through the air. An echo of a tune once loud but now forgotten.'

The hairs on the back of my neck stand on end. I can hear something. I can fucking hear something.

'But then it got louder. Clearer. A soft melody to compete with the deafening roar of Time.'

My skin prickles as somewhere in the distance I hear a song. It gets louder. And this isn't right. But I don't want it to stop.

'As he listened, it got louder still. He heard the stroke of a stringed instrument. And then another. And then another. The music surrounded him. It was music he had never heard before. It built up inside of him, a wild and harmonious crescendo. He felt it. Each pluck of a note reverberating through his being.'

My breathing deepens. I can feel it. I can feel the music as sure as I can feel her body close to mine. *'Fuck.'*

'He heard all the sounds of a magnificent symphony. It flowed through him. Music that had always been there, but that he'd never known.'

One of her hands rests on my chest and she moves the other to my neck. Her breath tickles my collarbone. My hands move to her waist, slipping through her open jacket and resting on the small of her back, pulling her closer to me. Her hair brushes against my chin.

'And he didn't want it to stop. He didn't want to hear the deafening beat of Time that pulsed through the land. He wanted to hear the music.'

I do want to hear it. This is impossible. It's not written. It can't be happening. But it is, and I don't want it to end.

'So he did not wind up his clockwork heart.

'No longer bound to Time, he went to find the woman with whom he had collided. The girl with the hurricane in her chest.'

I open my eyes and rest my forehead against hers. Her face is bright in the glare of the spotlight. The ghostly music is all around us.

'What happened when he found her?' I ask.

'Why don't you tell me the next part?'

I cannot tell stories. My power is not in words.

But I know what happens next.

I slide my hand into her hair, and I kiss her. Her lips part, inviting me in. She digs her fingers into my shoulders and pushes her body into mine, and I groan. She feels so warm, so soft, so *right* in my arms. I've never wanted someone like this.

I move my hand up her back while her fingers hook into the waistband of my jeans. I think the music might still be playing, but I can't tell. All I can focus on is the sound of her breathing, quick and shallow, as her mouth moves urgently against mine.

I want her to move her hands farther down, but I think I'll explode if she does. So I grab her wrists, ignoring the pain in my shoulder. I pull them behind her back and hold them there.

She tilts her head, and our lips part. Both of us are breathing hard. I need to get a hold of myself. I move my good hand up to the back of her neck.

'I told you you'd have to ask me, little Twist,' I say.

A breath catches in her throat. 'And I told you I wouldn't do as you told me.'

I run my thumb along her cheek. 'We'll see.'

She opens her mouth to reply, but I kiss her again. I tighten my grip around her wrists. And then someone coughs behind us.

'Am I interrupting?' says Raven.

I pull away and look over my shoulder. Raven's eyes are narrowed, her nose turned up in disgust. She's no longer wearing her jacket, and her muscular arms are tensed.

'Yes,' I say. 'Fuck off.'

'I wasn't asking you, *Blotter*,' she says as Elle lightly brushes me aside.

Her cheeks are red, and her neck is flushed. It takes the edge off the frustration that's building up inside of me. She can make impossible music play, but I have an effect on her too.

'No,' she says. 'Is everything okay?'

'Sylvia wants to see you,' says Raven as she walks away.

Elle straightens her jacket, then she nods and follows. She looks over her shoulder at me.

'Jay, grab a new top from the rack backstage. I'll meet you back at the shipping container. Okay?'

I raise an eyebrow. Seriously? She's thinks she can just leave me here? She thinks she can tell me what to do?

'You coming?' she says.

I swallow the rising frustration. Then I follow her.

She may think she can tell me what to do now. But once we're back at the shipping container, things are going to change.

Chapter Twenty
Elle

I step under the flap of fabric that leads backstage. I do not look back. I can hear his footsteps behind me though—strong, slow, steady.

I touch my chin. The skin feels rawer than usual, sore where his light stubble brushed against it. It is a new feeling. Different. When I lick my lips, I can taste him on them. There is something hot beneath my skin, lingering in my veins and twisting with the stories and the conflict inside of me.

I kissed a Blotter. Blotters killed my father. He is different.

Why do I want him so badly?

He ducks under the material a moment later. When I turn, my face comes close to his chest. Heat radiates off him, mingling with the scent of sweat and the alcohol I poured onto his wound. My gaze slowly travels up, tracing the tattoo that curls up his neck.

When I reach his face, his jaw is etched into a hard line, and his eyes are cold. I can't hold them for long. I gesture at the clothes rack.

'You can grab something from there,' I say. 'I won't be long.'

'Right.'

I need to be strong, invulnerable, when I talk to Sylvia. What I need to do will be hard without her. Yet if Raven tells her what she just witnessed, I don't think it will strengthen my story. I think it will tarnish it—tarnish me. A Twist in the arms of a Blotter. I think she will see it as an ink stain; an imperfection.

I like imperfections. I like the black mark in his left iris, and the faint scar across his eyebrow, and the dandelion seed on his skin. But this world does not. Sylvia does not.

I need to show her I have this under control.

I *do* have this under control.

Stories are true when we believe them.

I take a deep breath and feel his angry eyes boring into the back of my head as I head out of the tent to catch up with Raven.

Sylvia is waiting for me when I get to the shipping container she uses to conduct her business. Her pistol lies on the table in front of her, beside a pile of parchment and a bottle of ink. There's a map on the wall behind. It shows the outskirts of Draft One, and there are 'X's scribbled at the spots where The Darlings have been planting seeds about the Circus at the Edge of the World. They do it to keep the story in the tent powered up and to recruit new people who need to escape the Creators.

It's better than doing nothing. But it's not enough.

When we enter, Raven goes to stand on one side of her, resting her hand on the back of Sylvia's chair. On the other side of it stands Anna, and I wish she wasn't here right now.

She came to the Circus a couple of years after I did. A girl around my age with short black hair shaven close to her head and multiple piercings in her ears. There were stories she killed the factory boss she worked for in Draft Three. Sliced him open with one of the sharp blades that hang from her belt. No one knows what provoked her to do it, but it certainly didn't fit in with the One True Story.

That made her a Twist, like me. Maggie, the same woman who helped me escape the Final City, found her before she could be Cut and brought her here. She's never told us what happened; she lets her knives do the talking whenever she takes the Circus stage.

Even though we have these things in common, Anna has never liked me. I can't imagine my bringing a Blotter into her midst will have warmed her to me any more.

'Elle.' Sylvia assesses me from beneath the rim of the black hat. 'Hello, sweetheart.'

'Hi, Sylvia,' I say.

'What are you doing here?'

I have never shied from the spotlight, but with the three of them glaring at me, I think I feel a fraction of what Jay must have felt in that Circus tent.

'I can take down the Creators,' I say. 'But I need your help to do it.'

Sylvia laughs and leans forwards, steepling her fingers beneath her chin. Her shirtsleeves are rolled up, and there's a smudge of ink on her arm. 'Honey, you've been singing the same song for too long now. The tune's starting to get a little boring.'

'You know what I can do.'

'Dear little Elle, always thinking she can change the world.' She gets up, abandoning her cane, and walks around the table. 'I remember back when you were a child. Of course, I was a Primary back then, over in the Final City. Do you know how rare it is for a woman to be a Primary? Do you know how hard it is?' She leans back against the table and studies her nails. 'One mistake, one misunderstanding, one word that you are not fitting in with the Creators' story—that's all it takes.' She meets my eye. 'I always knew you'd be trouble. You and your crackpot father.'

'Don't speak of my father in that way.'

She walks towards me. 'Why not, honey? It's true. He was an old fool who got himself killed. And you're going to end up just like him.'

Heat rises, and I grit my teeth. 'Stop. Talking.'

'The old bastard had it coming.'

I slap her across the face. I don't mean to do it; it just happens. This isn't the way this was supposed to go. Raven tenses, and Anna's hand moves to one of the knives at her belt. Then Sylvia grabs me by the throat and slams me into the metal wall.

'I ought to have you thrown out of here.' Sylvia brings her face close to mine. 'See how well you do this time. See how long it takes for the Blotters to rip you apart now your time is up.'

'You won't do that.'

'Won't I, honey?'

'No.'

'How can you be so sure?'

'Because . . . somewhere inside, you care about me.'

She lets got of my neck, and I cough, wheezing for breath.

'Care about you?' Sylvia laughs as she steps back. 'I couldn't give two shits about you, darling. And you sure as anything don't give a shit about anyone here.'

'That's not true,' I say, touching my throat.

'You left,' she says.

'I'm back now.'

'Ah, yes, decided to grace us with your presence. I suppose we should be honoured.' She raises a finger as if she's had an idea. 'Although perhaps not. Perhaps we should be pretty *fucking* alarmed you've brought a Blotter along to our secret camp. All of our lives are in danger now too. But I suppose as long as dear little Elle has a nice time, that doesn't matter, does it? Had some fun in the real world? Found yourself a good fuck, did you?'

'That's not—'

'You've always been a selfish, ungrateful little brat, but I expected more of you than to roll over and fall at the feet of a *Blotter*.'

'I didn't—'

'You were kissing him, Elle,' Raven interjects. Her voice, thick and low, is barely audible, but it resonates around the sparse shipping container. 'His kind killed your father. His kind killed Sylvia's . . .' She tails off, and the missing word from her sentence hangs heavily around us. *Child*. His kind killed Sylvia's child.

My throat closes up, and I swallow to try to relieve some of the pressure. 'He's different,' I say quietly.

'Stupid girl,' says Sylvia.

'I know you're upset, but—'

'Upset? Ha!' She walks back to the table.

'You need to hear me out, Sylvia. You owe me that at least.'

She stills. 'Owe you?'

'Yes.'

'*Owe* you?'

'Yes.'

'*I thought you were dead.*' She lets the words hang between us, and as they do, they thaw and leave something heavy and painful in their place. '*You left. And we thought you were dead.*'

Words and stories are my strength, and yet now they are failing me. I left the Circus because I needed to. It was for the good of the people here. I'm the only one who is trying to do something; trying to change things.

So why is there a tightness in my chest? Why do I not want to look at the shine in Sylvia's eyes? Why is there a hard lump in the back of my throat making it hard to swallow?

'I . . . You wouldn't let me do what had to be done,' I say. 'You said if I left, I shouldn't come back.'

'Stupid girl. I was trying to stop you from leaving. I was trying to stop you from getting killed. Maggie and I smuggled you across the world. I practically raised you. For four years, I kept you safe while you gallivanted around telling stories and making trouble for yourself. And this is how you repay me? You disappear for nearly a month! No word, no messages, *nothing*. Do you know how that made me—?' She presses her lips together. 'And now you're here again because you want something. You're just like your father. We're all just pawns in your little games, aren't we?'

She sits back down at her desk and pinches the bridge of her nose. I search for the right thing to say, but everything catches in my throat and stagnates. I feel hollow, and I can't find the words to fill the emptiness.

'I didn't think . . .'

'You never do.'

'I'm sorry,' I say.

Sylvia's shoulders slump, and her head hangs low, and I see what I didn't see earlier. Exhaustion. Weariness. The fates of the Darlings like a weight on top of her.

'But I did it, Sylvia,' I press. 'You said I wouldn't be able to, but I did. I created. In the Creators' world. In Draft One. And I can do it again. Faster, with the help of the Darlings. And if you can get me to the—'

'I'm not having this discussion again, honey. You're putting my people in danger.'

'Your people are already *in* danger. Look at this place! People are starving. People are being killed. Every day, more citizens get Cut. And it's getting worse. Have you listened to what they're saying in the black markets? Have you stopped by a House of Truth lately? Have you felt the earthquakes or seen the fires in Draft One? I have. Every day for the past three weeks. They're saying the End is coming—the End written by the Creators. And guess what? We don't survive it. None of us out here do. But I can stop it. *We* can stop it.'

'*ENOUGH.*' She slams her palms against the table, and Raven flinches. 'That's the end of this discussion. You can stay the night. You will leave in the morning.'

'I will not.' I throw back my shoulders and stare her down. 'You do not have the authority to throw me out. This is *my* Circus.'

'And these are my people. *My* responsibility to keep safe. And what is your Circus without them? A dusty old tent. Take it with you. Burn it to the ground for all I care. But you will leave in the morning, and if you refuse, *my* people will make you.'

'Slyv,' says Raven, 'she's supposed to be dead. You can't throw her out—'

'She leaves in the morning, and she takes her Blotter'—she flicks her wrist dismissively—'with her.'

'Get rid of the Blotter, yeah. But Elle is one of us.'

'That's enough, Raven.'

Anna fingers the hilt of her blade. 'It's time to leave, Elle.'

'He's different, Sylvia,' I say.

'You said he was meant to kill you?'

'Yes. It was written.'

'How do you know it was written?' She steeples her fingers and rests her elbows on the table. 'Can you read the marks on the skin of those monsters? Did he tell you?'

I curl my fingers, digging my fingernails into my palm. 'He told me.'

'Right. And you trust him? Has it ever occurred to you, Elle, that it was written he would follow you here, thus bringing someone tainted by the Creators into our midst? Or that perhaps he was written to lead other Blotters to us? Has it ever occurred to you he is lying to you?'

'He's not.'

'You're naïve. You've always been naïve.'

'He's a Blotter, Sylvia,' I snap. 'They don't lie. They don't have a need to.'

Her expression darkens. 'No. I suppose not.'

'He can help us,' I press. 'Think of the story. Think of how it can power up *our* story. Make it stronger. A Blotter working with the Darlings.'

Her eyes glint. And there it is. The crack. The opportunity. She is curious about the Blotter. Because this has never happened before—a Blotter has never spared a life he was supposed to End. If people find out about this, it will give them hope. It will make them believe in us.

'A Blotter defying the Creators he is bound to,' I say. 'Think about it.'

Sylvia sighs, and the spark of interest is gone. 'Regardless, I don't want him here. He's a risk.'

'Sylvia—'

'Just go, Elle,' says Raven. Her dismissal feels like a slap, but when I meet her eye, she mouths, *I'll talk to her.*

I sigh. 'Fine.' I raise my hands. 'I'll speak with you in the morning.'

I don't look back as I leave the shipping container. I try to calm myself down as I head back through the camp. It's not her fault she thinks this way. She'll come around. She has to. And she won't make Jay and me leave here. I won't let that happen.

There are people crowding around the Circus tent as I pass, their voices excitable. When I spot the kids laughing and joking, a young girl with white-blonde hair in the centre of them, some of my bad mood shifts. It's the girl I saw in the black market last night. She made it.

'*But it was the Blotters who should have been afraid,*' she tells the kids. '*Because the dragon ate them!*'

I smile as I head in the opposite direction, through a pathway lit up by red-and-white blinking lights, the mist trailing around my feet. Jay is leaning against the side of our shipping container when I get there. He's changed into another vest, dusted with coal. It must have belonged to one of the miners. He's gripping his bad arm, and his expression is murderous.

'You're still angry,' I say as I approach.

'No shit.'

I have to stop myself from rolling my eyes. I've just had to deal with Sylvia trying to throw me out of *my* Circus, yet he is the one who has somehow found a reason to be annoyed.

He's not making things easy. I thought bringing him here would help, that the story of the Blotter who didn't do what was written would give the people hope. But we have all known loss at the hands of Blotters. In their eyes, I have brought a monster into our midst.

The fact Raven walked in on me kissing said monster has made things much worse.

'You're angry because you didn't get what you want,' I say.

'Oh, I'll get what I want, little Twist.' His eyes darken as he pushes off from the side of the shipping container, and I try to ignore the way my stomach tightens.

'So what is it then?'

He gestures with his head. I frown, my shoulder brushing his chest as I walk past him. When I turn the corner, the side of my lip tugs up, and I spot the source of Jay's bad mood.

'Maggie!' I say.

An old woman with frizzy white hair sits on the edge of the open doorway, scribbling in a notebook with her tongue poking out of the corner of her mouth. She's wearing bright green trousers and an embroidered patchwork jacket sewn together out of grey-and-black factory overalls.

A wide grin broadens across her face, revealing a gap where her front two teeth are missing. 'Well, well, well, if it isn't my little bumblebee.' She jumps down from the shipping container, and I sweep her into a hug, the top of her head only just reaching my chest. Like always, she smells like old books mixed with tobacco.

'They said you were dead, but not my little bumblebee, I said. I knew you'd show up.' She pats my back as she pulls away. 'I'd say I have plenty of stories to tell *you*, only I happened upon this strapping young gentleman when I got here. He very kindly offered to wait outside until you arrived.'

Jay folds his arms across his chest, his expression stony. I supress a laugh, and Maggie waggles her eyebrows. I can't imagine Jay kindly offering to do anything. But he's still here. And somehow, an elderly woman who is about a third of his size has managed to get him to wait outside.

There is hope for him yet.

'Come in, both of you,' she says, her grin widening. 'I want to know all of your stories. I have one for you too, bumblebee. Something important. About the Book of Truth you asked about.'

A spark of excitement ignites inside me as she slides up onto the shipping container and pushes herself to her feet. Jay puts a hand on my arm as I follow.

His jaw is set, and he shakes his head. 'I'm not a pet you can put on display.'

'Jay—'

He steps back. 'I'm going for a walk.'

Before I can stop him, he turns away and disappears into the mist.

Chapter Twenty-One
Jay

I walk away from the settlement and stop at the Edge of the World. I sit down. The thick mist cascades over my legs at the same speed as the thoughts running through my head.

I'm sick of being pushed around by Twists. And Darlings. And old women.

I got shot. My arm aches. Everyone hates me. And the Twist kissed me as if she wanted me and then fucked off without a second thought. I'm just a story to her, a Blotter too stupid to do what was written.

I'm pathetic. It'd be a mercy for the Creators to kill me.

I sit there for hours. I'm not going back. If she wants me, she can come and get me. If she doesn't, then I'm leaving. I don't care about her revolution. I don't care about what she's looking for in the Book of Truth. I don't care about that thing in the tent that's full of light and bees and feels dangerous and powerful and warm. It's only her I'm curious about. And it's not worth this.

Finally, a muffled footstep sounds behind me.

'Took your time, little—' I tense. It's not the Twist. I'd be able to smell her, honey and earth and leather. Instead, the air carries a musty scent that reminds me of the forbidden areas of the Citadel. It's that old woman. Maggie.

For fuck's sake.

'Hello, pet,' she says.

'I'm not a pet.' I used to be fearless. A killer. A soldier of the gods. Now, I'm acting like a sulky teenager to an old woman about a quarter of my size.

'No? A wolf then. Bred in captivity, like the ones in the Creators' menageries. But free now. And what will you do with your freedom?' With surprising agility for someone who looks ready to drop dead, she sits down beside me. 'Mind if I join you?'

Her short legs dangle over the Edge beside mine, and she stares out into the mist, massaging her thighs. I could tell her to fuck off, but her wide grin and kind eyes remind me a bit of one of the nannies who raised us in the Final City barracks. So I just grit my teeth.

What was that nanny's name? Marlena. She used to sneak us treats meant for the Tellers—sugared plums and fresh figs and dark chocolate. Her End was written on the skin of a Blotter from my cohort. He did it when we were seven, with a knife from the kitchens she stole food from.

I cried when it happened.

But Blotters don't cry. I learned that lesson that day. I never cried again.

'You're trying to decide whether to stay or go,' says Maggie.

'Yeah.'

'I suppose you're not used to making decisions, are you, pup?'

'I'm not a pup.'

'You're all pups to me.' She smiles. 'In my experience, decisions are harder to make the more we analyse them. But we listen to our gut, and it's almost as if the next move was written all along.'

'My next move isn't written. That's the fucking problem.'

'You didn't do what was written by the Creators. But tell me, little wolf pup, who created the Creators?'

I frown. 'What do you mean?'

'Oh, nothing. I just wonder sometimes—don't you?' She looks pensively out into the billowing white mist and sighs. 'You know, most of the books are gone. Many burned with their creators hundreds of years ago. But fires cannot quell stories. They spread like ash in the wind. And I've heard stories. I've heard stories of a Draft One, many centuries ago, unpopulated and covered with mountains peaked with snow. I've heard of a Draft Three where great evergreen forests grew from the earth instead of skyscrapers, and where wolves prowled free and hunted for rabbits instead of rubbish. Off the coast of Draft Four, it is said, the prison island was once a sand-covered paradise frequented only by strange and colourful birds and ships filled with rum.

'I have read stories too—written, they say, in the ashes of the women who burned with their books—that say the Edge of the World we sit within now was once a part of Draft One before the mist came and swallowed it.

'So my question is this: Who created *tha*t world, so different from this one we live in now? Was it the Creators?' She shakes her head. 'I don't think so, or they would have written about it in their Book of Truth.'

'How do you know those stories are true?'

'I don't. But I believe them. And that's enough, I think.'

'Why?'

'Because they give me hope, little wolf pup. Hope that the world could be better than it is now. Does it not give you hope?'

I sigh. 'I don't know.'

Her glassy blue eyes bore into my skull. 'Tell me, if it *was* written by some higher being that you were supposed to spare Elle and help her start her revolution, would it make you feel any better or worse?'

I shake my head. 'I don't know.'

She nods. 'With destiny comes purpose. But with freedom comes many choices, many paths, many potential endings. You need a purpose, little wolf pup, but not a destiny. Destiny is written for us. Purpose we write for ourselves.' She leans back on her gnarled hands, and her eyes glint with mischief. 'I think you should stay. Elle seems quite taken with you.'

'Right. I'm just her little pet, aren't I?'

Maggie chuckles. 'Maybe. Maybe not. Elle . . . she struggles to connect with people, you know? Her father kept her isolated when she was a child. She wasn't planned. Wasn't supposed to exist. He feared she would be taken from him, so he hid her so she'd be safe. She only had him and her stories for company until she was fourteen. When he died, she had no one at all.' Maggie smiles a toothless smile. 'Now, she has you.'

I'm not sure what to make of what she's saying. I don't want to be curious about the dangerous girl with white-blonde hair whose existence defies the gods and who made music play while I tasted her lips. I don't want to be curious about the girl who made me wait for her while she went off to talk to her stupid Circus friends as if I were some kind of puppy dog.

But, fuck, I am.

I run a hand over my mouth. 'She seemed happy to see you.'

'Yes. We smuggled her out of the Final City, Sylvia and I. Managed to stow away on one of the trains that run through the Drafts. I worked for her father, you see. She's fond of me. She liked my stories. But she's always put up a barrier, stopped herself from getting too close.' She chuckles. 'I'm an old sod now anyway. I can't quite compete with a strapping young lad like you.' She pats my thigh lightly. 'Yes, you'll be good for her, I think, little wolf pup.'

We sit in silence for a little longer before Maggie groans and pushes herself to her feet.

'I'm going to go and talk some sense into Sylvia and the others. Elle tells me she's kicking you out in the morning. Kicking my little bumblebee out of her own Circus.' She shakes her head. 'Over my dead body.'

'Why do you call her bumblebee?' The question leaves my lips before I can stop it.

Maggie smiles. 'Well, when she was a child, she used to tell a story about bees living in her roof. The story spread, got out of control, and one day, a whole swarm of them took over an entire wing of the house.' Maggie chuckles, her eyes glazed over in memory. 'Her father was furious. But for days, we had the sweetest honey.' She pats me on the head. 'Remember what I said. The more you think on a decision, the harder it becomes. But you already know, deep down, what your gut is telling you to do, don't you?'

'Yeah,' I say quietly.

'Good. Listen to it.' She turns away and hobbles back to camp.

I sit for a while longer, thinking about how fucked up this all is. Then I push myself to my feet too. I could be going mad, but I think the old woman may be right. It's my choice, but it feels as if I have no choice at all.

Maybe it's because I'm supposed to kill her and now I'm bound to her somehow. Maybe it's because she gets under my skin, and I want to frustrate her. Maybe it's because she's terrifying and beautiful and says she can create hurricanes and music and impossible doors. Maybe it's because she's going to get herself killed if she carries on with these stories about revolution.

Maybe I'm just curious.

I don't know.

But I have to stay with her. I can't leave. She'll die if I do.

She's sitting on the edge of the shipping container when I emerge from the mist. The camp is quiet now, and she looks as if she's deep in thought.

'You're back,' she says.

I sit down beside her. 'Yeah.'

She smiles, and something warm spreads across my chest.

'What are you so happy about?'

'Maggie has a lead on something I'm looking for,' she says. 'Something that can help me fight the Creators.'

I exhale. 'And what exactly do you think can help you fight the Creators?'

She looks up at me, smiling. 'A story.'

'Of course.' I stare at the graffitied wall of the trailer opposite. 'Crazy little Twist.'

'Do you want to know what story I'm looking for?'

'No. But I'm sure you're going to tell me.'

Her leg brushes against mine as she raises it, watching the mist coil around her combat boots. 'Each of the Creators wrote a section of the Book of Truth, so there are twelve sections in total. But there was a thirteenth Creator once.'

My grip on the floor tightens. I really don't want to be talking about this. 'The First Twist.'

'Yes. The Fallen Creator. Most don't even remember him now. The Creators made it that way. But I believe he wrote a story too, and there is version of the Book of Truth out there that has his story in it. I want to find it.'

'Why?'

'The Creators turned on one of their own because of it. I think it's the key to taking them down.'

'Hmm.'

'Maggie has heard stories of an underground library in Draft Four run by a story thief they call 'The Bard.' They say it is the biggest collection of forbidden books outside of the Citadel. And they say 'The Bard' worships the Fallen Creator, tells stories of him within the musty bookshelves and piles of parchment. If it's anywhere, Maggie says, it will be there.'

I groan. 'And you want to go and get it, yeah?'

'Yes.'

I lean back on my hands and look up into the foggy sky. We could get to Draft Four in a few days, but only if we could get a hold of a vehicle and manage to smuggle ourselves over the Draft borders. It would get us the fuck out of here, I suppose. But as much as I hate to admit it, she's safer at this stupid Circus, away from the Blotters and the Creators and the One True Story.

'It's too dangerous.'

'We'll stay here for a while first,' she says.

'There's that *we* again . . .'

'Maggie needs to refuel her van. And I want to plant some more seeds and work on Sylvia.' She gets up and yawns. 'I've given the shipping container to Maggie, but there's space for us in the Circus with the Darlings she smuggled here. I'm going to get some rest. You coming?'

Does she seriously expect me to sleep in a Circus tent with a bunch of people I don't know? It was supposed to be just me and her.

My jaw clenches. 'No.'

'You're seriously this stubborn?'

'Yeah.'

She sighs. 'Suit yourself.'

I spend the rest of the night outside, sitting against the wall of the shipping container, my fists clenched at my sides while she's in the tent, asleep. After what happened in the spotlight, my mouth on hers, her fingers on the fastening of my jeans, this isn't how I imagined spending tonight.

There I go again. Imagining.

No. Not imagining. *Planning.*

Planning what I'm going to do to her when I get her alone.

Maggie said I needed a purpose.

Making the Twist beg for it is purpose enough for me.

Chapter Twenty-Two
Jay

The week passes. And it's fucking awful.

Darlings head out to Draft One in the daytime, recruiting, trading in the black markets, stealing fuel and food, while the Twist tells the kids stories about dragons and a girl locked away alone in a tower and constantly bugs Sylvia, trying to get her to help out with her revolution.

The nights are worse. They all sit around in the Circus telling stories about phoenixes rising from the flames of burnt books, and singing about lost loves, and dancing to haunting tunes that come from nowhere as Elle creates music from nothing.

I hate it. But I can't stop myself from watching her as her cheeks flush and her hands gesture and her pupils dilate. They do that, I've noticed, when she tells her blasphemous stories.

They do that when she looks at me too.

She keeps trying to get me to sleep in the Circus tent with her at night. Alongside ten or so other people. I'm not doing it. It's not just because of the Darlings and that weird pulsating light she says is a story and the whispers that follow me; it's her. It's the torture of lying beside her, smelling her, feeling her. Remembering her mouth moving against mine. *Imagining* what I'll do to her when I get her alone. And I don't even know when that will be.

She's kept busy helping with the food rations and looking after the children and repairing clothes. There's only time for a few words, a few stories, a few lingering glances where her eyes trace my body and betray thoughts she's keeping to herself about what she wants from me. Nothing more.

No one speaks to me. Except for Sylvia and Raven who throw insults my way whenever they can. It takes all my strength not to lose my shit with them.

Maggie talks to me too as I help her to fix her shabby black van. There's fuck all else to do here, and she's the only person who doesn't look at me as if I'm a monster every time I get close. She tells me to give people time, not get angry they're keeping us apart.

But everyone is wating for me to fuck up; waiting for me to kill something.

I don't know what the fuck I'm still doing here.

On the fourth day, the Twist sneaks out into Draft One. I only know she's gone because I notice her absence like a hole. My feet lead me to the nearest black market—sprung up underground down an old mine shaft—in pursuit of her.

She's there. Of course she is. In the centre of a cave standing on a cargo box, hair wild and eyes bright in the darkness, her stories about yellow dandelions in a grey world travelling through the air like seeds as people listen.

She goes back the next two days as well—despite the fact I follow and grab her from the shadows each time, dragging her back to the mist while she tells me she's planting dandelion seeds and no one will hurt her here.

She drives me fucking crazy. She won't listen. She won't do as she's told. She won't take what she wants from me. My skin constantly itches and burns. She's like a virus, spreading poison that's going to get her killed.

I don't stop her from leaving the settlement though. Even though I could. Maybe it's because it finally gets me away from these people who hate me.

Maybe I like listening to her stories.

On the eighth day, we go through the same routine. Only, when we get back to the settlement, Elle is ordered to Sylvia's shipping container.

Sylvia sits behind her table when we enter, black hat askew on her head, with Raven and the knife girl standing on either side of her. When they see I'm with the Twist, Raven tightens her grip on the gun across her chest, and Sylvia's expression darkens.

'You've been busy, haven't you, sweetie?' she says. 'I hear you've been taking unauthorised trips to Draft One.'

Elle folds her arms across her chest. 'I told you, I need to plant the seeds.'

Sylvia slams her palms on the table so hard Raven flinches and Anna's hand reflexively moves to her knife. 'And I told you that you could stay so long as you remained within the camp.'

'Sylvia, it's fine—'

'Fine? Fine, is it? Well, as long as little Elle with her stories and visions of grandeur thinks it's fine to be gallivanting out into Draft One while the Creators are looking for her, I suppose I should stop worrying.' She narrows her eyes. 'You're not to leave the settlement again.'

'I don't answer to you.'

'Well, who do you answer to then, sweetie? Him?' She flicks her wrist at me.

'Watch it,' I say.

'Did someone say you could speak, Blotter?' asks Sylvia.

'Can I kill this bitch now, Elle?'

'*Bitch*. How creative,' says Sylvia. 'You know I've been called that a lot in my time, honey. I take it as a compliment. Because you know what it really means, right? It means a woman who hasn't conformed to her story. I guess that's quite hard for you to take in though, isn't it, Blotter? Someone not falling over their feet to do what you expect them to do. '

I step forwards.

'*Don't,*' says Elle.

My blood boils, and I'm struggling not to lose my shit at her, at these people, at this entire situation.

'No. I was mistaken, wasn't I?' Sylvia snarls. 'It's he who answers to you, isn't it? Follows you around like a little lost puppy. How sweet—'

I think I'm about to crack a tooth I'm clenching my jaw so hard. I'm going to kill her.

'Don't speak to him that way,' says Elle.

'I should have—'

There's gunfire outside. Sylvia stands abruptly, eyes widening, and grabs her pistol. Raven and Anna raise their weapons. I turn as Sylvia's door slides open.

Three Blotters stand on the other side.

They raise their guns.

Fuck.

Chapter Twenty-Three
Jay

I lurch forwards. Metal ricochets off metal. I grab the barrel of the gun in the centre and thrust it repeatedly into the Blotter's face. His nose cracks as he rains bullets. He stumbles, and I catch the look of surprise in his eyes.

Surprise. New for Blotters. Weird. *Different.*

I know the feeling, mate.

I twist his head and feel the satisfying snap of his neck. He crumples to the floor.

The other two are already on the ground beside him—one with a bullet hole in his head, the other a knife shuddering from his neck. The Darlings were lucky. The three dead on the floor hesitated when they saw me. Only for a split second. But it was enough.

The Twist.

I turn.

She's by the wall, behind Raven, who must have pushed her there. Her face is pale. There's something almost childlike about her expression—like she's lost. I've never seen her look like that before. Not when I came to kill her, not when the Blotters arrived in the black market, not even when I shoved her into the wardrobe of my bedsit.

She looks at me, and fuck, I want to take that look off her face. I want to tell her it'll be okay. It's just a few Blotters. I can handle it. I won't let anyone hurt her. And that fucks me up in the head, that urge to make her better. Because since when did I give a shit about some little Twist with a stupid idea about killing the gods?

I wrench the dead Blotter up by his vest. I pull the rifle and strap from over his head, dropping him in a pool of black, inky blood that splashes on my boots. I sling it over my body.

There's more screaming ahead, and I catch movement in the corner of my eye. The girl with the half-shaven head crouches beside me. She pulls her knife out of the Blotter's throat then sprints into the settlement. Raven follows, firing her gun and spraying black blood on the striped Circus tent.

That's new too, Blotters getting killed by Darlings. I've not heard of this happening. It cannot be written. It doesn't make sense.

Nothing makes sense anymore.

'You did this.' Sylvia's words are quiet, but they carry over the sound of the gunfire. She's on her feet, pointing her pistol at the open door of the shipping container. Her eyes are on Elle though.

'It's not possible,' says Elle. She stares out into the settlement, where people are screaming and dying.

'Elle,' I warn.

She sprints past me out into the carnage.

Oh, for fuck's sake.

'Blotter—' Sylvia starts.

'Fuck you.' I leap over the dead men on the floor and catch her by the entrance of the Circus tent, grabbing her arm and wrenching her towards me. 'What the fuck are you doing?'

'The children.'

'What?'

There's a loud male shriek. Out of the corner of my eye, I see a scrawny-looking guy get gunned down by a Blotter. His body crumples and is swallowed by the mist. Behind him, the forest painted onto the trailer is peppered with bullet holes.

'The shipping container at the other side of the tent. The kids hang out in there.' She pulls away, but I tighten my grip on her arm.

'And what are you going to do about it? You don't even have a weapon.'

She wrenches her arm out of my grasp. 'I don't need a weapon. I *am* a weapon. *There was a girl once. They said she was small, but she could touch the sky. She wrapped it around herself like a tornado—*'

I shake her arms and bring my face close to hers. 'Stop with the stories, Elle. Look around you. This is real life. We're going. Now.'

'No.'

'This place is fucked. These people are fucked. We need to go.'

A Blotter notices us—a tall, muscular blonde guy with death tattooed on his neck and shoulders. I recognize him. He's assigned to Draft One, like me. I've drank with him a few times in one of the taverns.

I let go of Elle, raise my rifle, and kill him.

'Elle.' I turn back, but I'm faced with the rippling fabric of the Circus tent. I let the gun drop against my chest, then I rub my face hard with my hands. I slip into the Circus tent entrance after her.

I jog through the spotlight, and I'm hit with the memory of our kiss a week ago, and the horrible sound of bees. Frustration writhes inside me. Why does she have to be so infuriating? Seconds later, I'm back in the camp, in the centre of the chaos and the screaming.

Where the fuck is she? People are running, panicking, looking for each other as Blotters hunt them down. I don't like to admit it, but I'm looking for Maggie too. Her time should have ended long ago, but she doesn't deserve to go like this.

Across the settlement, Raven is leading a group of kids around the edge of a shipping container. Is Elle with them too? Some long-haired guy, blood running down his face, barges into my bad shoulder as I make my way down one of the narrow pathways between trailers.

'Watch it.' I rub my arm absently as I pick up my pace, counting Blotters as I pass. There are at least ten, and they're not open firing anymore. They're working together, rounding people up, herding them towards the tent.

I've not seen such a large Blotter operation before. Usually, the Creators would send an earthquake or a fire to get rid of so many people.

It's because of her, the Twist, I'm sure of it.

They want to make sure they get her.

They won't fucking touch her.

The mist surrounding the settlement seems more agitated than usual. A whole wall of it billows in the air even though we're not at the Edge yet. Raven is sending the group of kids into it. She turns as I approach, her long braids whipping over her shoulder. We both raise our guns.

'Easy,' I say. 'I'm looking for Elle. Is she here?'

Raven's eyes flash. 'You brought the Blotters here.'

We circle each other slowly. I could kill her. But I won't unless she makes me. It would piss Elle off.

'Where is she?'

'You stay away from her.'

'Where the fuck is she?'

'You've got Elle fooled. She thinks her death is marked on your skin. She thinks your being here wasn't written. But of course it was. You were supposed to come here. You were supposed to find us, to lead them to us. Weren't you?'

A muscle twitches in my jaw. 'You have no idea what not killing her has cost me. You know fuck all.'

'I know everything I need to know. You're a *Blotter*.' Spit flies from her lips as she speaks. 'I should kill you.'

'You'd be dead before you pulled the trigger.'

A Blotter comes out of nowhere, raising his gun to hit her on the side of the head. I shoot him in the face, and he crumples to the ground. Raven's eyes widen, her gaze locking onto mine. And then we both turn and fire our weapons as six more run towards us.

My bullet hits the nearest, and then I charge forwards, dealing with three of them in seconds.

'Blotter!' Raven shouts. 'The kids.'

She's managed to disarm the Blotter she's fighting, but he's got his hands curled around her neck. She knees him in the crotch and wrenches out of his grasp. I shoot him in the head.

She catches my eye, breathing hard, as he falls to the floor.

'The other two went after the kids,' she says, moving her hands to her neck.

'How is that my problem?'

She looks at me as if I'm a piece of shit, then she turns and runs into the thick wall of mist.

And now I don't know what to do.

Elle will be pissed if the kids die. That was the reason she ran off like a maniac in the first place. Can she look after herself for a few minutes while I sort this out? Probably.

I sigh as I head after Raven.

The mist is thicker than usual, and I can barely see. There's a bang up ahead, and a woman cries out. *Shit.* I jog towards the noise, tripping over something on the floor and stumbling into the centre of a group. The teenage girl—Lucy, I think—swings a fist at my face. I throw her out of the way.

Someone is crying.

'Raven, get up.' A little girl's tear-thickened voice behind me. 'Please, get up.'

This isn't good. I spot a Blotter ahead, and I push against the flow of kids, heading away from the body on the floor. Before he knows what's coming, I grab his head and snap his neck. The other Blotter is on the other side of the group, a couple of heads higher than everyone else here. I shoot him, and he goes down too.

The kids scream at the gunshot, some of them throwing themselves on the floor, others getting too close to the Edge.

'All right, calm down,' I say as I head back. I shift the little crying kid out of the way and crouch down beside Raven. I exhale and arch an eyebrow. 'I thought you were dead.'

She props herself up on her elbows. 'You don't sound very concerned.' Begrudgingly, she takes my hand and pulls herself up. 'Bastard shot me in the leg,' she says through gritted teeth.

'Well, I'm not carrying you.'

The corner of her lip quirks. Lucy rushes to her side and pulls her arm over her neck.

'Elle's okay,' says Raven. 'I ran into her when I got the kids. She's been telling people there's a tornado coming.'

Course she has. I walk towards the camp.

'Blotter,' shouts Raven. 'Thank you.'

I raise a hand. 'Didn't do it for you.'

I edge along shipping container walls as I navigate back to the Circus. There's a crowd of people, scared and bleeding, cowering by the tent. I grab elbows and peer into faces as I make my way through them, searching for her.

The Blotters yell at each other over the heads of the crowd—twenty of them in total. They're searching for the Twist too. One of them yanks Sylvia forwards by her black ponytail and offers her the Creators' mercy if she gives Elle up. She spits in his face, and he forces her onto her knees.

I can't see Elle.

I can't see Maggie either.

As I reach the tent, though, a cool breeze tickles my skin, and I still.

Because this is the Edge of the World. The Creators can't send their weather here.

Silence falls over the Darlings even as the Blotters continue to shout.

The Blotters don't know.

But we know.

I turn. Elle is standing in the gap between two trailers. Her hands are by her sides, palms facing outwards. Her eyes are closed. And her mouth is moving furiously, whispering.

Behind her, the mist from the Edge creeps forwards.

'There's a tornado coming,' I hear someone murmur in the crowd.

Sylvia catches my eye. I believe it. So does she. So do the Darlings who are shifting, slowly, towards the refuge of the tent.

The breeze picks up. It whistles through the gaps between the shipping containers. It flaps the fabric of the tent. It carries the metallic scent of blood and makes the clouds at our feet dance.

Behind Elle, the mist rises, and her white hair whips her cheeks.

One of the Blotters notices her. But now, there is a tiny tornado behind her.

'What the fuck?' he says.

The other Blotters are realising something is not right too. As they scan the scene, the Darlings scramble to the tent for cover. One of the Blotters aims his gun at Elle, and I point mine at him.

But then Elle's eyes fly open.

For a moment, time seems to stop. Her pupils are dilated—small, burning ink wells in the centre of fire. Her hair is blown out of her face. Her cheeks are flushed.

She is beautiful. And she is fucking terrifying.

Then I fall to my knees, dropping the gun and raising my hands over my head as debris rains from the sky. I can't breathe. Elle moves her hands as if she's grabbing the sky, and the tornado rips, breaking into smaller twisters that hurl fully-grown men into trailers and snap them like kindling.

I try to raise my head. Dust scratches my cheeks, and my eyes water. Elle is still amongst the chaos. Unharmed. Whispering. Eyes blazing. Then she closes her mouth.

The twisters retreat to the Edge of the World.

When the air settles, the walls are all smeared with ink, and bodies lie in the mist. The Blotters are gone. All of them.

Ears ringing, I get up. Elle meets my eye across the settlement.

'Jay.' She mouths my name.

Then she crumples to the floor.

Chapter Twenty-Four
Elle

I'm lying down on something hard. There's a murmuring sound, but it's faraway. The air smells forgotten and familiar. Dreams ebb through my mind, and they're warm and safe. I cling onto them because when they abandon me, I know I won't like what is left in their place.

But I have to come back. I have to face it.

It flashes behind my eyelids. Blotters. Guns. Ink splattering the trailers. Bullets raining down. Screaming. Crying. Dead bodies littering the floor.

You did this, Sylvia is saying. *You did this.*

She's right.

I created the tornado. But I couldn't save them all.

Someone moves by my feet, and I open my eyes.

'Jay?' I cough as dust scratches the back of my throat.

'She wakes and her first thought is of the Blotter . . .'

It's Sylvia. I sit up.

I'm in the backstage area of the Circus tent, amongst the musty clothes racks and old wooden chests. People are crying and whispering outside. Sylvia sits on a chair at end of the table I'm lying on. She absently pulls her cane between her fingers.

I bite my lip, tasting salt and dust and the metallic tang of blood. 'Where is he?'

'He's assisting Raven with something for me.'

I hide my surprise that he's helping. I don't want her to discover how little I know about the Blotter I brought into her settlement.

'The children . . .?' I ask.

'All safe.' Her expression is unreadable, but relief crashes over me. 'Thanks to your Blotter, apparently.'

I raise my eyebrows, this time failing to hide my shock, and Sylvia chuckles. 'The world's turned upside down, hasn't it, sweetie? Blotters helping kids, Creators finding out all about our secret hideout, and you . . .'

'How many people?'

She takes off her hat and looks down at the rim. 'Sixteen dead at last count. The bodies are being lined up outside.'

The hollowness in my chest fills with darkness. Sixteen people. Dead.

I couldn't save them.

I led the Blotters here.

I did this.

'Who?' I say.

Sylvia reels off a list of names. I bring my knees to my chest and rub my face with both hands. There's grit on my face and it scrapes my skin. The pain feels good. It feels like *something*. Something to compete with the darkness.

When I look up again, Sylvia is watching me.

'They came here to find you, sweetie—the Blotters. Just like I said.'

'You can't make me feel worse than I already do.' My words sound empty. 'If that's why you're here, then you may as well go.'

'That's not why I'm here.' Her body deflates. 'I'm here to tell you it's not your fault.'

'You said—'

'I know what I said, sweetie. I blamed you for leaving and coming back. I blamed your Blotter for bringing them here. I blamed myself for not being able to protect my own people—' Her voice breaks, and she pinches the bridge of her nose to compose herself. 'But who killed those sixteen people? Maybe we have a part to play in it, but I didn't pull the trigger. Neither did the Blotter. Neither did you. We're all on borrowed time here and who is to blame for that?'

'The Creators.'

She inclines her head. 'What you did out there . . . I've seen your little tricks in the Circus. But I've never seen you do anything like that before. It was . . . it was extraordinary.' She exhales. 'It's not enough. And yet . . .'

I lean forwards slightly. 'It's our only option.'

'I'm willing to hear you out, sweetie,' she says. 'I'm not promising anything. But if you have a plan, I will hear it. We're all on borrowed time, and it seems the clock is finally catching up with us. If the End really is coming, and the Creators know we're here now, we don't stand much of a chance, do we?'

There are voices outside, and we both look at the entrance flap.

'Are you kidding? A Blotter standard Stet Rifle is a far superior gun to that piece of shit. No wonder you went and got yourself shot.'

'Fuck you, Blotter.' Raven ducks into the backstage area, supporting herself with a makeshift crutch. She's closely followed by Jay. He has a Blotter's body slung over his shoulders. When he sees me, he halts.

'You're awake.'

His arms are caked in dirt and ink, and there's a tear in his dusty vest exposing the ridges of his torso. His bullet wound from last week is almost healed, but it must still be bothering him because he's carrying most of the weight of the corpse with his other arm.

'I'm awake,' I say.

He chews his bottom lip. 'I wanted to stay . . . here . . . with you . . . But I didn't know when you were going to wake up. And Raven said . . . well . . . she wanted me to help with getting a Blotter body . . . so . . .'

He shifts slightly, and I smile despite the situation. I haven't seen him like this before. He's nervous, and it seems strange for someone his size.

'Yes, yes, very sweet. The Twist and the Blotter.' Sylvia waves her hand dismissively before I can reply. She nods at the dead body. 'Put him on the table.' She slips the hat back onto her head and rises from her chair, offering it to Raven who slumps into it and starts to massage the top of her leg.

'Are you okay?' I ask.

'Got shot. Hurts like a bitch. But yeah. You?'

I nod even though I'm not and she isn't either. As Jay drops the tattooed corpse onto the table, I slide onto the floor.

He catches my eye. 'What you did out there . . . That was fucking amazing.'

'Sylvia said you saved the kids.'

He runs his hand over the back of his neck. 'Yeah. I saved Raven too.'

'What? Shut the fuck up,' says Raven.

Jay's cool blue eyes don't move from mine, but the corner of his lip twitches.

'I suppose you're wondering why I wanted a dead Blotter,' says Sylvia.

'Not really,' says Jay.

'You want to see if it was written,' I say quietly.

She inclines her head. 'This place was supposed to exist beyond the reach of the Creators. We've never been bothered here before.

A CIRCUS OF INK

So the question is, what changed? Or was it always written that on this day, they would find us? I want to know how far outside the One True Story we're operating here. I want to know if this was predetermined, or if tonight, we were all a part of a huge twist—a mass deviation from what should have happened.' She nods at Jay. 'That's where you come in, Blotter.'

His shoulders tense. 'What do you want me to do about it?'

'You have tattoos covering your skin, sweetie. They map out your life. They tell you what to do, right?'

'Yeah. So?'

'I want to know if this was written, and I want to know if they expected Elle to kill them,' she says. 'Can you read the tattoos on this Blotter's skin?'

'I don't need to. If they were here, it was written. Blotters don't deviate.' He swallows. 'But they didn't know this was their Ending.'

'How do you know?' says Sylvia.

'I shot this guy. He hesitated. Blotters don't hesitate.' He's speaking to Sylvia, but he's looking at me. 'The guy whose neck I snapped, he was surprised. Blotter's don't get surprised. They didn't know they were going to die.'

I look at the body. The man's face is covered in ink, and there's a bullet hole in the centre of his forehead. It's hard to determine his age, but from his physique, he must be in his early twenties.

'If it were written on his skin that he'd come here and kill all those people, the Creators must have known we were here all along,' says Sylvia, her brow crumpled.

'No,' says Jay.

We all turn to him. He's looking at the corpse again.

'No?' says Sylvia.

He runs a hand over his mouth and takes a deep breath.

'Well? Come on. Spit it out, Bl—'

I raise my hand, shushing Sylvia.

His biceps are hard, and he curls and uncurls his fist at his side. It reminds me of the moment when he had his meltdown in his bedsit, when he was trying to decide if he should kill me or defy the Creators. Whatever he wants to say, he clearly sees it as crossing some kind of Blotter line. Which means it's important.

'Jay,' I say gently. 'What is it?'

He exhales and meets my eye. 'They change sometimes. The tattoos.'

A spark of hope or triumph or *something* ignites inside me as Raven frowns.

'The Book of Truth says everything is already written,' she says.

'I know what it says,' snaps Jay. 'But I'm telling you, the tattoos change sometimes.'

He looks at the body, then he points at a tattoo depicting twelve concentric circles on the Blotter's arm. There's a small triangle inked beside it. 'There. That's the Circus. That's what told him to come here. And it's new.'

'Are you sure?' says Sylvia.

'Yeah.'

'How?'

He drags his teeth over his bottom lip. Then he wipes away the dust caked onto his right forearm and shows me it. He has the same tattoo, only there's no triangle on the edge of his.

'All Blotters have this marking.'

I reach over the table and run my thumb along it. 'What does it mean?'

He pulls his arm back and puts his hand in his pocket. 'A map.'

'So the Creators don't know everything,' I say. 'They make changes to the One True Story.'

'It doesn't matter,' says Jay.

'It doesn't matter? Of course it matters!' I say. 'It means not everything is predetermined. It means we can change things. It means their story for us didn't go the way they planned, so they're being forced to react.'

'It means we need to get the fuck out of here before they come back,' says Raven. 'That's what it means.'

'No arguments there, honey,' says Sylvia. 'The Blotters drove to the Edge in their vans. Maggie's gone to see what we can salvage alongside her mobile library.'

Some of the tension in Jay's shoulders seems to release. I suppose he is pleased to be leaving this place. He's made no pretence he hates it here amongst the stories and people who do not worship his Creators.

But then he shakes his head. 'Where the fuck are you going to go? There's nowhere.'

'Thanks for that input, sweetie. Very helpful,' says Sylvia. 'But I have it under control. We'll follow the Edge, find a place to set up camp farther along.' She looks at me. 'I don't think it's us they're really looking for though.'

'You want us to leave.'

She inclines her head. 'But I said I'd hear you out. So tell me, sweetie, how do we fit into this plan of yours?'

'I need some help planting the seeds,' I say. 'That's all.'

She laughs a joyless laugh. 'That's all, is it, honey?'

'In Draft One, it took me a month for the story about the hurricane to spread enough for people to believe it. I need some help as we move through the other Drafts. The more people spreading my stories, the quicker and more powerful they'll be.' I hold her gaze, trying to show her with my eyes how sure I am of this. 'I can do this, Sylvia.'

Sylvia breathes out sharply, leaning on her cane. 'It wouldn't be the first time I've done something stupid on behalf of your family, I suppose.'

A flower of hope blooms in my chest. 'You'll help?'

'If the End is coming, we need to stop these bastards before they kill us all, don't we?' She sighs. 'There's a library in Draft Four. I don't know how long the Circus can hide out here along the Edge of the World, but the library could be a good new base for us. Stories grow faster in places where there are books. We'll recruit some volunteers. We'll take different routes through the Drafts, and I suppose we could plant some of your seeds along the way— *if* you can persuade some people to do it. I won't force anyone.' She arches an eyebrow. 'We're planting a new story about revolution, I presume?'

Jay tenses, and I smile. 'Yes.'

'You know your way through the Drafts, Blotter?'

He folds his arms. 'Course I do.'

'Good,' says Sylvia. 'You will escort Elle. By the Black Sea Bridge, there's a square—Creator Michael's. The library is close by. You can get her there?'

Jay inclines his head.

Sylvia puts two fingers into her mouth and whistles.

One of the Darlings, Rami, gracefully ducks through the entrance flap. He spent his childhood in Draft Seven as a pickpocket before joining a travelling crew of actors and crossing the wastelands with them. When they were killed, he made his way to the Circus. We have a bit of a history together even though it never led to anything serious, and he gives me a lopsided smile, creating dimples in his cheeks. Jay's eyes narrow on him. Rami turns to Sylvia.

'Yes, boss?'

'Can you put this'—she clicks her fingers at the dead body on the table—'with the others, sweetie?'

He nods and slings the body over his shoulder, although he does it with less ease than Jay. Then he flashes me another smile before heading out into the mist.

Sylvia sighs. 'Let's honour the dead. Then we need to get going before more Blotters come.' Her jaw sets, and she walks to the doorway leading into the auditorium. Her shoulders stiffen as if she's bracing herself for something. 'Elle, there's one more thing you should know. The story you've been growing, *our story*, about the Circus at the Edge of the World being a refuge for people like us . . .' She lifts the flap with her cane.

The inside of the auditorium is dark. It's gone. The story has died. Of course it has. Because I couldn't protect them.

There's a lump in the back of my throat, and I swallow, pushing it down. 'We'll create a new one.'

'Maybe,' she says.

Sylvia and Raven exit the tent, leaving Jay and I alone.

The air feels heavy. We haven't been properly alone since that night in the Circus. A Twist and a Blotter—two enemies—kissing. I wonder if it has ever happened before. I wonder if it will ever happen again.

He stares at me, arms folded across his chest. Then his expression softens. He steps forwards and puts his finger lightly beneath my chin to raise my gaze to his. He breathes out softly.

'You okay, little Twist?'

It's a question I can't answer. Physically, I am fine, but my insides feel heavy. Because people died. And I couldn't save them.

I don't want to feel like this. But I don't know how to stop it. I want *him* to stop it.

As he looks at me, his face darkens. He moves closer, and his body heat washes over me. I can't think; I can't focus. I just want the bad feeling inside to stop.

'Jay . . .' My voice sounds small.

'Little Twist.'

His hand slides up, his fingers curling around the back of my neck, his thumb rubbing circles on my skin. My heartbeat quickens as his eyes linger on my lips.

And I jerk back, almost knocking into the clothes rack, furious with myself. With him. How can I even have the thoughts I'm having when people died because of me?

'We need to go. They need me.'

I turn on my heel and stride out of the Circus to face what I have done.

As night falls, the bodies burn. The flames lick the air and dance with the mist in front of the Circus tent. The surviving Darlings stand in a semi-circle around the funeral pyre—around forty of them. The air is thick with grief and smoke and stories.

Jay stands beside me, his back stiff and arms folded across his chest. He doesn't want to be a part of this. Death is usual for Blotters. Emotion is not. I wonder if witnessing the aftermath of a Blotting makes him feel anything about the Blottings he has been a part of. I wonder if he feels as bad as me.

The Blotters came here for me. And sixteen people died.

It's my fault.

I don't think Jay cares much about the fates of these people. Not yet. But he helped the children. He carried the dead Blotter for Raven and Sylvia. He answered Sylvia's questions.

I have hope for him.

'This is fucking awful,' he says. *'Can we go?'*

'Soon. Be quiet.'

I turn back to the flames.

Usually, we would tell stories for hours about those we lost. But tonight, urgency prevails through the tears. We don't have time for it.

'Their bodies are gone, but may their stories live on,' says Sylvia, backlit by the fire, signalling the end of the funeral.

'May their stories live on.' All but Jay repeat the words back.

Then Sylvia, with a begrudging expression, invites me to speak.

It doesn't feel right to ask them to risk their lives while their loved ones burn behind me. But that is the way it must be. There's no time for anything else. So I step forwards and tell them what I want from them.

'It's time to put an End to their story. It's time to create our own story. It will be dangerous. I know it's a lot to ask. But we can continue to hide, to survive, to exist. Or we can *fight*. Come with me. Let's make them pay for what they've done.'

When no one responds, I sigh.

'I know you're afraid,' I say. 'But I know another girl who was afraid.

'*She had a hurricane raging in her chest. And with a travelling Circus, she travelled to the Final City. Together, they planted thousands of dandelion seeds that grew and spread around the world, forcing through the cracks, breaking through the pavement. Until the force of the Circus, and the dandelions, and their Story, was stronger than that of the Creators.*

'*And together, they changed the world.*'

'It's not true though,' says Anna. 'It's just a story.'

Despair hangs over the crowd like a shroud. But there is anger too—clenched fists, strained muscles, and set jaws. It gives me hope.

'But it *could* be true. Stories are true when we believe them. And I'm going to make them pay for what they did. Come with me.'

Raven hobbles forwards first. 'Well, obviously, I'm in.'

Rami nods. 'And you know I am too.'

A few more step forwards. Anita and Lucy, a couple of guys from Draft Five, and obviously Sylvia. It's not much, but it's enough. For now.

I catch Jay's eye, and he shrugs. Then Sylvia steps forwards again.

'Good. Elle and the Blotter are the biggest targets—they leave now. I don't want anyone else here put at risk. We meet in a week at the library.' She smiles thinly. 'Anna and Maggie will be in charge in my absence. Now, let's get going. It seems we have a revolution to start.'

Chapter Twenty-Five
Jay

I stroll around one of the three black Blotter vans parked by Maggie's mobile library. 'Blotter standard model from the Outer Drafts. So that's good, I suppose.' I catch a jagged scratch along the side. 'It'll be hard to get across the Draft borders in this though. Draft crossings are written.'

I kick the front tyre. It's softer than it should be.

'Bit fucked up as well. We won't get far . . .' Then I peer through the front window. 'Key's in the ignition at least.'

I run my palm over the side as I bring myself full circle back to the Twist.

She stands at the side of vehicle, rucksack at her feet, looking into the mist that has swallowed the Circus tent. I rub my hand on my jeans, wiping off the grime, then I turn her around.

'Hey. You listening to me, little Twist?'

'I was just thinking.' And there's that look again—the one I saw in Sylvia's shipping container. That lost look. I frown.

'What is it? You got what you wanted.'

Her forehead creases. 'You think this is what I wanted?'

'Well . . . yeah . . .'

She blows out hot air, and a strand of white hair dances in front of her face. Without thinking, I brush it back out of her eyes.

'What's wrong?'

'I couldn't save them all.' It sounds as if the words are hurting her as they come out. I don't like that. I don't know how the fuck this happened, but I don't like the thought of anything hurting her. I'd kill anyone who tried to touch her—I know that now. But I can't fight words, can I?

'Look, Elle,' I say. 'Those Darlings should have been dead a long time ago.'

It was the wrong thing to say. Fuck. She steps back, and her eyes blaze like angry stars.

'Is that what you think?' Her cheeks are flushed. 'Is that seriously what you think? That it's fine sixteen people were murdered? That it's all fine people lost their wives, their mothers, their friends, their families today—because the Creators wrote it that way?'

I rub my mouth. 'Elle, come on.'

'Don't you care? Don't you care they died screaming? But then I suppose you wouldn't. How many people have you killed, Jay?'

My jaw sets. 'You know what I am, little Twist. You've known since you met me.'

She steps into me, and I don't know if she's expecting me to move back, but I don't.

'If it were written, you'd have been a part of that massacre too, wouldn't you?' She pushes my chest. 'Answer me.'

I take her wrist, and she staggers into me, grabbing my vest with her free hand. She's breathing hard, and she looks fucking furious. She looks like a hurricane, a tornado, a raging storm confined within the frame of a woman.

I wonder what she will do. I wonder what she *can* do. I wonder if I'm the one who stands to get hurt here. Which is an odd feeling. No one hurts me.

For the briefest of moments, I wonder if I'd let her. Just to see. Just to know what it feels like to have her hurt me.

'Answer me,' she says.

'You don't want me to do that.'

She's looking at me as if she can't decide whether she wants to fuck me or kill me. I think both, maybe. I think my world changed the moment I arrived in her bedsit, but hers is only just changing now.

She's realised this isn't some little game. This isn't some neat little story she can tell in which everyone gets a happy ending.

This is real. This is life. This is the Creator's world, not ours.

People die. People follow the paths that have been written for them. People keep their heads down and get on with it because that's the only choice they have.

As we stare at each other, her breathing steadies. Her eyes are as wild and as lost and as angry as the stars. And I can see her searching for something in mine. Reaching for something that she can grab onto to stop herself from falling.

I hate it. I hate that she thinks it can be me.

'You know what I am, don't you, little Twist?' I say, bringing my face closer to hers. 'You know what I am, what I've done, what I'm capable of.'

I step forwards, pushing her back into the side of the battered van.

'Tell me. What am I, little Twist?'

She glares at me.

'What am I?'

'A Blotter.'

'Yeah. That's right. I'm not some little Darling, going around telling stories and playing nice with all the other little Darlings. And I never will be. So if that's what you want me to be . . . you can go find some other poor bastard to come on your crazy suicide mission with you.'

'You're wrong. You're more like them than you think.'

'You think I'm like a Darling? I don't act like a Darling, do I? I don't look like a Darling. I don't kiss like a Darling.'

She makes an angry sound in her throat.

'But then that's what this is about, isn't it? You want to know what it would be like with someone like me. But you need to pretend I'm a good person. You need to pretend I'm not a killer. You need to pretend I can be fixed.'

'That's not what this is.' She's breathing hard. 'You know nothing about me.' She glares at me, and I realise my breathing is heavy too. I can smell her—earth and smoke and sweetness. My eyes fall to her lips, pink and chapped. I tasted them once. Before the Blotters came. I want to taste her again. All of her. I'd drop to my knees right now if she asked me to.

I wanted to stop her from hurting a moment ago, yet now, I'm trying to hurt her. I don't know why. I don't know what I'm doing.

I sigh. 'What do you want from me, little Twist? Tell me what you want me to do.'

'I want you to care.'

'I'm here, aren't I?'

'You care that they died?'

I moisten my lips. 'I don't think you want me to answer that.'

She blinks and looks at the ground. I don't like that look on her face. It makes me feel like a dick again. I step back, and her clenched fist drops from my chest.

'Look, Elle. Just . . . just tell me what I need to do . . . or what I need to say, and I'll do it. Or say it . . . or whatever.' I rub the back of my neck. 'I'm not . . . I'm not good at this . . .'

'No shit.'

My lip twitches. 'Well?'

'Come on, kids. Time to go.' Maggie's voice interrupts us, and Elle's edges soften. The old woman emerges from the mist behind me, her patchwork jacket and white braid covered in dust.

'Couldn't have my little bumblebee and her wolf pup leaving without saying goodbye now, could I?'

I fold my arms, and a half-smile crosses Elle's face, her eyes boring into the side of my head as she hears the nickname. She'd better not get any ideas.

'Plus, I thought I'd give you a little help,' says Maggie. 'I've a connection in one of the Draft Two black markets. She's based in the factory district by the border. Ask for the Canary and tell her I sent you. She'll be there in three days' time, and she can get you across the river into Draft Three. It'll stop you from having to find a way over the bridge.'

'Thanks, Maggie,' says Elle. She bends to hug her. 'When will we see you again?'

'You'll be seeing me soon, I expect. I'm not one to turn down an adventure.'

When they pull apart, Elle takes a deep breath then grabs her rucksack and climbs into the van. Maggie moves towards me, her arms spread. I jump back, and she cackles, watery blue eyes glinting.

'Not a hugger, hmm? I guess some wolves aren't supposed to be tamed.' She steps back, arms dropping to her sides. 'But I have hope for you yet. You'll look after my bumblebee?'

'Yeah,' I say. 'I swear it.'

She nods, and something unreadable passes over her face. I think she's going to say something else, but then she smiles and steps back. 'Good luck.'

I want to wish her luck too, but that would be a weird thing for a Blotter to do. So I just nod and watch her as she heads back through the mist towards the Circus. I hope that she'll be okay. Then I get into the driver's seat.

Elle touches my thigh. 'You may say you don't care, but you saved a lot of people. I should have said something before. I'm upset about what happened. But you . . . you were . . . you helped, and . . .'

'It's not because—'

'But still, thank you,' she says before I can deflect the thanks I don't deserve.

'Yeah, well, you can thank me properly later.' I close the door and then meet her eye again. 'I can think of a few ways.'

Her eyes widen slightly as I rest my hands on the steering wheel. Silence hangs over us, but it's charged with something. We're finally going to be alone. Away from the Darlings, and the Circus, and the stories, and the constant noise.

'Where are we going then?' I say. My voice sounds weird, so I clear my throat. 'Draft Two border is a ten-hour drive. But we'll need to lie low for a bit to meet this Canary.'

She leans back against the tattered seat, frowning. Maybe it's because I'm a dick, but it makes me feel better that she's unsure about something for once.

'We could—'

'There's a guy in Draft Two.' I turn the key in the ignition. 'He runs a motel of sorts. For Blotters. Tends to turn a blind eye. We'll get a room there.'

The van grumbles into life.

'Why are you even here, Jay?' she says. 'If you think this is all for nothing? That it's a suicide mission? That there's no hope? That we're going to die?'

I shrug. 'Maybe I'm just curious.'

I put my foot down on the pedal, and we drive away from the Edge of the World.

Chapter Twenty-Six
Elle

Engine spluttering, we break through the wall of fog into the Creators' night. Rain patters on the roof. We're surrounded by crumbling skyscrapers and broken billboards that once showed Tellers reading from the Book of Truth. Now, they fizz with white noise.

I watch the tendrils of mist reaching for us through the rearview mirror. It's as if they're trying to pull us back to the Edge of the World.

It was my home once. It was safe.

I wonder if I will ever return. I wonder if there will ever be anything to return to.

The thought weighs heavily on my chest.

The Circus, as I knew it, is gone.

But not quite.

Because I will not leave its stories there to rot, to be swallowed by the mist. I carry them with me. So do the others. They will not be forgotten.

'May their stories live on.' My voice is quiet but firm as we turn a corner and leave it all behind. I expect Jay to say something, to tell me I'm being stupid or it doesn't matter, but he just glances at me and then turns his attention back to the road, one hand clenching the wheel, the other in a fist on his lap.

In the dark, his jawline is hard. The inked muscles of his arms are taut, and his chest rises and falls deeply. The sound of his heavy breathing mingles with the sound of the engine. He looks too big for the vehicle even though it was designed for people like him.

'You're tense,' I say.

'Course I'm tense. I'm driving a stolen Blotter van with a crazy little Twist in its passenger seat. And we're on a mission to—' He sighs and rubs his face, his hand scraping across his stubble. He can't say it out loud. To him, what we're doing is still treason. To him, this is defying the gods. To him, even after all he has seen, he still feels bound to the Creators. I wonder if that will ever change.

It will. It has to.

But right now, he doesn't care. He doesn't want to be here.

My skin prickles. 'On a mission to what?'

He swallows, and my gaze drops to his neck where tattoos curl around his throat like inky fingers. He shakes his head. 'Drop it.'

The air is charged, and it's hot and damp, and it smells like him. It feels like that moment before a storm breaks when something intangible hangs in the air that needs to be cleared. I want a rise out of him. I want to release this feeling that's building up inside my chest. It's too much to bear. I want the storm to come.

'We're on a mission to overthrow the Creators,' I say.

'Don't.'

'That's what we're doing, Jay.'

'Careful.'

'You're like me and the Darlings now.'

'Are you trying to antagonise me?'

'Yes.'

Our gazes lock. 'Well, stop it.'

He turns the steering wheel and takes us down another long road. I exhale and lean back in my seat.

'Okay.'

'Finally, she does as she's told.'

'I do what is in my best interests,' I say. 'Not what I'm told.'

'Well, I'm glad you've recognised pissing me off isn't in your best interests.'

I gaze out of the window as raindrops race down the scratched glass. I try not to think of his lips bruising mine, or that offer he made me, or that primal grunt he made when I pulled the bullet from his arm. I try not to think about sinking my teeth into his plump bottom lip, or digging my nails into his back, or making him lose control, and how that would make me feel better somehow.

I try to ignore the dull throb between my legs that thinking about doing these things provokes. It's not right. It's not right for me to be feeling like this after everything that has happened. It doesn't make sense.

I focus on what's important: the mission. I have seeds to plant.

I spent three weeks in Draft One, weaving stories for myself based on ID cards I bought from the black markets, slipping into the lives of those who no longer needed them. I moved around a lot—from the West where suffocating white mist creeps through the abandoned skyscrapers and the scent of the sea hangs in the air, to the Northern river, close to the bedsit where Jay found me.

I recognize one of the dark towers with the neon Sacred Stylus over its door as we pass it.

'There's a square up ahead,' I say. 'Next right.'

'So?'

'I want to stop there.'

'I'm driving us to the motel I told you about.'

'Fine. But stop here first.'

'Why?'

'There's something I need to do.'

'Not safe.'

I dig my fingernails into my palm and force myself to keep my tone even. 'There are no Blotters around.'

'Yeah, because a load of the Draft One Blotters were deployed to your *Circus*. Now they're dead.' He says 'Circus' as if the word feels strange in his mouth, and 'dead' as if it is familiar.

'Exactly,' I say. 'Less on the streets. So it's safe.'

'Don't be naïve. More are on their way.'

I take a deep breath, pushing down my growing rage. 'I need to stop. I'll jump out of the moving van if I have to.'

Jay shrugs. 'Go ahead.'

I grab his arm, and it hardens. Not for the first time, it occurs to me how strong he is. 'Jay. Please. It's important.'

He makes an irritated noise in his throat, then he swerves the van to the side of the road, spraying water onto the windows of the nearby building. 'You're a pain in my arse, little Twist. You have two minutes.'

I rummage through my rucksack and pull out a can of spray paint. 'Three.'

'Two min—' He notices what I'm holding, and his expression darkens. 'What are you doing?'

'Planting a seed.' I open the door and leap out onto the road.

'Two minutes,' he yells after me.

Boots splashing through the black, inky puddles, I run through a narrow alley between two buildings. The scaffolding overhead momentarily shelters me from the rain. At the end, I do a quick scan for any trouble, and then, heart in my throat, I run towards the concrete block in the centre. I step over the chains they use to bind the victims to it, and disgust creeps down my spine as I catch the metallic scent of blood in the air. Then I shake the forbidden can and spray the shape I want. The pink paint runs with the rain, so I trace it a couple of times.

Adrenaline surges through my body.

But I am not afraid. I cannot be afraid.

Stories are true when we believe them.

When I'm done, I step back. My heart races. Blood and death once marked this concrete killing block. Now, there is a symbol of hope, of change, of stories.

Now, there is a dandelion seed.

Stories will always grow. Like dandelions in the cracks in the pavement.

I glance at the hollow windows that look down into the square. I wonder how many people will see the image before the Blotters wash it away. I wonder if they will be surprised.

They will be. This is not written.

This is a story that does not belong to the Creators.

I imagine the others planting similar seeds as they journey towards the library. I imagine the new story that will grow. A story of revolution.

I smile.

Then I click the lid back onto the can and run back to the van. Jay puts his foot down on the accelerator as soon as I'm inside. He throws me a sideways look, assessing my wet hair and the spray paint I'm holding between my legs.

'I was—'

'Didn't ask. Don't want to know.'

Jay seems to know exactly where he's going. I wonder if it's the ink telling him; if it's something to do with that tattoo on his arm. We do not run into any trouble from the Blotters, although every now and then, he changes route to avoid an oncoming vehicle. I persuade him to let me stop a couple more times before we get close to the Draft Two border.

His knuckles whiten as we approach the crossing.

'If we get stopped at the bridge, I'll tell a story—' I say.

'No.'

'What do you mean, no?'

'I'm not having you causing a scene. If we get stopped, I'll kill them.'

'Oh, and that's not causing a scene . . .'

A muscle twitches in his jaw. 'We won't get stopped. Not where I'm taking us. There's a tavern close to the bridge. Blotters in the Outer Drafts are lax.' He shakes his head as though that's a bad thing. 'Unless things have changed, the Creators know where we are, and it's written that we're coming. Then we're fucked.'

We both tense as we reach the long bridge that stretches over the black water. True to Jay's word, though, it is unguarded. He puts his foot down on the accelerator, and we speed into Draft Two.

It is similar to Draft One—though there's less scaffolding propping up the towering skyscrapers, and there are more neon Styluses marking Houses of Truth. As we pass a billboard the length of the street, the hard voice of a Teller permeates the van. He's saying the End is coming and the curious will be punished.

We drive throughout the night. Jay lets me stop another two times to paint dandelion seeds. I push for a third, but it's clear he has reached his limit, and so I allow him to drive us to the Blotter motel.

He parks the battered van down an empty side street, away from the main road where a number of Blotter vehicles are stationed. We sit there for a moment, him clenching and unclenching the steering wheel with his big hands; me fiddling with the near empty paint can between my legs. It is thankfully still dark outside, but it has shifted from the inky hues of midnight to the watercolour grey that comes just before dawn. The rain falls hard, sheets of water cascading down the windscreen. It feels as if we are alone in the world; as if no one can see us.

Something in my stomach tightens at the look in Jay's eyes when he turns his head. 'You have paint on your face,' he says.

He removes his hand from the wheel and lets it hover for a moment. Then he leans over and rubs it off with his thumb. His scent hits me, salt and sweat and something primal that belongs only to him. His white vest hangs off his body, and I drop my gaze to his hard chest and the dandelion seed above his heart.

'Hey.' He places a finger underneath my chin and tilts my face up. 'My eyes are up here, little Twist.' He holds my gaze, then he sits back and smudges the paint against his thumb, looking at it with a mixture of distaste and wonder. He sighs. 'When we go inside, you keep your mouth shut, yeah?'

'You have a plan?'

'That *is* the plan. You being quiet.'

I frown. Blotters aren't known for making plans; they do what the ink tells them. And now he does not have a story to follow.

'And what will *you* be doing?'

'I'll be getting us a room.'

I put the spray can back into my rucksack. 'You're just going to walk in there and get a room for a Blotter and a Twist?'

'Yeah.'

'That may raise some questions.'

'It won't.'

'Why?'

'I've told you, the guy that runs it turns a blind eye.'

'To what?'

He rubs the back of his neck. 'Um . . . recreational activities . . .'

'What do you mean?'

He exhales. 'I'm going to tell him you're a girl I've brought here to fuck, Elle.'

I raise my eyebrows. 'You're actually going to tell him that?'

'Yeah.'

'What if he doesn't believe you?'

'He will.'

'I thought you couldn't tell stories.'

The corner of his lip twitches. 'Who says I'm telling a story?'

Before I can reply, he gets out of the van. I watch him for a moment as he rests his arm against the roof of the vehicle, then he looks up into the sky, letting the raindrops fall on his face.

I take a deep breath before grabbing my rucksack and climbing out after him.

Chapter Twenty-Seven
Jay

She comes to stand in front of me as I'm looking up into the bloated sky.

'I thought I had to ask you to fuck me,' she says.

She's drenched already. Her wild hair is tangled down her back, and her oversized leather jacket hangs heavily off her shoulders. Beads of water run down her chest, and her black vest clings to her small frame.

I rub my jaw. I'll be getting her out those clothes once we get inside.

'You'll ask me,' I say. 'Beg, more like.'

An image of her on her knees in front of me appears unbidden in my mind. I need to stop imagining things. It's weird. And wrong. I've been doing it non-stop since I met her. I lick my lips, tasting the rain on them. She drops her gaze to my body, eyes darkening on my chest where my tattoos are visible through my wet vest.

She steps forwards so one of her legs is in between mine. I can smell her scent, mingling with the aroma of wet concrete. My hands seem to find their way into her open leather jacket and onto her hips of their own accord.

'You don't believe I will. Not really,' she says.

'No?'

'No. I have never begged anyone in my entire life.'

I don't doubt it. I push off the van, bringing my body even closer to hers. She has to tilt her head back to meet my eyes. I slide my hand into her hair, cupping the side of her face, and brush my thumb against her wet cheek.

'Well then, it'll be a new experience for you, won't it, little Twist?' I drop my hands to my sides as her mouth falls open, then I step past her. 'You coming? I'm getting soaked out here.'

She falls into step beside me. I catch her looking at me before she fixes her gaze to the end of the alleyway. She wants me. It's obvious. And she'll get what she wants. I imagine the little Twist always gets what she wants.

I think I would have done it that first time we met if she'd asked for it—though it was not written; though I was meant to kill her. I'd have taken her on top of that small mattress on the floor, and I'd have had her rough and hard, her body pinned beneath mine, her legs over my shoulders, her hands balled into fists on the sheets that smelled like her sweat.

But I'll get what I want too. And after all the shit she's put me through—terrorists, and Circuses, and killing Blotters, and driving stolen vans, and *getting shot*—what I want is her begging me for it.

What I want is her doing what I tell her for once.

I pause at the end of the alley, placing my hand on the wall opposite to stop the Twist from walking onto the main street. The smell of stagnant water and shit is heavy in the air. The river is just ahead, and unlike the border between One and Two, there's a high-security gate blocking the steel bridge that crosses it. Blotters are stationed on either side.

'That's the place?' she says, looking at a flickering blue Stylus light marking a tall building on the corner of the street.

'Yeah.'

'We could take refuge in the black market Maggie told us about.'

'No. Blotters'll be after us soon. And that'll be the first place they look.'

It's true. It is. But I also want her alone in one of those rooms. And I want her in a place that's unfamiliar to her, so for once, I'm not the one who's completely out of their depth.

'It's getting light. We're taking one of these rooms,' I say.

She tenses but then nods. We head onwards.

'Remember the plan when we're in there,' I say.

'It's not much of a plan, Jay. You just told me to shut up.'

'Yeah. And you're going to, right? Because I'm knackered, I've been shot already since I've been with you, and I can't be arsed with killing everyone you manage to piss off when we get in there.'

'I won't say a word.'

I stare at her, raindrops rolling down her face and sticking her hair to her scalp, trying to work out whether she's taking the piss.

'Right. Good.'

I grab her arm. It must hurt, but she doesn't make a sound as I pull her towards the motel. The Blotters don't spare us a second glance. Their guard is down. I'm just a Blotter enjoying myself between jobs. They don't expect any Cuts tonight—it is not written in the ink that brands their skin.

Yet.

It won't be long before the Creators adapt their story accordingly. They found the Circus pretty fast. The Twist thinks we'll eventually get to the Final City, but that's insane. Maybe I should have just killed her like I was supposed to; maybe it would have been a small mercy. Because after all she's done, I can't see her death being quick and painless. Not now. Not after she's *created*.

They'll make an example of her. A story. One with a moral message: *Do not defy the Creators*.

I swallow hard, tightening my grip around her arm. No. I'll kill anyone who lays a finger on her. I'll make her see how stupid this plan is. And I'll keep her safe.

But where the fuck is safe for either of us now? This library she and Sylvia were talking about? I don't believe it.

We reach the concrete building as the first weak rays of light start to cross the river. I nudge Elle towards the revolving doors, pressing my body into her back as I reach over her shoulder to push the glass. For a moment, I feel her warmth against my chest. And then we're in the dingy lobby.

It's a shithole in here. It reeks of cigarette smoke, damp, and sewage, and there are stains all over the red carpet. Thankfully, it's empty except for the oily guy behind the wooden desk. He has slicked-back grey hair, and his watery eyes slither all over Elle. I hate this creep.

'Welcome, sir, welcome. And what can I do you for this evening? No request is too big for an agent of our beloved Creators.'

Elle's arm tenses beneath my fingers.

'Four nights. No interruptions,' I say.

'Yes, yes, of course, sir.' He shuffles, turning to the wall of hooks behind him. He takes a brass key from one. 'First floor, room on the left with the blue light.' He grins, exposing crooked yellow teeth as he glances at Elle again. 'Pretty little thing. I wouldn't mind a go on her myself.'

My jaw sets. The muscles in my arms tighten. I want to reach over and smash his face into the desk. I want to rip his fucking head off. I breathe hard, containing the storm. She wouldn't want me to do that.

'I heard a story about a man like you. Would you like to hear it?'

I jerk my head to the side. Elle holds his gaze.

For the love of the Creators . . .

'I told you to shut your mouth.' My voice is rough, and she flinches. Good. She needs to look scared of me. She needs to keep her mouth shut, not be spouting off forbidden words in a place like this. I drop her arm. I run my hand over my mouth. Then I step forwards and place both palms flat on the desk, bringing my face close to the guy's and smelling his rank, sour breath. I lower my voice. 'She's mine. Understood?'

His eyes widen. He's terrified. He should be.

'Yes, sir. Of course, sir. It was . . . meant as a compliment, sir.'

I grab the brass key. Then I snatch Elle's arm and drag her to the stairs across the room.

I'm pissed off. Pissed off at that creep, pissed off I couldn't kill him, pissed off Elle didn't do as she was told.

I march her up the stairs in silence and pull her down a long corridor. Cigarette smoke wafts beneath one of the doorways, and the sound of a woman moaning comes from another. I unlock a door halfway down, with a blue light blinking above, signalling it is vacant. I shove her inside.

'What the fuck did I tell you?' My voice is low as I lock the door behind me.

She turns to face me. 'I'm supposed to let him speak to me like that? Some guy who licks the arse of every Blotter in the Draft after they've spent a day killing his own people? Piece of shit.'

'You're *supposed* to do what you're told.' I bring my face close to hers. 'You're *not* supposed to start spouting off *stories* in public. We're on my turf now, little Twist. We're not at your little Circus anymore. This is the real world, and you're going to get yourself killed. Understand?' When she tries to look away, I grab her chin. *'Do you understand?'*

'Do not patronise me. I've survived this long.'

'Because it was written you would survive this long. Your time is up. Do you get that?' I moisten my bottom lip, and she looks as if she wants to bite me. Try it. *Little Twist?*'

'Yes. Fine.'

I let her go, and she turns away from me, breathing hard. I sigh as I lean against the wall, scanning the room as I calm myself down.

I've been here before, but not this room. They all look the same though. The only item of furniture other than the mattress on the floor by the barred window is the wonky dresser with a full ashtray and a cracked mirror on top of it. There's an ajar door to my left that leads into a bathroom reeking of piss, and black mould creeps up the striped wallpaper that peels from the walls.

It's similar to the bedsit I've been stationed in for the past four years. In my experience, most places in Drafts One to Three are like this. Shit, basically.

When Elle finally turns to face me again, her hair is wet, and rain drips off her jacket onto the carpet. There's an unreadable look on her face.

'I don't belong to you, Jay.'

I frown. 'What?'

'You told him I was yours.'

'So?'

'I don't belong to anyone. Not you. Not the Creators. Not anyone.'

Something tightens around my throat, and I crack my knuckles. 'Look, there was a situation, and I dealt with it, okay?'

'Blotters don't lie. You said I was yours.'

'Shut it.'

She swallows. 'I suppose you're used to hearing people talk about women like that.'

'I dealt with it.'

'Is that how you talk about women too, Jay?'

I step closer. 'Careful, little Twist.'

'Is that how you know about this place? You come here and share women with your Blotter friends?'

'Course I don't.'

She pushes my chest, but I don't move.

'You need to calm down,' I tell her, dropping my voice.

'What if I don't? What are you going to do?' She pushes me again.

This time, I grab her wrists and shove them behind her back, holding them there. She breathes in sharply. I walk until her back hits the wall. The weak morning light, distorted by the bars on the window, doesn't quite reach us, and we stand in shadow, her breathing shallow.

Her eyes blaze, and something relaxes inside of me. A slow smile spreads across my face.

'What?' she snaps.

'I like you angry, little Twist.'

'And why is that?'

I study her face: the flush in her cheeks, the slight parting of her mouth, the rise and fall of her chest. I drag my teeth over my bottom lip.

'I don't know. I guess because it shows you're human.'

She raises her eyebrows. 'Of course I'm human.'

I release her wrists and place one of my hands flat on the wall by her face. 'You going to tell me what's wrong? Or you going to carry on being a dick, picking fights you're not going to win?'

Her eyes don't move from mine, and all the anger ebbs away. It's replaced by something searching. Something lost. She looks at the puddle forming on the floor between us.

'Look at me,' I say.

Slowly, she does. 'It's been a long day.'

'Yeah.'

'The Circus, the Blotters . . .' She releases a breath. 'It wasn't supposed to be that way.'

'Well, believe it or not, things haven't been exactly going to plan for me either lately.'

Tentatively, she reaches for the tattoo that marks her death, slipping her fingers through the tear in my top. 'Do you regret it?'

I put my hand over hers, enveloping it and holding it to my chest. 'No.' I surprise myself at how quickly I say it, how certain I sound.

When her eyes meet mine, the lost look is still there, but there's something behind it. Something urgent. I lean closer, holding her hand against my pounding heart.

'Tell me what you need, little Twist.'

Chapter Twenty-Eight
Elle

One of his hands is flat on the wall by my face. The other curls around my fist, holding it to his wet chest. I feel his heart pounding beneath hard muscle. His eyes do not move from mine. His thigh is between my legs, pinning me to the wall as he towers over me.

And I'm hot. Too hot. He's like a furnace; the heat radiating from him fills the motel room. It stokes the fire building inside of me. My throat is tight with the effort it takes to contain it.

'Tell me what you need.' His voice is low and gruff as gravel.

I want to lose myself. I want to escape. I want to find a way to make this hurricane of guilt that rages in my chest disappear. I want him to take it away. I want to feel his hard body pushed against mine. I want to scratch my fingernails down his back and bite his bottom lip and know what his rough hands would feel like on my skin.

Yet he's a Blotter. He's a killer. People like him took my father. He doesn't care that people died at the Circus.

And I want him.

I want to make him bleed.

My gaze drops to his tattooed knuckles, then to his vest that clings to the hard ridges of his torso. He releases my hand and brings his finger to my chin, tilting it up so I meet his gaze.

'Look at me,' he says.

His eyes are dark and searching. I do not have my story tattooed onto my skin, but it's like he's trying to read me all the same. It makes my blood run even hotter. He has been guarded about his curiosity since we met. Yet now it is plain to see on his face.

He tilts his head to the side as he runs his thumb along my bottom lip, his breathing deepening as my mouth parts. And there are a million questions in his eyes, searching for answers as they scan my features. Questions he is no longer hiding.

I have imagined us being alone since we arrived at the Circus, I couldn't stop myself. But every scenario I concocted was rough and angry and hard, like Jay. But he is gentle as he traces my lips, and somewhere beyond the depths of ink and darkness, I see the man who might have existed if the Creators had not turned his blood into ink. Not the monster sent to kill me.

I respond to his touch with a question of my own, sliding my hand up his top and watching his jaw tighten in response. Still his eyes remain fixed on mine. Open. Wondering. But dark.

'You drive me crazy, you know that?' he says—his voice low.

'Yes,' I say. 'Why?'

He drags his teeth across his bottom lip and my stomach clenches. I want to bite his lip. I want to run my hands over his inked skin. I want to know what he looks like, what he sounds like, what he tastes like when he lets go.

But I am curious too. I want to know what he will do next.

'You make no sense.' He shakes his head. 'Nothing about you makes sense. I don't know what you're going to do. I don't know what you want.'

'You know what I want.'

His hand cups my cheek, his palm rough and calloused. A soldier's hand. Yet he is as gentle with me as he was when we first met, when I dared to step closer. His eyebrows knit together. 'Apart from treason, I have no fucking clue.'

Something in the air pulsates between us. It's like elastic. His body moves with it, his hard breath bringing him closer then farther away as he towers over me. I can smell him; sweat, dirt, and rain.

'I want you,' I say. 'But on my terms. Not yours.'

'Why?' he says.

'Isn't it the same for you?'

I can feel his restraint. His heartbeat is fast beneath my palm, his chest rising and falling. He swallows. The curiosity that brought us together is now holding us apart as he watches me. Waits to see what I'll do.

His eyes drop to my lips and I think he's going to snap. Then his hand curls into a fist against the wall by my face. 'I told you you'd have to ask me.'

'I told you I wouldn't.'

He makes a frustrated noise in his throat. Sliding his hand into my hair, he drops his lips to my neck and trails rough kisses along my collarbone. My breath hitches and I grip onto his shoulder, my body melting into his as though I was made to fit within his arms. His other hand grips the back of my thigh, pulling my closer.

'You're driving me crazy,' he whispers, his breath hot against my ear. 'I can't stop thinking about you. I can't stop *imagining*.' And there's a hint of anger in his voice, now, as he murmurs against my skin.

'You imagined?'

'I can't fucking stop.'

'What did you imagine?'

'All the things I was going to do to you.'

My insides tighten. I take a shaky breath. 'Show me.'

He pulls away and looks down at me. There's heat in his gaze as his eyebrows raise. He slides the coat off my shoulders.

'You want me to show you?' he asks.

'Yes."

Slowly, he peels off my top, his knuckles leaving a trail of fire on my skin. His eyes darken.

My heart beats a little quicker as I wonder what a Blotter would have imagined. Whether he is thinking of stripping me of my clothes and taking me against the wall, or over the dresser, in the ways that I imagine Blotters take their women.

He surprises me when he brushes my hair out of my face and kisses me softly. Frustratingly softly. I grip his shoulders and pull him closer, sliding my tongue against his, coaxing him to lose control. He makes a low sound and pushes me against the wall, his hands moving to my waist and pulling my body closer to his. All the while his kisses deepen, become more aggressive. I moan against his mouth as I feel his need, taste his desperation. It's not enough. I want more. Why isn't he giving me more?

As if answering my unasked question, he reaches behind me and unhooks my bra, and then his big hands are on me – running down my back, up my torso. I cry out and he pulls away, breathing hard, his forehead resting against mine. His jaw clenches as his gaze trails down my body.

He has fought to keep control of his emotions since the moment things did not go the way they were written. And I can see the animal behind his eyes, ready to break from its cage. But he is keeping it contained. I want him to let it go. I want to set it free.

'Show me,' I say, breathless.

I slide my hand down his stomach, trailing my fingers to the waistband of his jeans. He grits his teeth, watching as I unfasten the button. Slowly, I reach for the zip. I can feel him, hard, straining against the denim. He swallows fast.

Then he snatches my wrists, his grip like a vice. He tilts his head to the side, watching my face. Slowly, he drops his knees in front of me.

My breath hitches. 'What are you doing?' I say, and the waver in my voice betrays my surprise.

'Don't tell me the little Twist has been thrown off-guard.' He raises his eyebrow. "This is what you want, isn't it? Me to fall at your feet.'

'No,' I say.

The questions are in his eyes again as they hold mine.

'You try so hard to keep in control,' I say. 'You won't let go. I want you to let go.'

His grip tightens on my hips and his lips harden. 'You want me to lose control?'

I trace the burning damp ink that has bound him to my enemies his entire life and wonder how it can look so beautiful on him. 'Yes.'

'You may come to regret saying that, little Twist.' With excruciating slowness, he unties my boots and takes them off, then he unfastens the button of my jeans. I breathe in sharply, gripping onto the muscles of his shoulders as he pulls them off. His eyes jolt to the tattoo inked onto my ankle for a moment, but I pull his gaze up.

I touch the scar across his eyebrow, then I move my fingers to his mouth and trace his full lips. Something raw and vulnerable passes across his eyes. It occurs to me that perhaps someone who has lived with violence for their whole life has never had someone treat them gently before.

'But you're a hypocrite. Because you won't let go for me either, will you?' he says.

He drags his teeth across his bottom lip as he stares up at me, cheeks flushed, pupils dilated. He grips my inner thigh, his thumb achingly close to the place that throbs between my legs.

'You want to know what I keep imagining?' he says.

I swallow, my insides liquid, and nod. He hooks his thumbs into the sides of my underwear and gently pulls them down. When his eyes move up again, he groans. He slides his hands to my hips, and my pulse quickens.

Then he kisses me between my legs.

I cry out. First with surprise. Then with something else as he licks the most intimate part of me. 'What are you . . .?' My words trail off and end with a moan as he pulls my legs farther apart. 'Jay. Fuck—'

His eyes lock onto mine. There's a darkened curiosity behind them, as he moves his mouth. Every lick, every stroke, every lash, is a question that my body answers for him – my skin dampening with sweat, my breaths coming out short and sharp, pressure building beneath my legs. My fingernails dig into his shoulders, clinging onto the solidness of him, as he holds me steady.

The air is hot and charged. There's a hurricane building in my chest. A tornado. A fire. I grab the back of his head with both hands, pulling him close, moving my hips. He groans and the low sound vibrates through me. His mouth is hot, his fingers dig into my skin, his chest is moving up and down quickly like he has a hurricane inside him, too.

I can't stop looking at him. Inked and dangerous and on his knees before me, eyes dark and burning with questions. A crescendo is building inside me and he sees it. His tongue moves harder, faster.

I thought I controlled the hurricane, but I feel it taking over me. Wild. Dark. Enraged. It's too much to bear.

He slips his thumb inside me, and my back arches. I can't hold on anymore.

A raw cry tears from my lips as waves of pleasure ripple through. A low noise escapes from him too, hard and throaty. My knees buckle. I have to grab onto his shoulders to keep my balance. His breathing is ragged as he pulls back and his eyes fix on my face, pupils wide and blacker than ink.

He looks every bit the monster that killed the Blotters back in his bedsit.

Wild. Primal.

Hungry.

But I don't care anymore. If he is a monster, let him be my monster.

'Jay, please. . .'

Before I know what is happening, he's on his feet and I'm scooped up in his arms, his strong hands beneath my thighs, my legs tightening around his back.

And then we're on the mattress on the floor by the window, and I'm peeling off his vest, running my hands down the ink that stains his soul while he scrambles out of his jeans. When he looks at me, whatever restraint that masked his face before is gone. He's wearing the same expression he did when he killed the Blotters. A beautiful monster.

And when he is inside me, he isn't gentle. His hips thrust hard and fast and rough, provoking cries from my lips with each movement as my nails scrape down his back and my teeth sink into his chest. Yet I embrace the violence. I need it.

We move together, and something builds up as I grip onto him for life, the air hot around us.

'Ah, fuck,' he says as his body stiffens then shudders, a groan tearing from his lips. He crashes down on top of me, head sinking into the flattened pillow by my ear. 'Fuck,' he keeps saying.

Breathing fast, I slip my hand to the back of his neck, hot and damp, and hold him there.

His heart pounds, thunderous, to the same song as mine.

When he rolls off me onto his back, causing a dip in the springy mattress, he rubs his face with both hands. 'Fuck,' he mumbles, his voice throaty.

I touch his chest. 'You imagined that?'

The corner of his lip quirks. He rolls onto his side and brushes a strand of hair that's sticking to my cheek behind my ear. 'Something like that.'

'The thing you did with your mouth,' I say. 'Did you imagine that?'

'Yeah.'

I run my finger over his lips. 'Have you done that before?'

'No.' He pulls me closer to him, his hand on my lower back. 'But I told you I was curious to see what you tasted like.'

I bring my lips to his, and he kisses me softly. I cup both of his cheeks and study the blue and silver flecks in his irises, and that small ink-like blotch by his pupil.

'What else are you curious about?' I ask him.

He pulls me closer and shifts me onto my back, climbing on top of me and bringing his face back to mine.

Softly, he brushes his lips against my neck, then my collarbone, then my chest. He moves slowly down until he's by my feet. Then he kneels, the sunlight glinting off the black swirls and symbols inked onto his skin, and holds my ankle, studying it intently. He looks like a statue for a moment, impassive and impenetrable like the ones in Creators' Square in the Final City.

'Your tattoo.' He yanks me towards him, and I bite my lip to stop myself from crying out. 'Why do you have this?'

I shift into a sitting position, one leg on either side of him, and touch the identical dandelion seed that marks his skin right above my death warrant. 'I told you before,' I say. 'It reminds me of something my father used to say. Stories will always grow. Like dandelions in the cracks in the pavement.'

His eyes search for answers I don't have as he puts his hand on top of mine. 'Why do I have this?'

I shake my head, running my thumb over it. 'I don't know,' I say softly.

'I thought you had all the answers, little Twist.'

'I thought you knew what was written.'

'I don't. I don't know anything anymore.' He claims my mouth with his, slipping his hand into my tangled hair and pulling me roughly closer. Shifting on his knees, he lowers me onto my back, his kisses deepening as I wrap my arms around his shoulders. He groans.

'Nothing at all?' I murmur against his lips.

'Only you.'

Chapter Twenty-Nine
Jay

Fuck.

I face her on the mattress. I'm soaked with sweat. My breathing is hard, ragged. I grip the back of her neck, her damp hair tangled through my fingers. Her hand is on my chest, and she must be able to feel my heartbeat pounding beneath her palm.

She's close enough that her small nose rubs against mine. She smells like sweat and sex and honey. She smells like me too. I like that she smells of me.

Her amber eyes lock onto mine, and that look of wonder is still in there. I want to turn away from it. I want to tell her she's insane. She shouldn't be looking at me like that.

And yet I can't look away.

This is weird for me. I've never done this before. Never laid beside a girl and just looked at her, watched her. Never felt my heartbeat gradually slow beneath someone else's palm.

I'm a Blotter. That's not what we do. Love is not written into our stories or marked on our skin. We are bred. And we have needs. But there's no point in sticking around.

I reckon once I've come down from the high I'm on right now from thrusting inside of her as if my life depended on it—from releasing whatever's been building up inside of me since the moment I first laid eyes on her—I'm going to freak out. Because I don't know what happens next. I always know what happens next. But not now. Not with her.

And I reckon once she's come down from the high of falling apart beneath my body—once her breathing is settled and her skin has lost its pink flush—she'll realise her curiosity has been sated, and that'll be that.

But still, I can't look away.

'I knew you'd ask me, little Twist.'

'I didn't ask you. I was telling—'

I brush my lips against hers to shut her up. 'I know, but let's pretend. For my ego, yeah?' I murmur against her skin.

She laughs, and when she parts her mouth, I slip my tongue inside. She makes a soft sound in her throat, and her body melts into mine. I fucking love the sounds she makes.

When I pull away and my heart steadies, I notice how red the skin around her neck is, and the way her leg trembles between mine. My chest tightens.

'Did I hurt you?' I ask, and I realise it's the first time in my life I've ever asked someone that. She laughs, and I tense. 'What?'

She rests her hand on my cheek. 'You tried to kill me, and now you're worried you hurt me.' She smiles. 'It's just . . . strange . . . how this turned out, isn't it?'

'Yeah, it's fucking strange. That's what I've been trying to tell you all along.' I brush my thumb against her cheek. 'But I didn't try to kill you. If I'd tried, you'd be dead.'

'Are you sure about that?'

I'm not sure about anything anymore. 'I didn't try to kill you.'

She traces my eyebrow. 'Can I ask you something?'

'I suppose.'

'You have a scar,' she says.

'I'll probably have a few more by the time this is all over. You got me shot, remember?'

'You got yourself shot. How did you get it?'

'I was somewhere I shouldn't have been.'

'Where?'

'Doesn't matter.'

'It does to me.'

I exhale and look away. 'No, it doesn't, Elle.'

She pulls my gaze back to hers. 'Come on. Talk to me, Jay.'

The tension starts to build again. Because I don't want to talk about shit from the past. And yet I feel the insatiable need to live up to that wonder in her eyes, to give her what she wants.

'You're a pain in my arse, little Twist.' I brush the damp hair out of her face and give her a hard look. 'I got it when I was a child. Before I had ink in my veins. I was at the Citadel. Went somewhere I wasn't supposed to be. I was prone to man's first sin back then.'

She smiles. 'You're still curious, Jay.'

'Shut it. Anyway, I overheard a couple of Creators talking. One of them saw me. He wasn't too happy about it. And that's all there is to it.'

'He beat you?'

'Yeah.'

'What did you overhear?' She runs her thumb along my bottom lip and I bite it.

'Fuck knows. I was just a kid, Elle. It was an argument, I think. Something about ink'.

I roll her onto her side so I can't see the questions in her eyes and pull her into my body. She lies in silence for a moment. Then her stomach muscles tense against my hand.

'The One True Story says Blotters can't have children,' she says.

'We can breed,' I say. 'But only when it's written.'

She relaxes against my chest, and my lip twitches. As if I'd have done that with her if there were any chance it would result in such a thing.

'Who were your parents?' she asks.

I feel a tightness in my chest. I don't want to talk about this stuff.

'Don't know. Doesn't matter.'

'But you were born. Not created.'

'Yeah.'

She takes a deep breath. 'I never knew my mother either.'

'But you knew your father. The dandelion man.'

'Yes,' she says, and I hear the smile in her voice. 'There's something else I'm curious about.'

'Go on then.'

'Do Blotters dream?'

'What? No. Now, go to sleep,' I say to stop her from asking more questions. 'I'm knackered.'

'Fine. But not for long. I want to go to the black market before nightfall.'

I tense. 'We're not going to some illegal market when every Blotter in the Draft is going to be out looking for us.' I move closer to her, my mouth by her ear. 'We're going to wake up just before nightfall. I'm going to make you come again. And we're going to lie low until this meeting with the Canary or whatever her name was. Then we're getting the out of here. Yeah?'

She laughs. 'We'll see.'

'Yeah. We will.' I stroke her stomach, and soon, I feel sleep wash over her—her breathing slowing, her body relaxing. I smile. I never smile, but it seems I can't stop nowadays. When did I become so pathetic?

My eyelids are heavy when my body stiffens. The ink in my veins burns. I feel as if scalding metal is being pushed onto the spot above my heart, branding me like cattle. I try to calm my breathing. I try to make it stop.

She makes a muffled noise.

I wince. 'Shh. Go back to sleep.'

Her breathing steadies, and I pull her closer. I let out a long breath as the pain ebbs away.

The Blotter and the Twist. It won't end well. It can't.

But right now, with her asleep in my arms, it doesn't feel so bad. In fact, I think I might even feel a flicker of happiness somewhere in all the darkness—which is a novel fucking feeling. I exhale and kiss the back of her head.

'You'll be the death of me, little Twist.'

We spend the next three days in the motel. I spend the nights watching her at the nearby black market, making sure she doesn't get into any trouble. She makes it clear she'll go without me if I don't come, so what else am I supposed to do?

'Once, there was a world. And the world was grey . . .'

She tells the story standing on the bench of an old steel factory amongst stalls of forbidden things. The rank smell of the river drifts through the broken windows, and I can just about see the outline of Draft Three beyond it.

I keep my tattoos covered, but the small group of people who gather around her eye me cautiously as if they can sense what I am.

I'm dangerous.

They're idiots though.

I'm not as dangerous as her.

'No flowers had grown for centuries. The people had forsaken them for practical things like cities, and skyscrapers, and powerful men. They had forgotten what flowers were . . .'

A CIRCUS OF INK

She listens too, for word that her dandelion seeds are spreading.

I hear the whispers first, on the second night, as she talks to a larger group with faces smeared with dirt. A man talks in hushed tones to a vendor selling fake ID cards about a painted symbol on a killing block.

'But one day, there was a hurricane. The hurricane stirred something in the earth long forgotten . . .'

She gets bolder as the night gets darker, encouraged, I think, by the growing crowd—curious eyes that drink in her stories of flowers and storms and dragons. Her face glows, expressive, hands gesturing around her as she captivates audiences who should be afraid while the air smells like damp and home-brewed alcohol.

I get it though. The fascination. Because she tells me stories too, later, as we lie panting on the dirty mattress. She tells me about a girl locked away in a tower and a man with a clockwork heart, and I don't want to listen, but at the same time, I do.

'It was a dandelion clock. And as the winds blew, they started to spread its seeds . . .'

She insists on visiting other places in Draft Two as well, spreading more seeds. It's madness. And on the third night, before she heads to the black market, I have to drag her, struggling, with a paint can in her hand, away from a House of Truth she planned to graffiti.

The Sacred Stylus buzzes above its open doors, and there's a Teller inside the bare atrium of the tower, telling a crowd of people the story of the first sin—curiosity—and how all Twists must be Cut in order for the Creators to gift the people the foretold Ending.

It's only a matter of time before we're Cut. I don't know how the fuck I'm going to keep her safe. She's reckless. Naïve.

She's dangerous.

'And as the seeds took to the earth, they started to grow. When they bloomed, the world was no longer grey. It was full of colour. It was beautiful . . .'

It's on the third night that we run into the Canary, as Elle tells her stories standing on a crate by a smashed window, black mould creeping up the frame behind her and broken glass glittering in the firelight.

The Canary dresses like a man, in the grey uniform of the factories, and has dark hair tied back from a severe face. There's a tattoo of a songbird inked onto her skin beneath her sleeve. She tells us a story about a group of women in the old days who would sing songs to sailors to lure them to shore before stealing their ships as we share beer and stale bread in the factory's old breakroom.

Bullshit, I think. But she has a boat we can use to cross the river.

She tells us to meet her the following nightfall at a certain point along the riverbank. There are abandoned warehouses on the other side, she tells us, where we can shelter until we're ready to move on.

'And the people remembered what they had lost. They remembered what had been taken from them . . .'

Elle insists on telling her story one more time before we head back to the motel. She gathers the biggest crowd yet.

We shouldn't have stayed though. Strained grey light crawls up over the river when we leave, and there are more Blotters around than usual, patrolling the streets between the buildings and flickering billboards and standing by the steel bridge.

I don't understand why we've not been caught yet. It must not be written. But why?

I yank her arm roughly as I pull her inside the motel, past the sleazy guy behind the reception desk.

And yet it's just an act. I'm not angry. I'm not scared.

A CIRCUS OF INK

I think a part of me is glad I took her to the market—as dangerous as it was.

Elle's story rings in my ears.

'They remembered to fight.'

Chapter Thirty
Elle

Slowly, I open my eyes. Evening light strains through the barred window onto our bodies. It's our fourth night here, and we need to meet the Canary soon so we can pass across the river.

Jay is asleep, I think. His warm, steady breaths brush against the back of my neck. One of his tattooed arms lies heavily over my side, pinning me to the mattress. The other lies beneath my neck. His skin is damp, and his chest sticks to my back as it rises and falls.

What I'm feeling right now is not logical. Not when I'm supposed to be dead and people are coming to kill me. Not when I have *created*. Not when I have painted dandelion seeds on the killing blocks and killed Blotters with twisters and hurricanes. Not when I am lying naked beside the man who has my death inked onto his skin. It's a feeling I have not felt in a long time. Warm, it swells and spreads unbidden through my body.

I feel *safe*.

And it makes no sense.

Because I am not safe. Neither is Jay. Neither are Raven and Sylvia and the others who are travelling across the Drafts to meet us. None of us are safe.

We weren't before. And we aren't now.

It is dangerous for me to feel any other way.

Yet I don't want to push the feeling away. Not yet. I want to bask in its warmth the way I would bask in the glow of the Final City lights when I was a child, when my father would visit and tell me stories of dandelions and dragons and Circuses and little girls with hair wilder than hurricanes who could change the world; create their own destinies.

So I lie there as twilight trickles between the bars of the window onto the dirty bedsit and the springs of the mattress dig into my aching muscles. I sink into his cocoon of heat, his scent of salt and sweat. I let his rhythmic breaths wash over me, as steady and unfaltering as the beating of a clock. Every now and again, he twitches. He says Blotters don't dream, but I think he does. I wonder what he is dreaming about.

This is new to me. Being with a man this way.

I have had sex before—back at the Circus, not long before I left for Draft One. Clumsy and awkward: gnashing teeth and caught hair and hesitant hands. Rami and I had giggled after, hurriedly pulling on our clothes, cheeks flushed with embarrassment.

We had sex because we wanted to know what sex was like. Not because we wanted each other.

It wasn't like this—this insatiable urge to be closer to someone. This yearning to feel the heartbeat of another pounding to the same song. This need to use each other's bodies to purge ourselves of the building violence.

This feeling of finally finding something solid, something to cling onto while everything is chaos all around.

But it is dangerous to feel this way. I have things to do, and I cannot be distracted.

We need to get ready for our crossing into Draft Three.

So I shift beneath his arm.

The change in his breathing is instant. His muscles harden against my back. He flattens his hand on my stomach.

'Where do you think you're going, little Twist?' His words are thick through sleep, and they vibrate against my skin.

I try to shift him off me, but he's like a dead weight. Unmovable. Softly, he bites the back of my neck. I can feel him, hard, against the back of my thigh.

'I told you what was going to happen when we woke up,' he mumbles.

He did. This morning, when we fell asleep in each other's arms after the visit to the black market.

I swallow. It's almost nightfall, and shadows extend like fingers from the barred window. I need to go. I need to keep moving. I need to get into the next Draft.

I need to get to the library to find the Book of Truth I'm searching for.

But I don't move. Because I need him too.

'We need to get going,' I say.

I feel his smile against the back of my neck at the lack of conviction in my words. He slides his hand down my stomach and between my legs. My breathing hitches as he strokes me softly. The conflict between what I should want and what I actually want disappears. I just want him.

I press my body into his, reaching for the back of his neck and pulling his face to mine. He kisses me and groans against my mouth.

In a sudden movement, he grabs my thigh and puts my leg over his, spreading me open to give him more access. He shifts so he can see my face, his eyes dark with curiosity. Then he slips a finger inside of me, and I moan.

'*Fuck,*' he groans.

He is gentle at first, but then he moves his hand harder, faster. Short breaths tear from my lips. I move my hips against his hand, the room dissolving around me—*everything* dissolving around me. There's only him and the pressure building between my legs. It's too much.

'You *are* mine,' he says softly.

'Jay—'

'You said you weren't. But you are.'

I can't argue because I can't think; I can't focus. He nips my earlobe with his teeth.

'You're mine to protect.'

And then I'm falling, shattering. My back arches against his chest, and I cry out. His breathing is ragged, and I'm panting and wet. I can smell him, masculine and raw. Even though he's cupping me possessively and his fingers are there inside, he's still not close enough. He's never close enough.

I reach behind and take him in my hand. He groans as I guide him to me. There's a moment where I feel a mixture of pleasure and pain. Then the crescendo starts to build again as he thrusts into me.

Afterwards, when he stills and my body feels like liquid in his solid arms, he looks at me, his eyes refocusing. Hand around my neck, he kisses me, his mouth hot, his skin damp with sweat.

Then he pulls out and rolls onto his back. Both of us sigh.

I want to stay here like this. I want to spend the rest of the night in a tangle of limbs and muscle. I want to hear the noise he makes when he lets go again and again. I want to take charge for once, because he still hasn't let me fully take control of his body the way I want to. I want to see what would happen if I took him in my mouth. I want to study every inch of him, count the tattoos on his body and understand what they mean.

But we are in danger.

And I have things to do.

I shuffle off the mattress and tread barefoot across the threadbare carpet. My legs tremble a little, my skin wet and sensitive. He sits up too, knees up, resting his arms across them. He frowns as I hurry to the bathroom. When I come back, I pull some grey factory overalls out of my rucksack.

'We need to go,' I say.

His cheeks are flushed and his body covered in a sheen of sweat. He runs a hand across his mouth. 'Do you think this Canary will come through with the boat?'

'You don't trust her?' I ask as I pull on my clothes.

'No. She's operating outside of the One True Story. She's a Twist.'

'You still think Twists can't be trusted?'

'No one can be trusted.'

'You're wrong.'

He shakes his head, exasperated, opening his mouth to scorn me. But then a loud rumble vibrates like thunder through the small room, and he is on his feet, striding to the window.

'*Fuck,*' he says as I come to stand beside him.

There are black Blotter vans crossing the steel bridge over the river. A whole convoy of them coming towards us. A spark of panic ignites in my chest, and I try to push it away.

Jay's jaw clenches into a hard line. 'Fuck. They know we're here.'

Chapter Thirty-One
Jay

The walls are closing in on me. There's a weight pushing down on my chest. I can't breathe; I can't swallow.

It's not the bars on the window or the rumble of the Blotter vans crossing the river or the damp, suffocating air of the motel room that's making me feel as if I'm in a prison.

It's her.

I'm staring ahead, but I'm hyper-aware of her by my side. It's been the same since the moment I first laid eyes on her. I can always sense her, feel her, smell her. I think she says something, but all I can think about is what they'll do to her if they catch us.

If I were on my own, it wouldn't matter. I don't give a shit if I live or die. But I've never had to think about anyone other than myself before, and any decision I make could make things worse. I'm stuck. I don't know how to get the fuck out of this.

I grip onto the window ledge, cracking the plaster.

She touches my arm. 'Jay.' She shoves my jeans into my chest and raises an eyebrow. 'Get dressed.'

She looks wary. But not afraid.

She should be afraid.

'Jay,' she snaps when I don't move. 'Would you rather fight Blotters with your clothes on, or completely naked?'

I release a breath. 'Don't really give a fuck either way.' I snatch the jeans though and pull them on. My vest is folded on the dresser, and I grab it and pull it over my head.

I scan the room for something to help me and glance at the rucksack on the floor. The Twist has a knife in there. I open it and pull it out.

'If they don't know we're in the motel, it's safer here,' says Elle, staring out of the window. 'But if they do know, we need to go. Now.'

'Yeah, well, there's the dilemma . . .' I lace up my boots and then cross the room to tower behind her.

The vans have come to a halt on the bridge. There are ten in total. Two of the Blotters guarding the bridge approach the window of the first.

'What do you think we should do?' she says.

And that's the thing: I don't know. I don't make decisions. I just do what the ink tells me. There's a part of me that wonders if she's already made a decision and she's just winding me up, trying to make me do something she knows I can't do. She certainly looks as self-assured as always, with her straight posture and her shoulders pulled back. I crack my knuckles.

'Are you trying to piss me off? Because now's not the time.'

'Course I'm not.' She turns her head. 'Don't be defensive with me, Jay. It's not the time for that either.'

'Don't—' I frown and step forwards, my chest touching Elle's back. 'Is that the twat from downstairs?'

Together, we watch the shadow of a man walk towards a few of the Blotters on the bridge.

She stiffens against me. *'Piece of shit.'* Elle sounds so outraged that I smile. She can't comprehend that someone would sell out one of their own. Naïve little Twist. He's known there was something off about us ever since she started to tell him that story.

I told her to keep her mouth shut.

His actions have the opposite effect on me though. I feel as if I can breathe again. The fog in my brain clears. The decision's been made for us.

I grab her arm. 'Time to go.'

We cross the room, Elle throwing her rucksack over her shoulder as we pass it. I listen at the door and then turn the brass key in the lock. We head out into the murky corridor. We're halfway down the stairs when I push Elle back into the wall. There are men in the lobby.

'*Fourth door on the left, sirs. Please understand I thought he was one of you, sirs. I would never have . . .*'

'Shut up. Upstairs.'

Footsteps thud across the carpet.

'Get back to the room,' I say as a Blotter appears at the foot of the stairs.

I launch forwards before he can raise his gun. We land on the floor in a cloud of dust. I grab his head and smash it repeatedly into the floor. I'm seeing red, hearing nothing but my heartbeat, as I charge at the next. It's all a blur as I break a guy's jaw, stab someone in the gut, and slit the throat of another.

Then a gun clicks. 'Calm down, lad, or we'll kill the girl.'

I freeze.

'That's it, lad. Easy now.'

My breathing is ragged, a knife clenched in my fist. I try to focus. Try to clear the rage clouding my vision. There are eight more Blotters to kill. One of them stands over Elle.

My insides turn to ice, and my grip on the knife tightens.

She's on her knees with a gun pointed at the back of her head. Her breathing is quick. Her hair falls over her face, and there's a tear in her sleeve where someone has grabbed her. Her eyes lock onto mine.

'Get the fuck away from her.' My voice comes out like a growl.

'It's okay, lad. Calm down.'

The Blotter who spoke steps forwards from the tight circle surrounding us. He's old for a Blotter. Late forties, maybe, with a severe angular face and slicked-back sandy hair peppered with grey. Death curls up his arms and is painted on his chest and neck. He looks me up and down.

'Fascinating,' he says. 'You look just like a Blotter. It must have taken you a long time to ink your skin like that. Shame it will be wasted when we burn it off.'

'What the fuck are you talking about?'

His lips twist into a cold smile, and he holds out a hand. 'Give me the knife, lad.'

'I'd rather slice you open with it, mate.'

He shakes his head as though he's disappointed, but his eyes glint. 'There's no point fighting it. It is written.' He stares at me, waiting. 'No? Okay.' He looks over his shoulder. 'Kill her.'

Elle opens her mouth to speak, but I hurl the knife, and it embeds into the forehead of the Blotter about to shoot her. His eyes widen with surprise before he falls flat on his back.

The Blotter in front of me doesn't even flinch as the others raise their guns. 'Don't shoot.'

The air is charged. Blotters always know what is going on, but right now, no one knows what the fuck will happen next. Me included.

'So, this is your girl?' says the Blotter. His eyes linger on Elle for too long, and every muscle in my body tightens.

'Don't you look at her. Look at me,' I say.

He steps towards her. Her breathing quickens. Panic ignites in my gut because I don't know what he's going to do. I've seen her do incredible things, but there are no hurricanes here. No stories.

And she's so small compared to the men surrounding her. So breakable.

'Hey—' I say.

'I heard a story about a man like you,' she says, looking up to meet his eyes. 'He—'

The Blotter nods, and one of the others slaps her across the face. She falls down, and I lurch forwards, but the two behind me grab my arms and pull me back. The Blotter raises his hand before I can fight them off.

'I'd think very carefully about your next move, lad, if you don't want us to shoot her face off.'

I still, my breathing laboured.

'Good lad.' He chuckles. 'I can see why you're so taken with her. It's a pity an example needs to be made of you both.'

He nods, and one of the Blotters raises a plastic container and starts dowsing the carpet with fuel. My pulse quickens.

'Can't be having Twists masquerading as Blotters now, can we?' His eyes glint as he holds my gaze. He looks as if he's waiting for me to say something, but I have no clue what. Then he slips a box of matches out of his jeans pocket. The slimy motel twat whimpers, finally realising he's fucked himself over along with us.

'You've been told he's not a Botter,' says Elle.

The Blotter who hit her before strikes her again. She falls flat onto her hands.

'Touch her again, and I'll fucking kill you,' I say.

'No, you won't.'

Rage builds in my chest. I can barely contain it.

'Why do you think they told you to burn us and not shoot us?' Elle's eyes are locked on me now, a red mark across her cheek. The guy with the fuel sloshes it over her, and she coughs, spluttering and spitting on the carpet.

I'm going to rip his fucking head off.

'She's got quite a mouth on her, hasn't she?' says the grey-haired bastard. 'You will be burned because it is written.' He nods at the Blotter with the containers, and he comes towards me.

'Don't you fucking—' My threat is cut off as he throws the remainder of the fuel on me. I spit on the floor, the sour, artificial taste on my tongue.

'No. We will be burned because the Creators don't want you to see him bleed,' says Elle.

'Chain them to the desk,' says the Blotter. 'Let's be done with it.'

Elle's eyes slide to mine. 'They won't shoot you, Jay.'

She looks so fucking certain. So sure she's right. And what choice do we have?

I wrench my arms out of the grip of the two men holding me and knock the old guy aside. Elle stumbles to her feet towards me, and I grab her. She's right. No one shoots. Why? But then the grey-haired guy raises his matchbox.

I turn and tackle him to the ground with a roar. He puts his hands around my neck as I slam his wrist into the fuel-soaked carpet. The matchbox flies across the room, landing beside the revolving door.

'Elle!' I yell.

She's already running towards it. I charge after her, throwing two Blotters aside, and the air is filled with confused yelling. They don't know what's happening. This isn't going the way it was written. It's the only thing that keeps us alive.

'Just shoot them,' says one of the Blotters.

Elle is holding a match when I grab her by the waist and pull her towards the revolving doors. She lights it even though there's fuel all over her.

'What the fuck? Elle, come—'

She throws it as I pull her through the doors. The lobby goes up in flames as we stumble onto the pavement. There are Blotter vans parked all the way down the road and more coming over the bridge.

I catch movement out of the corner of my eye and pull Elle close to me, turning away from the motel as the reception desk hurtles through the window. The air is thick with heat and smoke and shouting.

Elle's cheeks are flushed, and her eyes are wide when I look down at her.

'*Run,*' she says.

Chapter Thirty-Two
Elle

Run.

We tear away from the river as more Blotters cross the bridge. A van skids down the road beside us, and a man with tattoos shoots out of the window. Jay pulls me down an alley between two towering buildings.

'Keep going,' he roars, rain running over his lips and into his mouth, mixing with the petrol.

The van door slams shut as we race ahead. Jay kicks over a bin to obstruct the path of the Blotter now pursuing us on foot. Shouts fill the air, mixing with the smoke. More are coming.

I can barely focus on our surroundings. My heartbeat pounds in my ears, and adrenaline pumps through my body. It's fueling me, but it makes me feel as if I'm underwater. My lungs scream for breath, and the air feels thick.

I don't know the route we take through the urine-scented alleys and backstreets, always keeping away from the roads, but Jay knows. He is a Blotter. The routes through this Draft Two labyrinth are imprinted in his mind by the ink in his veins.

Yet still, the Blotters follow us. They know their way too.

Jay keeps urging me to move faster, grabbing my arm and pulling, but he never moves from my side. He hasn't even broken a sweat. He's trained for this; I'm not. It's only the need to survive that keeps me going. I will not die. Not today.

There's a fire escape up ahead, against one of the skyscrapers lining the alley. Jay pulls me up it and smashes a third-floor window with his elbow. We climb through it into a thin, dark corridor.

Panting, I follow him through the building. We spill out of another door into another alley and continue to run.

And as my muscles scream, and the bottoms of my feet ache, and my lungs feel heavy with each breath of polluted air, Jay's pace slows. He comes to a stop beneath some scaffolding. There are voices round the corner, by the road, and he pushes me against the wall, my face level with his chest. But it is just a couple of civilians heading home after a day's work in the factories.

He sighs, resting his forehead against mine. I take big gulps of air, my side splitting, and grab onto his top to stop my legs from buckling. He's barely even breathless. When he meets my eyes, his full lips are hard, and his jaw is gritted as if he's in pain. He opens his mouth as if he's going to say something, but then he shakes his head.

He looks lost. Scared even.

When I asked him if he knew when he would die, his response was devoid of emotion. I don't think he's afraid to die. So who is he afraid for?

Me?

I put my hand on his chest. 'We're okay, Jay. I'm okay. This'll be okay.'

A breath escapes his lips. He steps back, taking away his heat, and looks at the long, dark road behind us. 'This isn't okay.'

'Jay—'

'Don't you get it?' He turns back to me and squeezes my shoulders. 'We've lost them for now, but they're going to kill you, little Twist. They won't stop. It is written that we die. You are going to die.'

I grab his arms, and his biceps harden against my fingers. 'It was written that you kill me too.'

'And?'

'You didn't.'

He moistens his bottom lip. There's a struggle going on behind his cool, ink-blotched eyes. Then he steps back and leans against the wall beside me. He tilts back his head and lets out a hard breath.

'I don't know what we do now.'

'We need to get into Draft Three. How far are we from the place we were supposed to meet the Canary?'

He runs a hand along his stubble. 'A few blocks. But we've missed it. We should have been there an hour ago.'

'We have to try. She could still be there.'

I take his hand and feel him give in, his rough fingers curling around mine.

Soon, we're walking through one of the Draft Two factory blocks. It's a mass of huge industrial buildings with dark paths cutting between. Noise bellows from their high barred windows: loud mechanical creaks, metal screeching, monotonous thuds that vibrate through my bones. There are people inside of them now. There are always people inside of them.

It's to keep us busy, I think. I've seen the magic and technology of the Final City. There, everything is quick and bright and efficient. I don't think there is need for these grey, never-sleeping buildings that suck souls and laughter and questions from people and chew on them with metal teeth until they are left hollow.

But people who are busy and aching and exhausted are less likely to find time to do other things. Such as dream, or pass on stories at the black markets, or question the so-called gods.

I follow the progress of the continuous streams of black smoke into the sky. The Creators put stars in the sky above the Citadel. Here, there is nothing but darkness.

'My father used to say that stars were made of dreams,' I say.

'They're not.'

I exhale, and my breath mists in front of my face. 'You lack imagination.'

'Yeah? Well, you lack a survival instinct.'

I narrow my eyes. 'I'm still alive, aren't I?'

'For now.'

Soon, the scent of the river adds to the smells of burning metal, industrial smoke, and the rain.

'How did you know the Blotters wouldn't shoot?' says Jay suddenly.

'If they'd shot you, you would have bled. If you'd bled, they would have known you were a Blotter.'

'So?'

'So the Creators are obviously spreading the story that you're not a Blotter. They were talking about you inking your own skin, remember? You're dangerous, Jay.'

'No shit.'

'No. Not because of what you have done for the Creators. You're dangerous because of what you represent. You're a hole in their story, a contradiction, something that doesn't make sense. You're supposed to enforce the One True Story. They can't let anyone know a Blotter can escape what is written. If anyone saw you bleed, they'd see the ink and they'd know the truth.'

He runs a hand across his mouth. 'If they'd shot us, we'd be dead. And this would be over. That's what the Creators want. They won't make that mistake again.'

Maybe he is right, but the river glints ahead, and relief washes over me. We walk to the riverbank and stare over the wide expanse of murky water. There are shadowy buildings on the other side of the river, and lights from the Draft Three skyscrapers blink in the distance.

I shiver, rubbing my arms, as I search for the Canary through the shadows.

'Are you sure this is the place?' I ask.

'Yeah.' Jay stiffens as the wind carries male shouting from somewhere within the factory block. 'Shit. We can't wait for her.'

Both of us look at the dark buildings behind us.

'Can you swim?' I ask.

Jay raises his eyebrows. 'You serious?'

'Yes.'

'We can't swim across the river.'

'Why not?'

He turns his head to me as I stare at the black stretch of water ahead. 'You know why.'

I know of the Creators' stories—spread like poison by the Tellers. Stories about creatures lurking in the rivers; stories about fatal undercurrents and drownings and danger. Stories about what would happen to anyone who illegally crossed the boundaries between the Drafts.

Stories are true when we believe them.

I pull my leather jacket closer to my body and swallow. 'It's not that wide.'

'Little Twist . . .' His tone is warning.

I glance over my shoulder. He looks menacing in the rain and the darkness. We cannot stay here. Even if we manage to lie low until tomorrow, the Draft will be swarming with Blotters by then. We need to get into the next Draft.

'What choice do we have, Jay?'

His features are like stone as he stares at me. Then his shoulders deflate. He walks forwards to join me.

'This is a really bad idea, little Twist,' he says.

Chapter Thirty-Three
Jay

The water is as black as ink. It's thick and glossy too.

It makes me think of my time in the Final City, in that room beneath the Citadel, surrounded by the Creators. Whispering. Weaving stories. The blood in my veins boiling.

Fuck.

I run a hand over my mouth. I don't want to go into that water.

Elle sits on the riverbank. She's mad. She has no idea what the Creators are capable of. I reckon even if we don't die from getting sucked to the depths or eaten by the monsters that lurk there, we'll probably get some disease from swimming through other people's piss and sewage and rot.

'Elle?'

She glances over her shoulder. Can't we go back to a couple of hours ago when I had my cock inside of her, my hands on her body, and my tongue in her mouth?

'Yes?'

'If we die, you'll never get to feel my cock inside of you again,' I say.

Her face remains impassive, but her breath hitches as she turns back to the river. 'We'd better stay alive then.'

I grin like a fucking idiot and run my hand over my mouth to hide it. I'm pathetic. *Is that all it takes to make you happy, Jay? You can ruin your life by not doing what was written, end up consorting with a group of terrorists, get shot, nearly get burned alive, and wind up about to swim across a big dirty river that'll probably kill you—but hey, a girl you like wants your cock, so it's all okay!*

Elle meets my eye, and she's breathing hard, her eyebrows knitting together. The smile dies from my lips. What are we doing? This is insane. She swallows, and her resolve hardens her soft features.

'Elle, this is a bad—'

She plunges into the river. I stare at the ripples, and time stretches on. She doesn't resurface. *Shit.* I put my hand on the ground and swing over the edge after her.

The water drags me down. It's thick and dark and as cold as ice. There's no world. No Circus. No stories. No Blotters or Creators or Twists. There's nothing. There's only ink.

I'm in one of the pools beneath the Citadel. The Creators are watching me as I drown. Two of them are arguing, I think. It's faraway. I can't breathe. My lungs scream. My muscles spasm as I'm sucked into the depths. I raise my arms, but I can't reach the surface. Black, sour ink seeps into my mouth. It curls up my nostrils. I don't know which direction is up or down.

But no, I'm not in the Citadel, am I? I'm in the river. I survived the Citadel, but I won't survive this. I'm going to die. This wasn't written. I have no purpose. There is nothing.

There's Elle.

I still. The fog in my mind starts to clear. The water lessens its grip on me. The bubbles leaving my lips are streaming upwards.

Something brushes my leg.

Panic stabs my heart like a blade. I kick hard, and I swim. Seconds later, I break through the surface of the water. The air burns my throat as I spit out black, murky water.

'ELLE?' Cold dread spreads across my chest. 'ELLE?'

I don't know what to do. I can't see her. There's a pit settling in my stomach, and it's so heavy I think it will drag me back down again.

'ELLE?'

The surface breaks a few metres away, and a tsunami of relief crashes over me. I propel through the water towards her. Her hair is sticking to her face, and there are streaks of brown across her cheeks. She's looking around frantically. When her eyes lock on mine, she looks as panicked and relieved as I feel. She grabs the back of my neck, pulling herself into my body.

'I thought you drowned,' she says. Her pale lips are tinted blue, and her quickened breaths mist in the small space between us. 'I thought you drowned. I couldn't find you. I thought you drowned.'

I put my hand flat on her back and pull her closer. I feel as if I'm suffocating all over again. My throat constricts, and my ribs close in on my lungs. Because it sounds as if she actually gives a shit. In fact, for the first time since I met her, she looks terrified.

'You were looking for me?' I say.

'Yes.'

I swallow hard. 'Shall we get the fuck out of here?'

She nods and lets go.

The water is thick and calm as we swim away from Draft Two. The current has taken us some way from the riverbank already. I can't help the trepidation that hangs over me though. Something brushed against my leg.

One hundred and fifty metres to go.

The bank gets closer. The Draft Three skyscrapers stretch into the sky, dark and foreboding.

One hundred metres to go.

I can't see my arms below the surface, and the air smells like sewers. The Twist's hair trails behind her over her rucksack, carried by the inky blackness.

Fifty metres to go.

'I knew it. There's nothing in the water.' Elle's voice is quiet, but it cuts through the still air.

She's wrong. She said stories are true when we believe them, and everyone believes there are monsters in the rivers.

'I wouldn't be so sure.'

Thirty metres to go.

My breathing is hard. My muscles tense with each stroke. I feel something, a change in the current, below my legs.

'Faster,' I say.

She looks over her shoulder, sees my expression, and quickens her pace.

Twenty metres to go.

The temperature drops, and something brushes against my leg again. I kick it.

Ten metres.

She senses it too. But we're almost there.

'Hurry up,' I say.

She drags herself up onto the riverbank, coughing black water onto the ground. She turns to me. Her eyes widen as something grabs my foot and pulls me down.

I inhale water, and my lungs burn, and I'm drowning again. I kick as hard as I can and tear through the surface of the water, gasping for breath.

'Jay!' Elle grabs my arm as I'm yanked down again.

She pulls, and I thrash against the current before grasping onto the riverbank. I taste the air. Elle has both hands under my arms now, her face flushed as she fights whatever is dragging me back into the water.

'Come on, Jay. Please.'

I wrench my upper body onto the concrete riverbank and kick again. This time, my boot makes impact with something hard. Whatever the fuck has a hold of me lets go, and I fall on top of Elle.

Her eyes widen on something behind my shoulder, and a shadow looms over us. I roll us both over as a huge black hand smacks the bank where we were moments before, something glistening around its little finger.

'WHAT THE FUCK?' I roar.

Then it's sucked down into the black water, leaving nothing but ripples in its wake.

I'm breathing hard, holding myself up on my forearms so I don't crush Elle. She rests her head on the ground, her chest rising and falling fast.

'What the fuck was that, Elle?'

She swallows.

'Ink,' she says. 'It looked like ink.'

Chapter Thirty-Four
Elle

It looked like ink.

My heart hammers so hard against my ribs I feel it might burst out of my chest. I can't control my breathing. Jay's face is inches from mine, his large body engulfing me. He's hot despite his wet clothes and the chill in the air. I should push him off me. I should get us out of here. We're not safe. Yet I don't want to move away from his heat. Not while cold adrenaline pumps through my body and river water seeps into my bones.

Jay's eyes are intense as they hold mine. He's trying to contain his emotion. His gaze drops to my lips, and I think he's going to kiss me—hot, hard, angry kisses as his body pushes me into the dirt. For a moment, I want him to. I want to grab his neck and sink my teeth into his bottom lip and taste his tongue. I want to dig my nails into his shoulders and hear his low, primal grunt vibrate against my mouth.

I want to feel him. I want to make sure he's really here. Because I thought I'd lost him. I thought he was dead.

I want to take out my anger on him too.

Because I don't like how much the prospect of his loss hit me—how something cold and dark scraped and hollowed my insides as my muscles screamed and my heart pounded like a frightened animal.

I am not afraid.

Stories are true when we believe them.

'Ink? What the fuck, Elle?'

'I don't know.'

'What do you mean, you don't know?'

'I mean I don't understand it either.'

'Fuck.'

The cold river breeze brings with it the faint sound of shouting from Draft Two. The Blotters must still be searching the factories for us. He looks over his shoulder, and I touch his chest, feel his skin burning beneath the sopping wet material. He breathes in sharply, and his gaze snaps back to mine.

'We need to go,' I say.

'Yeah.' He moistens his full lips. 'Yeah.'

He pushes himself to his knees, taking away his damp heat, then he gets to his feet. I jump up too, grabbing my rucksack laying haphazard on the ground. By the time I've swung it over my shoulder, Jay has turned away, a large, menacing silhouette against the backdrop of concrete skyscrapers across the river, water dripping from his clothes, jeans clinging to his thick legs. He's looking warily into the depths.

He really is curious for a Blotter.

My attention is drawn to the black marks on the bank of the river. Were the monsters of ink created by the Creators many years ago, protecting the borders from those trying to illegally pass through? Or do the Creators know we are here?

I have so many questions. Their answers are not tangible; they are muffled and confused—forgotten words on the tips of tongues, nameless melodies drifting through memories. I don't understand. I want to understand.

But we're not safe. I get back up and grab Jay's arm. 'Let's go.'

'Yeah. Right.'

Ahead, a collection of abandoned warehouses look out onto the river. I try not to shiver as we walk towards them. I don't want to look weak, but my breath mists in front of my face, and my feet squelch.

We'll be okay. We've made it into Draft Three. I can see the skyscrapers puncturing the starless sky in the distance. We'll shelter for a while and figure out what to do next.

'Ink. For fuck's sake.' The line of Jay's jaw is hard, and I feel the tension in his muscles as his shoulder brushes against mine. His face is wet, and his vest clings to his chest. He's obviously had enough.

I have an urge to reach for him, to run my hand down the side of his face. I want to retrace the scar across his eyebrow, the memory of the pain he does not want to talk about. A mark that's different to the symbols inked on his skin, but the mark of a Creator all the same. A Creator who thought nothing of beating a child. Why would he? Why would the Creators who deny us the stars think twice about hurting someone innocent?

My eyes flick to the black tattoos curling up Jay's arms and neck. He is not innocent anymore, yet the thought of losing him physically hurts me. Why is that? How could I be so stupid to have let myself feel this way?

Fearing what he will see in my eyes, I fix them ahead on the mass of derelict buildings by the bank of the river.

'We'll dry off a bit and figure out what to do next,' I say.

'Right.' The word comes out gruff and forced.

I touch his arm. 'It's going to be okay, Jay.'

'No, little Twist. It's not.'

He's wrong. I'll make him see that. Once we're inside, we can figure this all out.

I take us down a path between two vast concrete buildings and stop by the door of one of them. When I try to open it, though, it doesn't budge.

I push again, and the lock rattles. I swallow the emotion building in my chest, but my throat is tight. I clench the handle so hard it hurts and try again and again. *Why won't it open?*

'Little Twist . . .'

I barge my shoulder into it, feeling my skin bruise beneath my sodden jacket. And still, it doesn't shift.

'Hey—'

Rage burns through my body, and I'm going to scream. I slam myself into the wood.

'Elle!'

I'm lifted off my feet and pushed into the wall. Jay's body engulfs me. He tightens his grip around my arms.

'What the fuck, Elle?'

'Get off me,' I say.

'No.'

My chest heaves. *'Get off me.'*

'No.'

I meet his eye, and his face softens. He releases a breath that tickles my skin. It does nothing to ease the hurricane building in my chest.

'I can't open the door,' I say.

'No shit. What's wrong with you?'

'I'm cold.'

'You're acting like a maniac because you're cold?'

'Yes.'

'That's not the reason.' There's a glint of amusement in his eyes now. It makes me want to lash out at him—bite him, tear my fingernails down his back—something, anything to relieve this pressure in my chest. 'Look at me, little Twist.' He puts a finger under my chin. The humour is gone now, and only darkness remains. 'I think you're acting like a maniac because you're scared. And you should be.'

'I'm not afraid.' I take a deep breath. 'But we were almost burned alive, and we had to run for hours, and there was that thing in the river. And I thought you. . . I thought you drowned. And I'm cold and wet. And all those people died at the Circus. And I need to think. I want to go inside. I want to go inside so I can think.'

Jay stares at me for a minute. 'Okay.'

'Okay?'

He steps back, and I shiver as the cold wind hits my skin. 'Let's go inside.'

He's more relaxed than before. It's as though my loss of control gave him an opportunity to take it. He barges into the door, and it crashes open as if it's made of paper. He nods at the entrance, a curious look on his face.

I release a breath as I walk past him. 'Thank you.'

It's dark. There are cargo boxes on the floor and a stairway ahead that leads to a balcony overlooking the main space. Jay comes up behind me, warm and solid.

'Happy now?' he asks.

'Yes.' I sigh as I glance through the shadows at the row of doors on one side of the space. I walk towards them. 'Or I will be. Let's . . . let's see if there are any heaters or anything in the rooms. Then—'

Jay abruptly hooks an arm around my waist and wrenches me into his body. A strangled sound escapes my lips, and he clamps his other hand over my mouth. My whole body tenses.

He bends down to my ear, his soft, rough words tickling my skin. *'We're not alone.'*

Chapter Thirty-Five
Elle

My breathing quickens as I catch the moving silhouettes on the balcony. Jay is like a statue behind me, still and solid. The only thing that reveals he isn't made of stone is his heart beating fast against my back. One of his hands holds my stomach; the other clamps over my mouth. His muscles are tensed.

'Let her go, Blotter,' says a woman.

And then beams of light criss-cross the darkness and spotlight us. The woman steps forwards and leans on the balcony railing. I squint up at her. She's mid-thirties maybe. Her dark hair is pulled back from her face to reveal a scar across her cheek, and she's dressed in black. Teenagers stand on either side of her, holding torches. She's aiming a pistol at Jay's head.

'Walk away, Blotter, and we'll let you live,' she says.

Jay's arm tightens around my waist. 'Point that thing away from me, and I'll let *you* live.'

I grab his wrist and try to pull his hand off my mouth. They're clearly not a threat, but he doesn't seem to notice.

'I'm afraid we can't do that, Blotter. Last warning.'

I bite Jay's palm, tasting salt and flesh. He doesn't react for a moment. Then he drops his hand. He keeps the other wrapped around my waist.

'That's it. Nice and slow. Now, send her over here and you can be on your way.'

'Are you serious—?'

'It's okay,' I say, and all the torches point at me. 'It's not what it looks like.'

I don't manage to hide the shiver that comes from the water in my boots and my hair, even though Jay is like a furnace behind me. It makes me sound weak, and I steady it before saying anything else. I notice the woman has a tattoo on her muscular arm.

'You're Darlings, right?' I say. 'We are too.'

Jay tenses as the light moves to his face. '*He's* a Darling?'

'No—' he says, and I elbow him in the side.

'He would have killed me by now if he weren't.'

She frowns. 'How is that possible? And why are you wet?'

I breathe out slowly. 'It's a long story. We've come from the Circus at the Edge of the World. And—'

'It's real?' A hint of hope breaks through the hardness of her tone.

'Yes. But Blotters found it.' A whisper travels around the balcony, and the energy shifts from hope to sadness. I sigh. 'You were looking for it.'

'Yes. We were.'

'We've had a rough night,' I say. 'And we're dangerous to be around. But if we could just shelter awhile and get some food and fresh clothes, if you have any, it would be appreciated. In exchange, we'll tell you our story.'

The woman stares at us, eyes unreadable and glinting in the beam of the torch. Jay, clearly tiring of this situation, runs his thumb across the wet material of my top. I grab his wrist and still his hand. These people could help us.

Then she puts the gun in a holster on her belt. 'Angie and Philip, get a fire going. Jamie, see what food we have to spare. Peter, come with me.'

The teenagers spring into action, and the woman walks down the stairs. A tall, skinny boy with curly ginger hair follows her.

'Thank you,' I say as they approach.

'It's no problem. But if you're dangerous, you can't stay long,' she says. 'I have people to protect, and if we can't get to the Circus, we may be stuck here longer than I hoped. I'm Priya, by the way.'

'Elle,' I say. 'And this is Jay.'

Her gaze lingers on his arm where death marks his skin. Then she looks at his hand, gentle on my stomach. 'Elle, come with me. Peter, take our guest Jay and find him something dry to wear.'

Peter's face drains of whatever colour it had, and I give Jay a warning look.

'*Be nice,*' I say as he looks at Peter distastefully. I grab his arm, and he brings his gaze back to mine. '*I'm serious, Jay.*'

Priya shakes her head as I follow her to one of the doors. 'A Blotter and a Darling. That sounds like quite a story.'

Ten minutes later, I'm standing in an old storeroom beneath the dim light of a buzzing bulb, waiting for Jay. I'm almost dry in a fresh white T-shirt a couple of sizes too big for me and a pair of shabby but dry grey worker trousers. My wet clothes hang off the side of an old wooden crate, and there's a puddle of water collecting beneath them.

I wander around the space, the concrete cold against my feet, studying the dusty boxes and the remnants of past Darlings who must have stayed here. There are a couple of food bar wrappers, a holey sock, and a box of matches.

Then I empty my rucksack, lining the items by a metal chair in the corner so they can dry. One of the spray paint cans leaks onto my hand as I set it down, leaving a glossy blue blob on my palm. I use it to draw a small dandelion seed on the grey wall with my fingertip.

The door shuts, and I turn.

Jay stands there. They've given him trousers like mine and a long-sleeved black shirt. It's a little tight around his chest and shoulders, but the colour suits him. It emphasises the blue of his irises and the darkness of his hair.

He notices the smudged painting on the wall, and his expression darkens. 'What are you doing?'

'Painting.'

Something stirs inside me as I take in the rise and fall of his chest. This evening, I've faced Blotters and fire and that thing in the river. I thought I'd lost him. I've been wound up and on edge since. From the way he's looking at me, I can tell he feels the same.

'Painting?' His voice is rough. 'Can I not leave you alone for five minutes without you doing something illegal?'

'It seems not.'

He stiffens, his large body dominating the doorway. Then he crosses the space between us, and his masculine scent washes over me. I grab the front of his shirt, and he moves a hand to the back of my neck and pulls me closer.

And then his mouth is on mine, hot and greedy. My back crashes into the wall beside the painted dandelion seed, and I sink my teeth into his bottom lip. He groans against my mouth as I reach for his trousers and clumsily pull down his zipper. I take him, hot and hard, in my hand.

In a sudden movement, he yanks down my trousers and grabs me beneath my thighs, hoisting me up against the wall as if I weigh nothing. I tighten my legs around his back, and my fingers dig into his shoulders. A low, raw sound rumbles deep inside of him.

Fuck, Elle. What are you doing to me?'

I kiss him harder. Pressure builds between my legs, and I rock my hips against his body, desperate for the friction. One hand holding me up against the wall, he shifts between my legs and slips my underwear to the side with his fingers. He groans when he touches me.

And then he pushes inside. My cry is echoed by his low, raw groan. His forehead falls against mine, hot and damp. His movements are slow at first, but they become faster and more urgent as my pulse quickens. I dig my nails into his shoulders, and his eyes focus on mine, dark with heat and curiosity.

'I need you to come for me.' His voice is strained.

I pull his face closer, and he moans against my mouth. The low, gentle sound along with his body rocking against mine does something to me. It builds until it takes over my body in powerful, hard waves. I cry out as I melt into him, and it's not long before he joins me in release, a low animal sound escaping his lips and adding to mine.

Gradually, he stills. He holds me, both of us breathing hard, and his eyes don't move from mine. His expression is softer than usual, relaxed. Then he pulls out of me and slowly lowers me to the ground.

I release a breath. My mind feels all fuzzy and blank, and I search for something to say.

'So . . . you . . . you got some dry clothes then?' I sound breathless.

His lip twitches as he looks down at top. 'Yeah.'

'You weren't horrible to Peter, I hope.'

'Nah. But the kid's fucking terrified of me.'

I laugh. 'You're not so scary.'

He smiles. It lightens his face and makes him look younger and softer. He shrugs. And the way he is looking at me, his gaze like an anchor, causes that same spark of panic I felt when I was in the water.

The last time I felt panic like that was when Maggie smuggled me out of the house in the middle of the night and told me we had to leave my father. He was the only person I ever loved, and when he was taken from me, it was as if something was ripped from my body. My heart, maybe. I can't withstand pain like that again.

My mouth dries, and I look over his shoulder at the door.

There is something happening between us. Something dangerous. Something that cannot last. Nothing in this world is supposed to last.

My death is written on his skin.

The Creators want us both dead.

I swallow. 'I . . . uh . . . They'll be waiting for us.'

'So?'

'I want to know how Priya got here. It could help us get to the library.' I give him a light push and pull up my trousers. 'Come on. I said we'd tell them our story.'

His expression darkens. I feel his eyes boring into the back of my head as I brush past him and walk to the door.

Chapter Thirty-Six
Jay

Is she fucking serious? She wants to spend time with a bunch of kids and a terrorist? Now?

I pull up my trousers. When she reaches the door, she turns to look over her shoulder. There's a light sheen of sweat on her face, and her cheeks are still flushed. I lean against the wall and fold my arms across my chest.

I felt a moment of relief as her nails dug into my skin and her legs tightened around my back. I felt a moment of quiet as I tore a cry from her lips and held her body against the wall. But now, I feel it again—the thoughts nagging at my brain, the frustration building in my chest, the itch raging beneath my skin. And the ink burning in my veins.

'We've got dry clothes, little Twist. We've got what you wanted. Let's just get some food and get across Draft Three. Try to find this library you've been going on about. Come on.'

'We will. But Priya might have information that can help us. *You* come on.'

'No, she won't.'

'She might.'

'It's pointless.'

'It's not.'

I'm not going out there. I'm not spending my time with a bunch of kids who'll probably shit themselves the moment I walk out of this room, and a Darling who thought she could threaten me.

'Jay.' She looks at me as though I'm a child misbehaving.

I shake my head.

She exhales. 'Fine. Suit yourself.'

'Little Twist . . .'

She turns and heads into the warehouse, closing the door behind her and leaving me alone.

I stand there, and something squeezes around my throat so tight I can hardly fucking breathe. I don't want to go out there.

Creators. Blotters. Twists. Darlings. Circuses and dandelion seeds and revolution and fire. Not doing what is written. Hurricanes and tornados. Monsters in the river. Death. Stories. Ink. Elle. Elle and that misplaced wonder in her eyes. Fucking. Feeling. Feeling something. Feeling something that's not certain, not empty, not hollow like before—but not freedom. I don't feel free. I feel full. Too full. The weight of it crushes down on my chest. It's crippling. I can't move with it. Too many decisions. Too many outcomes. Too many questions. It's so fucking heavy.

There's too much.

Too much time. Too much time to fill. Stagnant and stale. It drags on and on and on and on.

And yet there's too little time, each second slipping away until it's gone forever.

I can't stop it. I can't go back. I can't go forwards either. I'm trapped.

It's too much.

I just want everything to be still for one fucking minute. Just want everything to start moving and making sense.

I don't know what I want. That's the problem, isn't it? There's too much to lose.

I look at the little dandelion seed she painted on the concrete. Illegal. Forbidden. Curious. It's a shit painting. It doesn't look much like a dandelion seed—it's smudged and fat and the wrong colour.

It's weird, really, when I think about it—that the Creators would forbid ink and paint and stories. That something as small as this shitty painting could be dangerous.

But it is dangerous. And it's not weird. Because it *is* a dandelion seed. But it isn't.

It's a painting about her father, somehow, and her stories, and her stupid revolution. It means something more than what it is.

Lightly, I touch it, then I look at the wet blue paint on my finger. I draw the shape of the dandelion seed in the air. Then I touch the wall with my fingertip, my heartbeat racing.

I wipe my hand against my jeans and stuff it in my pocket.

What am I doing? This is insane. I can't paint something on the wall.

Yet I've defied the Creators and killed Blotters. I've followed a Twist and told a story in a Circus. I've swum across a forbidden river.

What was that thing in the river anyway? It stirs a memory, but I can't quite grab onto it.

I sit down against the wall, legs spread, forearms resting on my knees. I stare at the door. I don't move for an hour as I try to get rid of the tight feeling in my throat and all of the thoughts and words and questions that feel as if they're choking me.

I don't know what I want.

Except that's not true, is it?

I exhale, rub my mouth, and get up. I walk past the cargo boxes and forbidden crap from the Twist's rucksack she's lined up by the wall. I flex my fingers and put my hand on the door handle.

I do know what I want.

I want her.

I head out into the warehouse.

'Once, there was a world. And the world was dark. And so dark was the world that people were afraid to dream,' she's saying as I quietly close the door. 'And in this world, there was a factory . . .'

They're sitting on dusty cargo boxes and broken plastic chairs around a fire cracking in a metal bin on the floor. There are six teenagers and Priya, all leaning towards Elle, their attention rapt.

Slowly, I make my way over to them.

'The factory was run by a man. The man never told his workers what the factory really did, so they did not know they were working on a machine that stole the stars.'

A smile spreads across her face as I approach. Peter, the ginger kid, looks as if he's about to shit himself when I sit down on the crate between him and Priya.

'One day, a group of teenagers started work at the factory.'

Priya leans towards me, passing me a few of the cheap processed food bars they eat in the Outer Drafts and a flask.

'We got off on the wrong foot, Blotter.' She speaks quietly as the kids turn their attention back to Elle and her story.

I nod, not looking at her as I unwrap one of the bars—grains fortified with artificial protein and vitamins. Tastes like shit, but better than nothing.

'She told me what happened. That you didn't do what was written. She said you saved her and the kids at the Circus. That's pretty decent.'

'Yeah? And what did you tell her?'

'The teenagers noticed something about the people who worked the machine. They started to become different. Tired. Less.'

Priya's lip twitches. 'Okay. Straight to the point.' She reaches for a flask between her boots and takes a sip. 'I told her about the Underground railroad we used to get across the Draft unseen.'

'They realised it was the machine. It was doing something to them. To the world. To the night. It was stealing dreams and spreading darkness.'

I unwrap the next bar. 'If there were an Underground railroad, I'd know about it.'

'No. It's been forgotten by most. Not functioning anymore, obviously. Most of it's barricaded or flooded or worse. But so long as you take the right route and head in the right direction, you can get into Draft Four.'

'So one day, they rebelled. They fought the man. And they broke the machine.'

'And you know the right direction?'

'Yes. I've drawn it out for Elle.'

I shake my head and bite off half of the nutrition bar. 'It makes no sense.'

'And yet here we are.'

'Suddenly, on breaking the machine, all the stars that had been stolen scattered out into the night.'

Elle's eyes glint as they catch mine. I lift up my flask to her and then take a sip of tepid water.

'A million dreams lit up the sky. And the world changed. It was no longer dark, but filled with light.'

My lip twitches. What a load of crap. And yet I like it. I like the sound of her voice. Her words seem to ease something inside of me.

'And all because of a group of teenagers who dared to dream,' she says. Her face lights up as the kids start to talk to her. I can't take my eyes off her. I watch the way her eyebrows move when she speaks and note the peculiar straightness of her back. Her hair is wild, and her eyes glint with wonder.

How is this happening? How am I falling for a Twist? How am I falling for a Twist who tells stories about dreams and factories and stars?

As I watch her, she gets to her feet and meets Priya's gaze. 'We'll get a couple of hours' rest and then move on. Thank you. For everything.'

Priya nods and gives her a half-smile. 'Likewise.'

Elle crosses the circle and stops by my side. She lightly touches my shoulder, and I feel the heaviness again. The weight. I don't want to lose her. But we won't make it out of this alive.

'Coming?' she says.

'Yeah.'

Together, we head back to the storeroom. As soon as I close the door behind us, she turns and looks up at me. Lightly, she touches the dandelion seed on my chest. My skin hums at her touch.

'Are you okay?' she says.

'Yeah. No. Maybe.' I exhale. 'I don't fucking know, Elle.'

Vulnerability flashes across her face. It's the same vulnerability I saw when we were in the river. She closes her fingers, scrunching my shirt in her fist.

'Yeah. Me too.' She sighs. 'I'm glad you're here, Jay.'

The heaviness lifts just for a second. I envelop her small fingers in mine and hold them to my chest.

'Yeah. Me too,' I say.

And despite everything—defying the gods, and not doing what was written, and getting involved in a revolution, and setting myself up for what will likely be a horrible death—it's true.

I am glad I'm here. With her.

Chapter Thirty-Seven
Elle

Jay's heart thumps beneath my fingers. Our eyes lock. Something seems to push and pull in the air between us, taut. Our bodies move with it. Slowly, I undo the buttons of his shirt, revealing the hard, tattooed muscle beneath. His breathing deepens as I trace one of the black shapes that stop just above his belly button.

'What does it mean?' I ask.

He touches my cheek and shakes his head. 'You don't want to know.'

I slide the shoulders of his shirt down, and it drops to the ground behind him. His scent washes over me as I brush my lips against his chest, tasting the salt on his skin. He tenses then relaxes.

'Elle,' he says.

He kisses me. And it is different than before. Not hard and urgent but slow and deep, his tongue hot as it moves against mine.

And when he picks me up and takes me to the corner of the room and we have sex on top of the sleeping bags laid on the floor, that is what it is like too. Slow and deep.

Afterwards, while we lie on our backs looking up at the damp spots on the ceiling, panting and covered in sweat, something between us feels different. It's suffocating.

Because Jay knows just as well as I do that it is not wise to become attached to anyone in this world.

But somehow, even though I am a Twist and he is a Blotter, even though it was written that he would kill me, even though he is bound by ink to those I seek to destroy, I am attached to him.

I don't want to lose him.

When I catch the raw glimmer of fear in his eyes, just for a moment before he looks away, I know he feels it too.

We rest for a few hours, say our goodbyes to Priya and the children, and then set off.

It's just before dawn, and the dark has faded to a milky grey. The faint wheeze of the factories drifts over the river with the scent of stagnant water, but the shadows here are quiet. Ahead, the skyline is jagged with tall buildings.

A heavy silence surrounds us as we navigate the warehouse district. Jay's arms are taut with tension, and there's a lump in the back of my throat. Something is different between us. The stakes are higher somehow.

I do not want to lose him. This was not supposed to happen this way.

I try not to let it distract me as I quickly spray a couple more dandelion seeds onto the abandoned buildings.

When we reach the road, Jay pauses and curls his fingers around my arm. It cuts directly through the Draft, and the first of the skyscrapers stand before us, black and glinting as the sun starts to rise. There's a faint thrum of engines in the distance—Blotter vehicles, or perhaps the goods vehicles distributing food from the factories.

'How much farther?' he asks.

Priya's scribbled map sits in my pocket, but I do not need to consult it. I memorised the route to the entrance of the underground network before we set off.

'Not much. She said there's an entrance by the warehouses.'

'It's getting light.'

'I know.'

He lets go of me and runs a hand over his light stubble. When he exhales, his hot breath mists in the air in front of his face. 'We should have set off earlier.'

'We're almost there, Jay. I promise.'

For a second, our eyes meet. Then, almost imperceptibly, he inclines his head.

I lead him down the road, sticking to the shadows. We slip past a group of people with their backs to us, lined on the pavement looking up at the recording of a Teller talking about The End. Ahead, large heavy goods vehicles are parked in the middle of the street. We hurry past.

I take us through an alley, and Creator Michael's severe face looks down at us from a billboard the length of one of the buildings. The muscles in Jay's jaw tighten.

'Did you meet him?' I ask. 'Michael?'

'Yeah, I met him. He was my Patron.'

'Patron?'

'Every Blotter has one. The Creator who's in charge of writing their story.' He shrugs a heavy shoulder. 'I dunno. I dunno how it works. Doesn't matter anymore, does it?'

Ahead, there are two rusty doors in the ground by a row of bins at the end of the alley. Some of the darkness lifts.

'There!' I say. There's a thick chain wrapped around the handles. Priya didn't mention this. I crouch down, locating a metal padlock. 'If I had a hairpin, I could pick the lock.' I look over my shoulder at Jay's hulking figure.

'Yeah, well, unfortunately, I'm not wearing my hair in my pretty updo today, so I don't know why you're looking at me like that, little Twist.' He rubs the back of his neck and turns his gaze warily upwards to the surrounding skyscrapers. Some of the lights flicker on as the dawn approaches.

I grab my rucksack and start rummaging through the damp contents. Maybe there's something in here that can help.

'Run.' Jay's tone turns my blood cold.

I look up, and my heart stops. There's a Teller standing at the other end of the alley. He's large and hooded, wearing robes the colour of blood. He raises his gun.

Jay yanks me to my feet and pushes me behind him. *'Run.'*

'No.'

I won't leave him.

Jay throws me against the wall as the Teller shoots. I stumble, winded for a moment. Then the two of us dart down the alley to the left, my hip knocking one of the bins. A crackling noise follows us, but I don't have time to figure out what it is.

The Teller's boots thud after us, steady and slow. It's more menacing somehow than if he ran. What does he know that we don't? We turn the corner into a backstreet, and Jay stops and pushes me behind him. He roars, lunging forwards, and I cry out when I hear the click of a gun.

Jay falls to his knees and slumps, lifeless, to the ground.

I'm back in that river again, ice-cold water crashing over my head, and everything is faraway. Through my blurred vision, I see there's a Teller ahead, leaning against the same heavy goods vehicle we saw earlier. He has a gun and a radio in his hands. My heart pounds. Footsteps approach from behind.

I try to breathe. I try to think. But I'm too cold.

Jay is dead.

A hot scream builds in my stomach, thawing the ice that has its hold on my limbs. I charge. Someone grabs me from behind and clamps a hand over my mouth. I smell damp and must and old parchment. This cannot be the end. I buck against him, kicking and screaming.

The hooded figure ahead pulls down his hood.

I still. Long brown hair spills over the front of her robes, and a pretty heart-shaped face with turquoise eyes and soft plump lips is revealed. It makes no sense. Women are not permitted to be Tellers.

'You must be Elle. We've been waiting for you.' Her eyes glint mischievously in the shadows. 'I'm Mary, although you may have heard of me by another name.' She nods at the man holding me. 'That's my brother, Tom.'

'Pleased to meet you, ma'am.' His voice is cheerful—a sharp contrast to the strong, vice-like grip he has around my waist.

'And I take it this is Jay. Sylvia told us about him.' Mary looks down at him sprawled at her feet and then lifts up her weapon. 'Sorry about that. Tranquiliser gun. Didn't much fancy my chances against a Blotter. Not looking forward to when he wakes up, but I've heard he's pretty sweet on you, so perhaps you can smooth things over for me.' She slides up the door at the back of the goods vehicle.

My heartbeat will not stop its relentless thrumming in my ear. The woman's words seem to float in the air around me. I can't seem to catch them. Nothing makes sense.

And then I notice the gentle rise and fall of Jay's back as he breathes, his cheek pressed against the pavement. I release a breath, and the world comes into focus.

'Mary.' My mouth is dry. I swallow. 'You're the Bard. You run the library.'

She smiles, and dimples spring into her cheeks. 'Guilty as charged.' She nods at Tom, and he releases me. My legs tremble as

A CIRCUS OF INK

I look at her clothes questioningly. 'Ah, the robes. I can understand your confusion. Tom's idea. It works quite nicely. Of course, when we encounter Blotters, they can tell something's slightly off. Instinctive—something to do with the ink that bonds them to the Creators, we think. But they also know not to question a Teller, so it makes getting around the Draft undetected a little easier.'

'You're going to drive us to the library,' I say.

'Yes. We can get you across the border. Now, come on. It won't be long before Blotters realise you're here. We don't have much time. Tom, can you get Jay inside?'

'Yes, ma'am!'

'Wait,' I say.

Tom halts.

'How did you know we were here?' I ask.

'Sylvia and some of her lot arrived earlier,' says Mary. 'Told us you were coming and you might need some help. So we've been listening to some of the Teller broadcasts. Not much out there about you for now—they obviously want to keep you quiet. But we heard one of them telling a story about a false Blotter and his slut in Draft Three—his words, not mine—killing innocent people. The best route into Draft Four is the underground railway, so we parked up here last night to wait for you.'

There's warmth in her face and mischief in her eyes, and it reassures me. So I climb into the vehicle and settle down on the floor by the partition at the back. Tom hauls one of Jay's big arms over his equally broad shoulders and pulls him to his feet. With a grunt, he places him down on the ground beside me and plucks a dart from Jay's neck.

His hood is down now, and when he smiles at me I see a shock of blond hair, a big, cheerful mouth that's slightly too wide for his face, and glinting eyes the same colour as Mary's. He jumps onto the pavement beside her.

'Ready?' she says.

I glance at Jay, noting the peaceful expression on his face and the comforting rise and fall of his chest. I touch his shoulder, and he makes a low sound in his throat. He's not going to be happy when he wakes up. But we're okay.

I smile. 'Yes.'

'See you at the library.' Mary winks then pulls down the metal door, plunging us into darkness.

Part Three

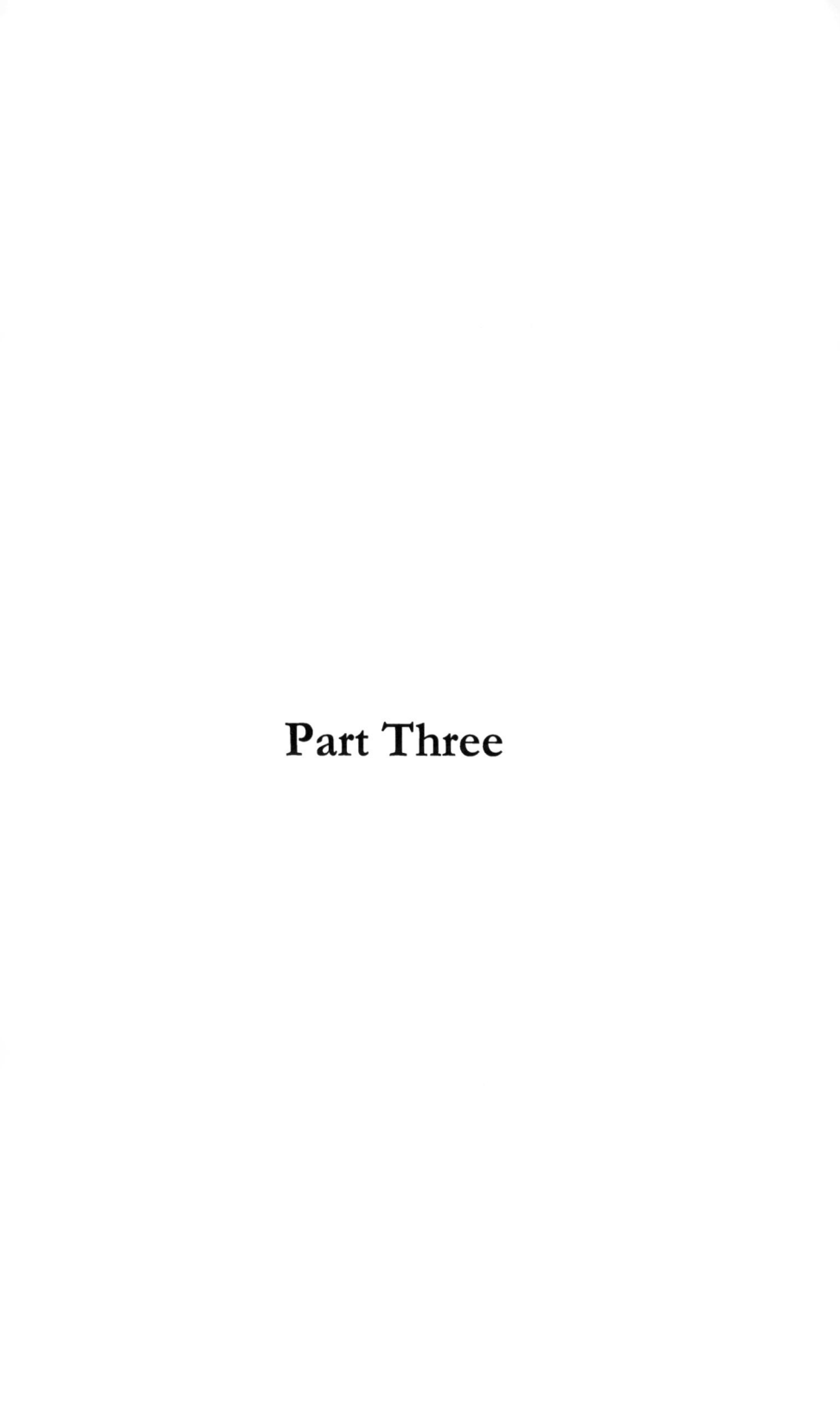

Chapter Thirty-Eight
Jay

I breathe in sharply.

My head is throbbing. My heart's beating fast.

I open my eyes. Spots dance across my vision, and after I blink a few times, a high ceiling comes into focus. I'm lying down on something soft. And this isn't right.

Where the fuck am I?

I jolt upright.

I'm on a bed. There's a door opposite, and the floor is made of small black-and-white chequered tiles. My muscles tighten. This room doesn't feel as if it belongs in the Outer Drafts. It reminds me of the Citadel.

My throat constricts as it all comes back to me. The Tellers, the big vehicle, the gun, and Elle. There's a hard weight pressing down on my chest. Where is Elle?

I throw myself off the bed. The room sways, and I slam my hand onto the edge of a scratched bedside table, gripping the varnished wood to steady myself. I move the other to my heart and rub the tattoo branded over it.

She's not dead. She can't be dead. I'd fucking know if she were dead. I would know. She's not. No fucking way.

I'm breathing fast, and the room's swimming around me. I swallow hard, pushing down the panic. I need to calm the fuck down. I can't protect her if I can't get control over myself. I close my eyes for a second. Then I look around properly.

I'm in a bedroom that could belong to the Citadel in the Final City. I'm leaning next to a high bed with a thick cream quilt and swirling leaves carved in its black headboard. There's a gold candlestick by my spread palm, and the doorknob is made of gleaming brass.

But there are chips in the chequered floor tiles. There's an ink stain on the scuffed desk. White plaster peels from the walls, and there's a hard pool of candle wax beside the handprint I just left in the dust.

This room is a stale memory of whatever it once was.

When I steady my breathing, the air is damp and heavy. There are no windows. I'm underground. And is that a book on the other bedside table?

It doesn't make sense. I have no clue where I am.

All I know is that I need to find Elle. I push away the thought of what the Tellers might be doing to her. We're bound by ink. I was supposed to kill her. If she were dead, surely I'd feel it. Surely this unbearable pressure in my veins would lessen. Surely my chest wouldn't hurt so fucking much.

I walk to the door. Someone is approaching, so I flatten myself against the wall, blinking hard to keep my focus. I get ready to kill something.

The door opens, and blood pumps hot through my body as I grab the invader. Beyond the thudding heartbeat in my ears, there's a familiar voice, distorted and breathless. But my body moves faster than my mind.

I've thrust her against the wall, wrists pinned above her head, before it all crashes into focus.

Except I didn't kill her, did I? My hands aren't squeezed around her throat. She isn't screaming. I didn't hurt her, even though I have instinctively killed and hurt people bigger than her.

So maybe I did know it was her. Maybe I just wanted to feel her skin against my skin. Maybe I just wanted to hold her against the wall and feel the reassuring heat of her body pushed against mine.

Her breath is hot and fast on my neck. 'Jay, what are you doing?'

Our gazes lock, and the soft relief ebbing through my body turns into something more familiar. Something more hostile.

She's not hurt. In fact, she looks far from it. She smells like soap and honey, and her skin has been scrubbed clean of all the grime from the river. Her long hair is damp. She's changed clothes too, and she's wearing a simple beige dress that skims the tops of her knees.

I grit my teeth to stop myself from completely losing my shit. *What. The. Fuck?*'

'We're at the library.'

'The Tellers—'

'They weren't Tellers.'

'What?'

'Jay, I can see you're feeling a little confused—'

'Oh, you can tell?'

'—but I'm going to need you to calm down.'

'How about I'll calm the fuck down when you tell me what's going on?'

I tighten my grip around her wrists, but she doesn't flinch. 'It was The Bard, the one Maggie told us about. Mary and her brother. They were dressed as Tellers. They brought us here.'

I rest my forehead against hers as I process what she's saying. She's fine, we're at some library, we were somehow taken here by two Darlings dressed up like Tellers. She's safe. She's not dead.

And they obviously take me for an idiot.

I slowly meet her gaze. 'They shot me.'

'It was a tranquiliser. They were under the impression you might be a little . . . difficult.' Her amber eyes glint, and irritation prickles beneath my skin.

'Is this amusing to you?'

She bites her bottom lip and composes her features. 'I shouldn't have left you on your own. I'm sorry. I really am. We got here a couple of hours ago. I didn't know when you were going to wake up.'

'Right.'

'And Sylvia and some of the others are already here, so I was—'

'So a whole bunch of your crazy Circus folk have seen me unconscious. Bet that gave you all a good laugh.'

'Jay, that's not what happened, at all—'

'Which one shot me? Mary or her brother?'

'What? That's not important.'

'Well, I want to know.'

'They only did it to defend themselves. They helped us.'

'*Which. One?*'

She tries to push me away, but I don't move. I want her to feel helpless. I want her as angry as I am right now. When a pink flush creeps over her cheeks and neck and her eyes narrow, I feel a burst of satisfaction that I'm having the desired effect on her.

But then she sighs. 'Look, I'm not going to tell you just so you can decide which one of them you're going to be more of an arsehole to. So just . . . get over it. Okay?'

'Get over it?'

'Yes.'

I glare at her, and she glares right back, her eyes fierce and curious and challenging as if she's wondering what I'm going to do next. And I don't fucking know what I'm going to do next. Why is she so annoying?

I exhale as I release her wrists, and some of the frustration escapes me in a long, weary breath. Yeah. She's made a mug out of me. But she's safe. The Tellers didn't get her. I didn't fuck up as badly as I thought.

'I'll just have to be an arsehole to both of them then, won't I?' I say.

'I wouldn't expect anything less of you.' The corner of her lip lifts. Then she takes a small step forwards and presses her forehead against my chest. Confused, I touch the back of her neck. Somehow, holding her and feeling her warmth, the tension in my muscles ebbs away.

'You . . . er . . . you okay?' I mumble into her hair.

She pulls away, and her eyes catch mine. Something raw and vulnerable flickers behind them. I stare at a spot of peeling plaster on the wall behind her, not wanting to see that emotion. She clears her throat and smiles, and it's as if I imagined it.

'Yes. I was waiting for you before I went to get the book I've been looking for. Do you want to come with me?'

I rub the back of my neck. Do I want to walk around some book-filled terrorist base with her weird Circus friends while looking for a message from the First Twist?

I exhale. 'Yeah. Okay.'

Chapter Thirty-Nine
Jay

I follow her across the room, and my eyes linger on the thin material of her dress as it skims her legs. She glances over her shoulder when she reaches the door.

'Hey, my eyes are up here.'

'Yeah. But your arse is down there.'

She stares at me. I stare back. My lip twitches.

'I take it you've cheered up then?' she says.

'Not sure, really.'

Have I cheered up? Yeah, the hot anger has subsided into something cooler. But I'm not sure if that constitutes as feeling cheerful. I don't want to kill something anymore, but I don't want to be around any of her Circus friends either.

I halt in the doorway as her bare feet slap against the tiled floor. The cold, persistent feeling of wrongness spreads in my chest. It could be dread. Dread about that vulnerability I caught in her eye, maybe. Or dread that I don't belong here, and soon, she's going to realise it. Dread that I probably can't save her.

But there's something else as well. Something more imminent. I look down the long, narrow corridor, registering the fancy-looking candle holders in the walls, and the high ceiling, and the chequered floor tiles. This doesn't feel like Draft Four. It feels like the Final City. A sense of the Creators seems to hang in the musty air.

When Elle realises I'm not following her, she turns, and her brow furrows. 'What's wrong?'

'I dunno. This place. It reminds me . . .' I frown and look up and down the corridor, the candles flicking shadows along the walls.

'Of the Citadel?' she says.

'Yeah.'

'Me too.'

'It feels . . .' The words catch in my throat, and I shake my head. 'What *is* this place?'

'I told you, we're at the library.'

'But why is it here? Was it always a library? How—?'

A slow smile spreads across her face, and I give her a hard look. 'What?'

'Nothing. Just . . . you,' she says. 'So curious for a Blotter.'

I fold my arms. 'And you, so annoying for a Twist.'

But she's right. I *am* curious. Curious about this place. Curious about the things she can do. Curious about her. I thought it would all disappear once I released my tension inside of her, but it hasn't. It's still here, persistent and relentless and irritating. And it's getting even worse.

Curiosity never did anyone any good. It never did me any good. This story doesn't end well for either of us.

'I like that you're curious,' she says.

'Oh, shut up.' I catch up with her in a few strides, and a smile plays on her lips again.

'I don't know for sure why the library is here,' she says. 'I have a theory. Mary probably knows more. You should ask her.'

'Are you trying to get me to make friends, little Twist? Because I don't make friends.'

'That's surprising. You're always so pleasant to everyone.'

'Funny.'

'Am I not your friend?'

I run a hand over my mouth. 'No. You're an annoying pain in my arse.'

Her laughter fills the dark, and I smile like an idiot as we walk through an arched doorway into an empty hall. I look up at the high, domed ceiling. The air tastes like must, and I'm sure we're underground.

But how can a building this big be underground? And why would it have a domed ceiling? Why would the Creators have made it? And why would it exist in Draft Four?

It makes no sense to me.

'How would you know what the inside of the Citadel was like anyway, little Twist?'

'My father told me stories—'

'Right. Course he did.'

'—and they show it sometimes, on the billboards.'

We walk through one of the doorways into another corridor. There are voices coming from a room at the end. I tense.

As if sensing the shift in my mood, Elle shoots me a warning look. It would be adorable if I hadn't seen her create tornados with her words or set a room full of Blotters alight with a match.

'Be nice,' she says.

When I don't reply, her eyes narrow.

Jay . . .'

I raise my hands. 'Fine. Just so long as—'

'Thank you.'

She walks through the arched doorway without letting me finish.

We're in a candlelit room that looks like one of the council meeting rooms in the Citadel. Unlike the Citadel, though, where twelve oil paintings are displayed around the room in ornate gold frames, the far wall is a mural of the sea. Cobwebs drape from the chandelier that hangs from the ceiling. And my breath mists in front of my face.

There are five people sitting at the long oval table in the centre, and they all fall silent and turn to face us.

'Ah, so the Blotter awakens,' says Sylvia.

'Oh, it's you,' I say.

I recognise two others from the Circus too. Anita, the woman with long dark hair who ran the infirmary, and Rami, who smiles warmly at Elle. I narrow my eyes and step closer to her. There's something about this guy that rubs me up the wrong way.

'Jay, it's so nice to finally meet you.' A woman with wavy brown hair stands up and walks over, her hand extended. 'I'm Mary.'

She looks as if she's in her mid-twenties, with irritatingly curious eyes the same colour as her long-sleeved turquoise top.

When I don't shake her hand, she drops her arm to her side and nods to the blond guy at the table. 'This is my brother, Tom,' she says.

He grins. 'All right, mate,' he says.

'Sorry about the tranquiliser,' says Mary. Elle tenses beside me. 'One of our book thieves used to work at one of the Creators' menageries before we took them on.'

I drag my teeth over my bottom lip. 'You were the one who shot me.'

The atmosphere in the room changes, and Tom slowly gets up, his chair scraping against the mosaiced floor tiles. His eyes darken. He looks as if he's preparing himself for a fight he could never win even though he is almost as big as me. It pisses me off. Yeah, I'm annoyed at being shot, but I'm not going to hurt her. I may be a monster, but only because I was written that way.

'Yeah,' she says. 'We okay?'

Elle is practically holding her breath beside me, and that pisses me off too. Is that seriously what she still thinks of me?

I exhale. 'Yeah. We're okay.'

Mary smiles. 'Good.' She turns to Elle. 'You were looking for a story written by the First Twist?'

Yes,' she says, and she sounds almost urgent before she smiles, composing herself. 'Yes. Please.'

'Great! Let's go.'

Elle lightly touches my arm then follows Mary out of the room. Feeling Sylvia's eyes on me, I head after her into a narrow corridor. The muscles in my jaw tighten when I walk into the vast space at the end.

There are books everywhere. They climb up the circular walls on either side of me, leather-bound and dusty. The shelves creak beneath their weight. I've burnt books during black market raids, but I've never seen so many in one place before. Not even in the Citadel. I think there may have been rooms like this there, but they were restricted—open only to the Creators.

My heart pounds, and my mouth is completely dry. This is wrong. Yet I can't look away from the labyrinth of dark, narrow paths that lead through the forbidden ink and parchment. Elle disappears into it.

'It's quite something, huh?' says Sylvia as the others walk past.

I swallow hard. 'How . . .?'

'A Blotter asking questions. I never thought I'd see the day. You going to stand there gawping, or you going to step up and help your girlfriend? She's going to need your support in a minute.'

I close my eyes and breathe out slowly. I hate this woman. Then I fall into step beside her. I run a hand over my mouth. 'Raven,' I say. 'She's not here.'

'No.' Sylvia's eyes darken. 'Neither is Lucy. But they're tough. They'll get here.'

We follow the others into a small room. The ceiling is so low my head almost brushes it.

'Like it?' says Mary. Two of the walls are lined with shelves cluttered with papers, books, and parchment. But Elle and the Darlings are clustered around something on the far wall. 'I painted it myself.'

'I . . . I'd almost forgotten what he looked like.' Elle sounds as if she's in pain. I don't like it.

'You knew him?' says Mary.

I push through the group to stand beside her.

'He is . . . he *was* my father,' she says softly.

My heart stops. Waves of darkness crash over me. Something heavy pushes down on my chest, and I can't fucking breathe.

There's a painting of one of the Creators on the wall. The Fallen Creator.

Her father.

His greying hair, sharp chin, and brown eyes blur as the room swims around me.

There's a watery film over Elle's eyes when she meets mine. I can't do anything. I can't say anything. She coughs, blinks, and then turns back to the painting. She's talking to Mary, but their voices fade to nothing. I can't focus on them. I need to get the fuck out of this room. I can't fucking breathe.

I step back. No one seems to notice as I leave. The books and shelves blur together, and I find myself back in the room we started in. I put my hands on the table and take deep breaths.

Get a grip on yourself, Jay.

I close my eyes and try to process it.

Elle's father was a Creator. Of course he was. It all makes sense. The story about the clockmaker and the grey world and the dandelion. The story about the man who first spread the seeds of the Circus. The way Sylvia referred to him as a crackpot. The reason Elle knows so much about the Final City. Her naïvety. The way she knows how to tell stories too.

'You knew Elle's father, didn't you, Blotter?'

The door clicks shut behind me. I stand upright. Slowly, I turn to face Sylvia. Her lips are pursed in a hard line.

'Everyone knows him. He was a Creator. The Fallen Creator. The First Twist.'

'Yes. But you *knew* him. Didn't you?'

I hold her gaze. Then I incline my head.

'How?'

I moisten my lips. 'I met him twice. Once—' I exhale. 'Once when he gave me this scar.' I touch my eyebrow. Then I look at the chequered floor between my boots and rub the back of my neck.

'And the second time?' she asks.

She already knows what I'm going to say. I know she does.

I meet her eye. 'The second time when I killed him.'

She stares at me, and her lips harden. Then she nods. 'Elle can never know,' she says.

She turns on her heel and strides out of the room.

Chapter Forty
Elle

My fingertips skim over the dusty tomes lining the shelves. When I close my eyes, I smell him in the air: old parchment and cigars and peppermint. Something aches inside of me. It's relentless and consuming.

I miss him.

I miss him so much.

'Do you know what you're looking for?'

I open my eyes and turn. The others have gone. Jay too. I don't know when that happened. But Mary sits casually in a chair by the painting of my father. I can't look at it. In this room full of his things, his absence feels like a tangible thing; a hungry mouth waiting to swallow me.

'Yes,' I say. 'I'm looking for a Book of Truth. One that's not in circulation anymore. I think he wrote a story in it. One that got him killed.'

She leans forwards, resting her forearms on her black trousers for a moment. Then she nods and gets to her feet. 'There's nothing like that in here. But we have a collection of them. Maybe the one you're looking for is amongst them.'

She walks past me, stirring the stale air. I momentarily lock eyes with my father. Then I tear myself away and follow Mary back into the main room of the library.

'How do you have all these books?' I ask as I fall into step beside her.

'Well, I was born here. As was my mother. And my grandmother. And my grandmother's mother.' Our way is lit by glowing table lamps, and our boots leave footprints in the dust as we navigate the narrow paths. 'My family has been based her for decades—centuries maybe. We record people's stories and rescue books from fires.'

'Stories will always grow,' I say.

'Stories will always grow,' she repeats.

'Jay says this place reminds him of the Citadel.' I glance up at the domed ceiling and the gold railing that circles the gallery up there. 'The Creators lived here once, didn't they? That's why some of my father's stories are here. They ban books for the rest of us. They have libraries of their own.'

Mary nods. 'I'm not sure how many generations back it was, but one of my ancestors worked in the Citadel. She made a record of it. We think the Citadel she spoke of was this building. Only, it wasn't considered Draft Four back then; it was the Final City. But then the Creators moved on and built something better. They hid this place under the earth to be forgotten.'

I think about the underground railway we were heading towards and Jay's insistence it didn't exist. Did the Creators hide that too?

'But it wasn't forgotten,' I say.

'By most, it was. History belongs to those who write it after all.' She smiles. 'But not by all.'

'There are cracks in everything.'

'Yes.' We walk through a small doorway, and Mary flicks on a light. 'Ah. Here we are.'

We're in a hexagonal room filled with books. The Sacred Stylus is embossed on many of them in glinting gold or bronze or silver. The Book of Truth. Thousands of them. All of them filled with the One True Story, the words of my enemy.

'Tom wanted to burn them.' Mary leans against the doorframe and crosses her arms. 'But I don't like the idea of burning books. Even these. Need any help?'

'No,' I say. 'Thank you.'

She grins, flashing white teeth. 'I'm so glad you said that. I don't much fancy going through this lot. Tom's going to head out to see if he can intercept the rest of your Circus friends. I'll go prepare us some food so we can all eat together when they get here. You know where you're going to start?'

'If it's here, my father will have left me a sign. I'll know it when I see it.'

She smiles and heads back into the library.

It must be about an hour of pacing the room and pulling tomes from the shelves before I see the dandelion seed scribbled onto the spine of one of the books. My pulse quickens as I slide it off the shelf and crumple, cross-legged, onto the floor.

There is a symbol on the first page: thirteen concentric circles with thirteen black lines cutting through from a blot in the centre to the edges. It looks a little like the tattoo on Jay's arm. The one he said was a map.

I frown, running a finger along it. Then, hand shaking, I flick through the pages, catching glimpses of the One True Story. There's the story about how the Creators made the world out of ink and words, a parable about a greedy smuggler who was killed in the river, the promise that if we follow the One True Story our souls will be saved when the Ending is upon us.

Then I turn the page on a dried dandelion. My heart jolts.

Something burns behind my eyes. This has to be it. I place the small, withered flower onto the chequered floor. Heart beating fast, I read the words my father left for me to find.

'*Once, there was a world, and the world was grey.*

But before that, there was a different world. A world that was full of colour.

Dandelion seeds were carried by the breeze, and wherever they landed, a dandelion would grow.

In this world, there were some who wondered what else could be grown amongst the fields of flowers. Their creations started small: a bee, a door, a storm, a Circus. But like their creations, their ambitions grew too. And before long, there was War between those who were starting to understand their power, and those who were trying to cling onto it.

The War lasted for many years, and as it raged across the land, flowers were culled to make way for instruments of destruction. In the darkness that remained, the men who clung onto power planted something else. A new story.

They told the world dandelions were weeds, not flowers, to be uprooted and destroyed. And gradually—so gradually no one even seemed to notice—they rid the world of colour altogether until all was grey, and only their story remained, carried instead of dandelion seeds by the breeze.

'*As time went by, they grew and revised and amended their story. They made themselves gods. They reinforced their story with Ink to give it power. And then they hid the Ink so no one else could use it.*

Because they knew a truth many had forgotten.

Whoever controls the Ink controls the Story.

Whoever controls the Story controls the world.'

Chapter Forty-One
Elle

Jay is lying on the bed when I make it back to the room, hands clasped behind his head as he stares vacantly at the ceiling. He's fully clothed, and his muddy boots have left marks on the cream bedspread. He doesn't look up when I close the door behind me, but he tenses, his breathing stopping momentarily.

I hurry over and kneel on the mattress beside him, placing the book down on the sheets. A smile spreads across my face. 'I found the story I was looking for.'

He swallows hard then glances at me. His eyes are cold. He turns his attention back to the ceiling. 'Oh.'

'Don't you want to know what it is?'

'I don't know, Elle. Do I?' He exhales a long, weary breath and sits upright. He swings his legs over the side of the bed and puts his head in his hands.

'Jay?' I shuffle closer and place a hand tentatively on his shoulder, feeling the knots in his muscles. 'You're upset.'

When he doesn't reply, I sigh. I think I know what this is about. Most records of my father are gone. His stories were deleted from the Book of Truth, the buildings with his face on them were destroyed, and any devout followers of his were Cut from the One True Story. My father exists only as a footnote in the Creators' story now. They call him the First Twist and say he existed only to tempt people into straying from the true path.

Most forgot his name and his face when the new version of the One True Story washed over them.

But Jay is a Blotter.

'You recognised the painting, didn't you?' I drag my teeth over my bottom lip. 'Only a few people know he's my father, Jay. It was drilled into me since I was born to never tell. I needed to survive. But I wish you hadn't found out that way. I guess it was surprising.'

'Yeah, it was pretty fucking surprising.' Tension radiates from his hunched-up body.

I run my thumb along his shoulder. 'You were going to find out at some point. And . . . well . . . I . . .' The words catch in my throat, and I'm unsure whether I can say it. Then I breathe out softly. 'I *trust* you, Jay. I should have told you.'

And it is true. I *do* trust him. I have always looked out for myself; I've never really let anyone get close to me before. And yet somehow, even though this man was sent to kill me, I trust him.

'Yeah, you should have. It would have saved a lot of trouble.' He stands up abruptly, and I'm stung.

'What do you mean by that?'

When his eyes hit mine, there's pain behind them—hot, malleable pain I can't understand. He looks away. Runs a hand across his mouth. Then he paces in front of me.

My father told me a story about a wolf with a thorn stuck in his paw once. The wolf lashed out because it was in pain until someone pulled it out. But I do not know what is hurting Jay. I do not know how to make it better.

I do not understand.

I push myself up and stand on the bed so my eyes are level with his. 'Jay? What's wrong?'

He looks away from me then nods. 'I got you to your stupid library.'

My insides freeze. All the warmth I felt after reading my father's story drains from my body. 'What do you mean?'

'You know what I mean. I'm going. I'm out. I should never have come in the first place.'

'You mean you should have killed me?'

His eyes blaze. 'No. That's not what I mean, and you know it.'

'Well, what then?'

He steps back, taking away the heat from his body.

'No, Jay. You're not leaving.'

He smiles, but his lips are hard, and there is no warmth in his ink-blotched eyes. 'Right. and you're going to stop me, are you, little Twist?'

'Yes.'

'And how the fuck are you going to do that? Create a hurricane to trap me here? A tornado? An impossible cage to lock me in? No. Because you can't do that out here, can you, little Twist?'

'Stop being a dick.'

'Don't you get it, little Twist? I *am* a dick. I've always been a dick. Stop trying to *fucking fix me.*'

'I'm not trying to *fix you.*'

'Yes, you are.'

'Do you think you're the only one who has problems? Who feels pain? Do you think you're special because you're a Blotter and things didn't work out the way you planned? Do you think things worked out for any of us either, Jay? The only person I loved was killed. Sylvia lost her *child*. Raven's girlfriend was murdered. We're all broken here.'

I'm breathing hard, and so is he. He rubs his face with both hands.

'FUCK.'

'My father being a Creator changes nothing.'

He drops his arms to his sides. His face is red, and there's a watery film over his eyes. 'It changes *everything.*'

'*Why?*' I grab his hand and move it to my waist, then I take his face in my hands. He doesn't pull away when I rest my forehead against his. His skin is hot, and his short breaths mingle with mine.

'*Jay, what's wrong? Why are you being like this?*'

He meets my eye, and there's something painfully vulnerable in those hard pools of blue. 'I'm going,' he says. It's not the hard, impenetrable voice of the Blotter I met in my bedsit, but I hear the finality in it all the same.

I try to swallow the panic rising in my chest.

No. I don't need him. I'm fine. It's fine.

'But I don't want you to.' My voice comes out as a whisper.

'I have to.'

'Why?'

'I just do.'

'No.' I step closer so our noses touch. *Jay . . .* ' I brush my lips against his. He doesn't kiss me back. *Jay, what's the matter? Talk to me.*'

'I don't belong here, Elle.'

I kiss him again, and a low, hollow sound vibrates against my mouth. 'Yes. You do,' I say.

'I've done terrible things.'

'That's what this is about? I know.'

'You don't know the half of it.'

'You've done good things too. You didn't do what was written. You saved my life. You helped Raven. You saved all the kids at the Circus. And now you're feeling guilty about the bad stuff. And that's good, Jay. It shows you're human.'

'*I'm not. I'm a fucking monster.*'

'*No, you're not.*' Holding his face, I brush my lips against his again, and this time, his mouth part slightly. His grip tightens around my waist.

'You can't change your past, Jay. It's done. But you can change your future.' I nip his bottom lip with my teeth.

He makes a low sound, and his other hand moves to my waist. Some of the tension in his chest eases as if he's giving in. But then he inhales sharply through his nose. 'Elle. I can't.'

'Yes. You can.' I move my thumb against the side of his face. He closes his eyes. '*Fuck.*'

'I know you don't think you belong here. But you do. And it's dangerous for you out there now, because you *are* one of us. You can't leave. They'll kill you. Please. Stay with me.' I brush my lips against his again. '*Stay with me. Please.*'

Finally, he kisses me back. He groans as his mouth moves against mine. One of his big hands slides up my back, and he pulls me into him.

'*Stay with me,*' I say as his kisses deepen and his mouth moves urgently against mine. His grip on me tightens until it's almost painful, and I don't care.

'*Stay with me.*' I hear the panic in my voice, and I hate it. I don't need anybody. I don't. I can do this alone. I can. '*Please stay with me.*'

I know he can hear that I'm panicking too. I hate that he hears it. But something dissolves in his chest. He lifts me off the bed and holds me in his strong arms.

'*I'm here,*' he says.

Chapter Forty-Two
Jay

I taste her. I taste every fucking inch of her.

Head between her legs, I devour her until she throws her head back against the mattress and cries out my name.

Then I make her do it again with my fingers.

And then I take her with her legs over my shoulders and her hands balled up in the sheets.

And with every thrust, I try to forget. I try to get it out.

That bad.

Fucking.

Feeling.

Building.

In my.

Chest.

Fuck.

And when I release a low, guttural cry that comes from somewhere deep inside and scrapes hard against my throat, it comes out with it. That bad feeling. Just for a few seconds.

No thoughts. No emotions.

Just relief. Lightness. Bliss.

But when I crash down on top of her, sinking my head into her neck and feeling her heartbeat pounding against my chest, it starts to build up again. Hollow and heavy at the same time. A shadow. Growing. Spreading. Dark like the ink I can't get out of me.

'*Jay.*' Her fingertips move against the back of my neck, and I groan into her skin. I inhale her scent of sweat and sex and soap. I taste her on my tongue. I let her take over my senses as my heart pounds and my breathing steadies.

And I force the bad feeling to the pit of my stomach so it won't destroy everything. It settles, cold and hard, and feels too heavy. But I have to hold it there. What else am I supposed to do?

'You're staying then.' She's not asking a question, yet her words lack their usual conviction as they tickle my ear.

I breathe out slowly. 'Yeah.'

Even just saying it makes me feel better. Eases something. Lightens the weight. Because I've made the decision: I'm not leaving her.

Not now. Not ever. I'll keep her safe.

She breathes out softly too, breath warm against my skin. 'I thought you said I couldn't make you stay.'

I lean on my forearms and look into her eyes. 'Yeah, well, I didn't know you were going to get naked, did I, little Twist?'

The corner of her lip tugs upward. 'So that's all it takes?'

I shake my head. 'That's not the reason.'

Her face darkens as she registers my expression.

'I know.' She says the words hurriedly. As if she doesn't want me to say it, why I stayed. And that's fine by me. I don't want to say it either. I don't want to admit it was the plea I heard in her voice—the vulnerability, the panic in the way her hands clung to my face and her lips moved against mine—that crumbled my resolve against doing the right thing.

Or maybe it's just that I'm a selfish bastard. Maybe it's just that I didn't want to leave her. And I don't want to say that either.

Hurt her if I stay. Hurt her if I go.

I'm fucked anyway, so I may as well do what I want. Even though it'll probably destroy us both in the end.

My eyes drop to her lips. They're red and swollen. I shift my hand and run my thumb along them. She looks at me a moment longer. Then she shuffles beneath me.

'You haven't asked me what I found in the library,' she says. 'The story in my father's section of the Book of Truth.'

I roll onto my back to release her, planting my feet on the cold tiles. She props herself up on her elbow.

'Yeah, well, I was a bit busy between your legs.'

I focus on a spot of damp on the ceiling. I don't want to know about the message from her father. Not anymore. Not now I know who he was. I don't want to hear about him. I don't want to talk about him. I don't want to think about him. I want him out of my mind.

I grab my jeans and pull them on. She pushes a book onto my lap and then gets dressed. She looks at me expectantly.

I exhale and pick it up. 'What's this then?'

She flips it open about halfway through. There's a dead flower wedged into the spine.

'Let me guess. A dandelion.'

Her amber eyes are bright against her flushed skin. I should have left. Course I should. But I like that I did that to her—the pinkened skin, the sheen of sweat, the flush on her neck. I smell myself on her as she stands in front of me, her sweat mingled with mine.

She smiles. 'Read it.' She nods at the pages. 'Read the story.'

I scratch the back of my neck. 'I . . . er . . . I can't read, little Twist.'

Her cheeks flush. 'Oh, right. Course. Sorry.' I see the pity in her face.

'We don't all have the privilege of a Creator father, do we, little Twist?' My voice comes out rougher than I meant it to, but she doesn't flinch. What am I doing bringing up her father anyway?

'I can teach you, if you like,' she says. 'I taught Raven. Kind of. And some of the kids at the Circus.'

'No.'

She takes the book out of my hands. 'Okay. Suit yourself.'

I let out a hot breath. 'Go on then. Let's get this over with. What does it say?'

A smile tickles her lips. And she starts to read.

'Once, there was a world. And the world was grey.'

I watch her as she tells the story—the way her face animates, her eyebrows moving with each intonation of her voice. I don't know if she thinks this story means something or if she's just happy because her father wrote it.

But as I start to understand the words she's repeating, I am glad I stayed.

Because they're dangerous. They're going to add fuel to her stupid ideas about revolution and overthrowing the Creators.

'As time went by, they grew and revised and amended their story. They made themselves gods. They reinforced their story with Ink to give it power. And then they hid the Ink so no one else could use it. Because they knew a truth many had forgotten.' Her eyes meet mine. *'Whoever controls the Ink controls the Story. Whoever controls the Story controls the world.'*

She smiles expectantly. 'Don't you see what this means?'

'I think it means you're going to get yourself into trouble, little Twist.'

She shakes her head then taps the page. 'It means the world wasn't always this way. It means the Creators aren't special. And it means the Creators didn't create the world; they stole it. This story changes everything!'

I exhale and shake my head. 'It doesn't, little Twist.'

'Course it does.'

'How? Are you going to tell people *this* story? Do you really think they're going to believe you?'

Her smile falters just for a moment before she shakes her head. 'You're missing something. The power doesn't belong to them. They just monopolised it.'

'So?'

She rolls her eyes and then pats my arm. 'Come on, put your top on. I want to show the others.'

With that, she turns on her heel and heads to the door.

'Ink!' she says. 'It's all about ink! Come on.'

I rub my face. I don't want to go out there. I don't want to have to face Sylvia again.

'No. Not now,' I say.

She looks over her shoulder at me, and her brow furrows with uncharacteristic worry.

I sigh. 'Look, I told you I'm staying. I'm not leaving. I just. . . I'll be out in a minute.' I raise an eyebrow. 'Okay?'

She releases a breath then nods. 'Okay. I'll see you out there.' She heads out of the room with an irritating skip in her step. She's got the book nestled beneath her arm that will most likely be the end of us all.

Chapter Forty-Three
Elle

'Whoever controls the Story controls the world,' I say.

Tom thought he heard news about Raven and Lucy, so headed out to find them, leaving Mary, Anita, Rami, and Sylvia behind in the council room. The Circus ringleader frowns.

'So we all had the power of stories once, huh? Back in the day? Guess that somewhat ruins the little chosen-one complex you've got going on, doesn't it, sweetie?' She exhales and shakes her head. 'I don't know why you're looking so pleased. It doesn't change anything.'

'Of course it does.'

Sylvia gestures to the book, and I slide it over the table. She grabs it.

'It's not just the story that changes everything,' I say. 'The bit about the Ink . . .'

'And then they hid the Ink.' Sylvia shrugs. 'No shit. They forbade ink, didn't they? That's not new informa—'

'There's more to it than that.' I slam my palms on the table, and Rami flinches beside me. 'Do you know how Blotters are made?'

'Made?' Mary leans forwards on her elbows.

'Yes. They're not born with ink in their veins. And they're not created by the Creators either. They're made that—' My breath catches in my throat as his heat washes over me. My skin hums at his presence. He smells hot and masculine, like sex. My pulse quickens.

Sylvia looks over my shoulder and raises an eyebrow. 'Elle was just telling us how you were made a Blotter.'

He breathes out slowly through his nose. I catch the movement of his arm out of the corner of my eye and hear the scrape of his hand against his stubble as he runs it across his mouth.

'Right.' The word comes out hard. I tense as I recall his reluctance in telling me about his Blotter Ceremony in the first place. 'She was, was she?' Jay sits down, throwing his arm over the back of his chair, and looks up at me.

'Not about you specifically,' I say. 'I wanted to tell them about the ink. You said there was a pool of ink in the Citadel.'

He visibly tenses. 'So?'

'They hid the ink,' says Mary. 'Whoever controls the ink controls the story . . .' She chews her lip, and I see the cogs turning behind her eyes. 'You think it's related? You think Jay's pool of ink is the ink they hid?'

'Maybe.'

Anita leans back, her long black hair sweeping over the back of her chair. 'What? You think they have some kind of pool of magic ink?'

'I've always been able to create. I was doing it as a child, but my stories would always get away from me. I'd lose control of them or struggle to get people to believe. That story says the Creators used Ink to reinforce their story. What if that's what I've been missing? What if that's why their story is so powerful? The Ink.'

'Hmm,' says Sylvia.

I run my fingers through my tangled hair. I know this is important. I know I'm right. Sylvia continues to look through the book.

'What's this?' she says.

'What?'

She slides the book back over the table but is looking at Jay. It's open on the cover page—the one with thirteen concentric circles drawn on it, with the thirteen lines cutting from the centre. It's similar to the symbol Jay has tattooed on his arm. He cracks his knuckles then takes the book.

'Your map, right, Blotter?' she says.

'Yeah. But . . .'

I reach for his arm and brush my fingertips across the black symbol tattooed onto his skin with the other. Thirteen concentric circles, but without the lines coming from the centre.

His eyes burn into mine.

'The circles?' I say.

'Each of the Drafts exists within one of the circles. The Final City is in the middle.' He pulls his arm gently out of my grasp and turns back to the page.

'But the lines?'

His brow furrows. 'Lines of ink,' he says softly. He looks lost in thought, and I touch his shoulder.

'What is it?'

He shakes his head, looking down at the table. 'Reminds me of something. Something I overheard as a boy. About lines of ink beneath the world.'

'What about them?'

He shakes his head. 'I dunno, little Twist.'

I run my fingertip across one of the lines as it joins the black dot in the centre. 'Lines of ink that join in the centre, in the Final City.' I look up at the others. 'When we swam across the river, something attacked us, grabbed Jay's leg.'

A CIRCUS OF INK

'There are monsters in the rivers,' says Sylvia. 'Everyone knows that.'

'It was ink.'

'Sweetie . . .'

'No. Listen. What if . . . what if there are lines of this Ink running beneath the world?' My words tumble out fast and breathless. 'Whoever controls the Ink controls the Story.' I tap the book. 'What if one of the Creators caught wind of where we were and somehow controlled the Ink? Used it to create a hand? To grab Jay?'

Sylvia, Anita, and Rami stare at me blankly. Mary seems pensive. Jay just looks confused.

'So what if that were true?' says Sylvia finally. 'It just makes everything worse. If the Creators can literally manipulate this Ink, what's to stop them from manipulating it into—I don't know, something to kill us?'

'I don't know,' I say. 'But you're missing the point. If they get their power from these lines of Ink and the main source of it is in the Citadel, maybe we could take that power away from them.'

'Power can't be taken from men like that, sweetie.' Sylvia sighs and rubs the dark smudges beneath her eyes. 'Maybe there's something in what you're saying. Maybe this Ink is real, and maybe there's power in it. But people believe in the Creators' stories. They live by them. They spread them. They enforce them. And they die by them. Maybe once, the Creators needed the Ink, but I don't think they need it anymore.'

'But if we can get a hold of it, *we* can use it. Why else would they have hidden it? I can create, but it's harder out here. It took me almost a month to plant the seeds for the hurricane, and that was in Draft One. When we get to the Inner Drafts, when we get to the Final City—'

'We're not going to the Final City,' Jay and Sylvia speak at the same time.

'—it'll be harder still. Maybe the Ink would help. Whoever controls the Ink controls the Story. That's what my father said.'

'Sweetie . . .'

'It's worth looking into, Sylv.' Mary smiles, and I nod gratefully. 'We can—'

Urgent footsteps approach, and we all turn to the door as Tom bursts into the room wearing his Teller robes. Seconds later, Lucy, the fifteen-year-old from the Circus, stumbles into the room after him. Something hardens inside of me. Blood streams from her nose, her eyes are black and bruised, and her dirty blonde hair is matted.

Sylvia gets to her feet, and I cross the room.

'Lucy . . . what happened?' I ask as I grab her arms.

She's trembling. 'They caught us. I got away, but—' She swallows. 'They've got Raven. They're taking her to one of the killing blocks. They're going to execute her.' Her bloodshot eyes lock onto mine, and she looks lost. 'Tonight.'

Chapter Forty-Four
Jay

I tap my fingers against the table as chaos erupts around me.

Elle's face drains of colour as she hurries the teenager to a chair. Tom heads back through the door. The others pace the room, barking questions and raising their voices.

It's exhausting. And it's pointless.

They want to save Raven. They won't save her. It's already too late.

The thought of her being killed is heavier than I expect it to be. Why would I care if another Darling is Cut by the Creators? I've killed enough myself.

'Quiet!' Sylvia slams her cane against the table, and everyone shuts up. Her lips are hard with tension, and she takes a couple of deep breaths before swallowing. 'Who caught her? Blotters?'

'No. Just . . . just people. From the Draft.' Lucy narrows her eyes. 'Bastards.'

Elle's face whitens. 'It wasn't Blotters who did this?'

Tom comes back into the room and places a radio on the table. He fiddles with the dial, and a male voice comes from the speaker.

'*. . . plot coordinated by Darlings who have twisted from the One True Story. So filled with hate are they, so lacking in thanks for all the Creators have done, they seek only to destroy—*'

Elle's jaw sets. 'How can people believe—?'

'Shh!' Sylvia hisses.

'*Today, the Blotters rounded up these abominations. They will be Cut from the One True Story at midnight by the Black Sea Bridge. Come join us as they—*'

Noise erupts as Tom turns off the radio. Rami and Elle are yapping about heading to the Bridge. Anita is comforting the kid. Mary's saying something to her brother. Only Sylvia remains quiet. She meets my eyes, and for a moment, it's as if we're the only people in the room.

'It's a trap,' I say.

'Yes. You're probably right, Blotter.'

Silence falls, and the others turn to look at us. I hold Sylvia's gaze. I don't know what she wants from me. I don't like it. She knows what I did. She knows the shadow that lives inside of me.

Elle glares at us both then shakes her head. 'No. I know what you're going to say, but we're not leaving Raven to die.'

Sylvia closes her eyes. When she opens them again, her expression has shifted; become harder. 'I'm not risking any more lives.'

Elle spins around to face her. 'I'm bringing her back.'

'No. You're not.'

'Yes—'

Sylvia slams her hand on the table. 'I was made the leader of our little group, honey, and that means making the difficult choices sometimes.'

'Difficult choice? This is Raven we're talking about.' She sucks in a breath then lets it out slowly. 'Look, we're wasting time arguing when we should be coming up with a plan. Mary—you know where the Black Sea is . . .'

I rub the bridge of my nose, blocking out her voice as she fumbles for some bullshit plan. It won't work. There's no way a group of Darlings can stop this. We're talking about Blotters here, and Creators, and a Draft Four high-security area. The Creators obviously expect us to go to the bridge—why else would there be a broadcast about it on the radio? They've written our deaths. It'll be on the skins of every Blotter in the area. They won't fuck up again.

I run a hand over my mouth. 'I'll go.'

Everyone looks at me.

Some of the weight that's been crushing my chest lightens. The Twist won't give this up; she won't allow the Darlings to do nothing. So I'll go. And if I die, then I die. And then what I did dies with me. And that'll be that.

I won't survive this anyway.

'They'll be keeping her in a holding cell near the killing block,' I say. 'I know where it is. They're all laid out the same. If I can get in there before midnight, I can break her out.'

Elle raises her eyebrow. 'You'd do that for Raven?'

'No. I'd do that for you.'

Something shifts in the air, becomes uncomfortable.

'How would you get in?' says Elle. 'They'll kill you.'

'I'm a Blotter. I'll walk in. I'm the only one here who can.'

'They're looking for you.'

'You said they were looking for a fake Blotter. I'm not fake.'

She bites her cheek, and I can tell she's thinking about it. 'They wouldn't be expecting it. Raven's death is written at midnight. I presume that's when they'll have written our deaths too. If it's a trap.'

'Yeah. Right.'

'It's just . . . if they catch you.'

'I'll kill them.'

'It's not safe.'

'Nothing's safe.'

'I'll come with you. You can say I'm a prisoner.'

'Unnecessary risk.'

'I know. It's just—' She's breathing quickly, as if her chest contains one of her tornados. 'No—'

'No? I'm the best option you—'

She holds up her hand to silence me. 'I know. Just . . . quiet. I'm thinking.'

I clench my fist and rest it by my mouth. Even now, with the taste of her lingering on my lips and her smell fading on my skin, she still finds a way to drive me fucking crazy.

When Elle looks at the others, the emotion is gone from her face. We're back at the Circus when she saved me, in control, in command. Her head is high, and her breathing is steady.

'We'll cause a distraction,' she says. 'Draw some of the Blotters out so the way is clear for Jay to get out.'

'No,' I say. 'There's no—'

'Shh.'

Sylvia is drumming her fingers against the table, her eyes fixed on Elle. 'What are you thinking, sweetie?'

'We spread some more dandelion seeds.'

Sylvia frowns. 'It'll be dangerous.'

'Yes. That's why I'm not letting Jay do this alone.'

I stand up so I'm towering above her. 'Letting?'

'Yes. Letting.'

My lip twitches despite everything that's going on and everything that's about to happen. 'And you could stop me, could—?'

'Okay. That's enough of that.' Sylvia gets up. 'Reconvene in the entrance hall in thirty minutes. Mary, load up the van. We'll need weapons, petrol, and all the paint you can spare.'

Before she follows the others out of the room, Sylvia stops in front of me. This close, I can see the creases in her black jacket and the smudges beneath her eyes. I can smell that slight note of fear in her sweat too. She's tired and afraid, though she is doing a good job of hiding it.

'You sure you can do this, Blotter?'

I hold her gaze, and I think we understand each other: Either I bring back the Darling, or I die. Either outcome works. And we keep Elle safe. Can I do this?

'Yeah.'

She nods. 'Okay. Let's go get our girl back.'

She leaves me and Elle alone. I exhale slowly. It's strange. I know I'm going to my death, but it relaxes me somehow. The inevitability of it maybe. The newfound purpose. The fact that when I die, the shadows die with me.

'You're not leaving me. You know that, right?' says Elle.

I can't meet her gaze. Instead, I look at the foaming sea that vandalises the wall behind her. It shouldn't be here—it's forbidden and unnatural, but it's beautiful too, in a way.

She puts her hand on my chest, just above my heart. I swallow as I tilt my head down and move my hands to her hips. She's warm, and when our eyes meet, hers are filled with fiery, misplaced belief. The darkness comes back. She shouldn't look at me like that. She needs to prepare herself.

'Elle, listen—'

'You're coming back to me.'

She slides her palms up my chest then clasps her hands around the back of my neck. She pulls my mouth to hers. I groan as I kiss her back, sinking my fingers into her hips and pulling her closer. I want this bad feeling to go away. But I want to come back to her too.

I rest my forehead against hers.

'If you get caught, I'll come and get you. You know that, right?' she says.

Something clenches in my gut. I don't want it to be true. It's too heavy to bear.

But her words flood me with another sensation too. Unbidden and warm, it spreads through all the ink and the darkness and fills up the hollow spaces inside my body. I don't know what this feeling is, but I know she's telling the truth. She *will* come for me.

'You shouldn't do that.' My words are gruff, and they scrape against my tightening throat.

'But I will.'

I pull her into my chest. 'I know.' I lightly brush my lips against the top of her head. 'Crazy little Twist.'

The road to the promenade is empty, but I can hear voices ahead.

I walk along it with my hands stuffed into the pockets of my jeans. It's dark. Small droplets of water sting my face, carried by a wind that howls against the off-white skyscrapers. The air smells like the ocean—salt and rotting vegetation—and waves crash against the cliffs in the distance.

When I get to the end of the road, I lean against the wall of a House of Truth. I drag my teeth over my bottom lip and taste salt and the kiss I took from Elle before the van drove off. There are at least a hundred people already gathered in the square ahead. They're congregating around the raised platform in front of the sea where Raven will be executed in a few hours. The white stone statue of Creator Michael looms over them.

I count around twenty Blotters. Some are stationed at the entrance of the Black Sea Bridge that stretches across the ocean. Others are moving through the crowd.

I breathe out slowly. If I get caught, Elle will come for me. It raises the stakes. Makes this harder. I need to actually succeed.

I remove my hands from my pockets, crack my knuckles, and walk towards the high-security cell that's built into the foot of the bridge. I changed into a vest, so my tattoos are visible, and people cower away from me. No one is guarding the doors when I get there. I put my hand on the ice-cold handle, ready for someone to stop me. Then I push it down.

The door screams as it scrapes open.

I step into an empty corridor and frown. It's unusual for one of these places to be completely unguarded. Where is everyone? I push the door closed with my back, and all is silent. The air carries a metallic scent.

Something's not right.

Muscles tight, I turn around. There are two dead Blotters in an alcove to the left, their heads twisted at unnatural angles. *What the fuck?*

I'm stepping away from them when something plunges into my neck from behind. With a start, I turn, grabbing onto the vest of a man as my legs give way beneath me.

'Hello, lad,' he says.

That Blotter from the motel swims in and out of focus above me as I land on my knees. Everything's going blurry, but I can make out the syringe in his hand. I blink.

Fight. Have to fight it.

'I thought it was about time we had a chat.' He crouches down, and I swipe my fist at him but miss.

'*Fuck . . . you,*' I mumble.

He produces a small penknife from his pocket and flicks out the blade. His lips twist into a smile. 'But first,' he says. 'I want to see you bleed.'

Everything goes black.

Chapter Forty-Five
Jay

Everything is dark. Peaceful. Water is dripping somewhere.

Drip. Drip. Drip.

I breathe in time with it.

Drip. Drip. Drip.

It reminds me of something. The sound. Something from when I was young, maybe. Ink. I think it reminds me of ink.

Drip. Drip. Drip.

It starts to piss me off though.

Drip. Drip. Drip.

It starts to bore into my skull.

Drip. Drip. Drip.

And *fuck,* my head is killing me. Throbbing.

Drip. Drip. Drip.

I groan and thrust my hand to my temple.

Only I don't. I can't. I can't move.

My eyes jolt open.

'Hello, lad.'

I jerk forwards. Something metal bites into my wrists, which are bound behind my back. My ankles are tied to the chair legs, bolted to the concrete floor. I'm in a small, dark room. There are no windows and one door. A pipe is dripping from the ceiling.

The Blotter from the motel is here, leaning against a wooden bench littered with sharp objects. A smile spreads across his face and pulls at the burn mark across his cheek. His eyes linger on my chest as it heaves up and down.

'Calm down, lad.'

Drip. Drip. Drip.

He picks up his penknife and turns the blade to the dim light coming from a buzzing bulb.

I don't understand. I don't understand why I'm not dead. I don't understand why two other Blotters were dead at the door. I don't understand why he seems to be enjoying himself. He's playing with me. But Blotters don't play. We kill.

'What the fuck are you doing?' I say, and my mouth is dry.

'You're surprised.'

He crosses the room and stops so close to me I can smell his sweat. He grabs my chin between his finger and thumb and forces me to look at him. All the while, that dripping sound bores into my skull, and the handcuffs bite into my wrists.

'You're curious too,' he says. 'Curious about what I want. Curious about what I'm going to do to you.'

His eyes move with interest over my face, then down my neck, lingering for too long on my chest and body. I swallow.

'My eyes are up here, mate.'

He chuckles. 'Curiosity. And surprise. Such unusual traits.'

'If you're going to kill me, just get on with it. I don't need to hear your fucking monologue.'

He lets go of me. 'I told you, I want to chat first. And with the unfortunate ends that met the two Blotters standing guard, we have ourselves a little privacy. For now at least. You see, *I'm* curious too.' He studies his knife. 'When I cut you open, what will

I see? Blood? Or Ink? They say you're nothing but a misbehaving Twist, but I don't believe that. You *are* a Blotter, aren't you, lad?'

'Ye—'

'*Shh.* You'll ruin the surprise.' He pulls down my vest, and my breathing roughens.

'Get the fuck off me.'

I'm going to kill him. I'm going to kill this bastard.

Except I'm not, am I? I can't move.

Drip. Drip. Drip.

I control myself. It doesn't matter. I just need him to do it fast. I need her to know it's a lost cause. If I'm dead, she won't come for me.

'Get on with it then,' I say.

He studies my chest then moves his fingertip over the dandelion seed etched above my heart. My skin crawls. I jerk back, but there's nowhere to go. The Blotter pushes the cool, flat side of the blade against my skin.

A gruff sound vibrates against my throat as he slices through my flesh. When he's done, he raises the knife and holds it to the light so he can study the glossy substance covering it.

Ink runs down the blade. It drips onto the floor by his boots.

Drip. Drip. Drip.

A smile broadens on his face. 'I thought so.'

Slowly, I meet his gaze. 'What do you want?'

He wipes the knife against his vest. 'I told you, I'm curious.'

He grabs another chair from across the room and drags it in front of me. He sits down, his posture casual as though we're two Blotters in a tavern after a day of Cuts. He fiddles with his penknife.

'I could just kill you now. But aren't you curious about what I'm curious about?' he asks.

I stare at the floor marked with my blood. There's a part of me that just wants this to be over. There's a part of me that wants him to kill me and be done with it. Then it ends. All of it. This hollow fucking feeling, this weight in my stomach, this constant feeling of being too empty and too full at the same time.

But another part of me is curious. Another part of me wants to live. Another part of me wants to get back to *her*.

You're coming back to me. You know that, right?

Slowly, I meet his gaze. 'Yeah.'

My voice is so quiet it's barely audible, but the Blotter grins. 'You don't disappoint, lad. I'm curious about your girl.'

My muscles tense, and it sends a sharp pain through my chest. 'You stay the fuck away from her.'

He chuckles. 'I'm curious about you too. We crossed paths once before, you know—'

'In the motel.'

'Before that. You were just a little lad at the time—I doubt you remember me. You'd just taken quite the beating.' He looks at the scar that cuts across my eyebrow. The one Elle's father gave me. 'I remember though. I was in my thirties at the time.'

I look pointedly at his greying hair. 'You do look a bit past it, mate.'

'Yes, lad. I'm old for a Blotter, I know. They don't usually let us live so long. But you see, the Creators have become rather fond of me. And that being the case, I've spent a lot of time in the Citadel. When you've done that for so long . . . well, lad, you start to learn things. Things you shouldn't know. You get an eye for the bullshit. There was no hurricane scheduled for the Draft One black market that day. The Creators took credit for it, said they'd written it into the One True Story, but they didn't. Did they?'

He looks at the knife in his hands, turning it over between his fingers. 'I remember when the Creator who gave you that scar started to change some of his opinions. It was about nineteen years ago, give or take, wasn't it?' He looks up slowly. 'How old is your girl, lad? I'd say she's about nineteen years, give or take. I imagine something as precious, as innocent, as a baby could cause a father to look at the world in a different way. What do you think?'

My fists clench behind my back. I remember her story about the clockmaker—a cruel man who changed when he was given the dandelion seed.

'Another curious thing. You were assigned to Draft One around five years ago, weren't you? That's a strange move for a big lad like you. Wasn't that around the time the same Creator who gave you that scar'—he points the blade at my eyebrow—'was executed?'

I swallow hard, fighting against the tightening of my throat and the rising weight in my gut.

'And isn't Michael your patron?' He touches Michael's mark—a cross—on my bicep with the tip of his blade. 'He was the one who had the most to lose if that particular Creator who gave you that scar was allowed to continue spreading his new stories. Am I getting close to the truth?'

I purse my lips together. I'm not telling this bastard anything.

'There are ways I can make you talk, you know?'

'No,' I say, 'there aren't.'

He sighs. 'There's no need to play the hero, lad. There's no point. There are no heroes; no villains. No right; no wrong. No good or evil. There are only stories. And those with the power to wield them.'

'What do you want?'

'I want your girl to come for you.'

I jerk forwards, but the bastard doesn't so much as flinch. 'You stay the fuck away from her.'

'A Blotter and a Twist. Such a curious thing. But she'll come for you, won't she, lad?'

There are voices in the corridor. His gaze moves back down to my body.

'I wonder what stories I could find written on your skin.' He stands up and flicks the blade back into its case. 'Perhaps another time. If you survive tonight.' He turns and walks to the bench across the room then returns with a small medical kit. 'But for now, let's get you cleaned up. For appearances. Can't have the others knowing what you really are.'

'Fuck off,' I say through gritted teeth as he cleans the ink from my chest then tapes some gauze over the wound.

He's setting the kit back down again when the door bursts open and two Blotters enter the room.

'All right, lads,' he says. 'Caught us the fake Blotter. He killed the two guards outside, got a hold of a knife, and tried it with me too. Put him in the cell next to the Darlings. I need to find a Teller so we can amend the story that's being broadcast through the Draft. At midnight, he's going to burn with the others.' He looks over his shoulder at me and smiles. 'And we want to make sure his friend knows we have him.'

'*No.*' I thrash in the chair, the handcuffs biting my wrists and my blood pounding in my ears. 'Fuck you.'

He walks to the door.

'Wait!' I roar. 'I'll tell you anything you need to know. Just kill me now. Kill me now.'

'Oh, and I'd tranquilise him first if I were you,' he says as he exits the room. 'He's a little upset about what we're going to do to his girlfriend.'

Chapter Forty-Six
Jay

My cheek is pressed against the floor. The air is damp. My chest throbs, and my eyelids are heavy. I groan. I feel like shit.

Where am I? What time is it?

I blink a few times. Then it all comes back to me.

Elle.

I get up, and my legs aren't working properly. I stumble forwards and slam my hands against the stone wall to get my balance. I close my eyes and take deep breaths. I need to get it together.

It's twenty minutes past eleven. I feel it in the ink pounding through my veins.

I have forty minutes until I die.

I have forty minutes until she comes for me.

Fuck.

'What are you doing here, Blotter?'

Raven is standing in the cell beside mine, looking at me through the bars. There's congealed blood on her forehead, and it glints in the flaming torchlight. She doesn't look impressed to see me.

'I'm here to rescue you.' My mouth is dry, and I clear my throat.

'Yeah? How's that going for you?'

'Pretty fucking shit.'

The corner of her lip quirks up.

I exhale and slide down the wall into a sitting position, resting my forearms on my raised knees. Raven does the same. She's close enough I can smell her sweat. It's slightly acrid, fear sweat. She looks calm though.

'I hear we face the firing squad at midnight,' she says.

I look up at the damp ceiling and sigh. 'They can't let anyone see me bleed. They're burning us now instead.'

She raises her eyebrows. 'Oh. Well, thanks a fucking lot, Blotter.'

My lips twitch. I laugh. Then Raven laughs. It builds until I'm laughing so hard the muscles in my stomach hurt and my eyes water, and tears roll down Raven's face. I don't even know what's so fucking funny.

When it finally fades, we just sit there side by side in the damp cell, waiting for death.

'Do you think she'll come for us?' Raven says.

'Yeah.' I run a hand over my mouth. 'But I wish she wouldn't.'

'She's with Sylv?'

'Yeah.'

'Good,' she says. 'Maybe she'll stop her.'

'Hope so.'

Her dark eyes bore into the side of my skull. 'You really care about her, don't you, Blotter?'

'Yeah.'

She exhales. 'You know, there's something that occurred to me as I was moving through the Draft.'

'What?'

'It was written that you would kill Elle. And you're connected to the Creators by the ink in your veins, right?' She looks at me searchingly, and I keep my gaze fixed on the barred door ahead. 'Why haven't they killed you?'

'I don't fucking know.' I exhale and rub my face. 'The ink inside of me has changed. I feel it burning sometimes. They're killing me slowly, I think. I don't fucking know why. It doesn't matter anymore, does it?'

'You knew you would die when you didn't end her life.'

'Yeah.'

'And you did it anyway,' she says. 'Why?'

'I don't know, do I?' I drag my teeth over my bottom lip. 'When I met her, she . . . she surprised me, I guess. I was curious about her. I hadn't felt that since I was a kid. It made me feel . . . human.'

She nods as though that makes any kind of sense. 'You know, that tattoo you have on your chest—the dandelion seed—it's strange. Her father—'

'I know.' I don't want to talk about her father. 'You have a tattoo too.'

I glance at the constellation inked onto half her shoulder and chest, partially concealed by her black braids and tank top. 'What does it mean?' I ask.

She frowns. 'Elle was right. You really are curious for a Blotter.'

I turn my attention back to the barred wall ahead. 'I was only asking.'

I don't even know why I asked. I don't know why I'm talking to Raven about any of this stuff. It's not as if I really give a shit. Maybe I'm just distracting myself. Maybe I don't want to think about what's going to happen.

I don't want to imagine what will happen if they catch her. I don't want her to see me burn. I don't want anyone to lay a finger on her.

And I don't want to be a selfish bastard. I don't want to *want* to see her again before I die.

'It's for my girlfriend. The tattoo,' says Raven, and her voice is thick. She sighs. 'She was called Star. She was my version of Elle. The one who got me into this whole sorry mess.'

'She must have been a pain in the arse.'

She smiles. 'Yeah. She was infuriating. But she helped me hear the music.'

I think about the first time I kissed Elle. 'What, literally?'

Raven laughs. 'No. Not literally, Blotter. But the first time I saw her, she was working in a strip club—one of those seedy joints men use to treat women like pieces of meat. I'm sure you know the places I'm talking about.'

I scratch my jaw.

'She was a dancer, dancing to those awful repetitive beats they play. Only, when she danced, it was as if . . . it was as if she wasn't dancing for those dirty fuckers with their hands on their dicks; it was as if she were dancing for herself. And when she danced, it was as if she was hearing something else too. It was as if she were hearing *music*. It was beautiful. *She* was beautiful.'

She tilts her head back against the wall.

'I ended up getting a job there, working behind the bar, and when the shift was over, we would dance together. Then I started to hear it too. The music. But my story was to marry a man and look after his house and bear his children. So when she told me about a Circus at the Edge of the World, where we could be together outside of the story the Creators had written for us, I followed her there.'

'But she died?'

She swallows hard. 'She was killed.'

I run a hand over my mouth. 'Blotters?'

'No. One of the owners of the club. He followed us. Shot her.' She rubs the back of her neck. 'I managed to get her to the Circus before she died. So at least she got to see it. But I never did get the chance to kill that cunt.' She exhales. 'I guess now, I never will.'

'I'm sorry you didn't get to kill him.'

'I don't know why the fuck I'm telling you all this.'

'Probably because we're going to die.'

'Yeah. Probably.' She bites her bottom lip. 'Elle told me a story once. She said that when we die, we join the stars.'

'Yeah? She told me the stars were dreams.'

Raven snorts. 'What a load of bullshit.'

I chuckle. 'Yeah.'

She turns her head to me. 'What do you think happens when we die?'

'Nothing. It just ends.'

Raven sighs. 'Yeah. I think that too. It'd be nice though. It'd be nice if I could see her again. Up in the stars.'

I think of Elle, and I close my eyes, something tightening in my throat. 'Yeah.'

Chapter Forty-Seven
Elle

We move from street to street. We paint big neon dandelion seeds on the sides of skyscrapers then hurtle away in Mary's van, always staying ahead of the Blotters.

I expected stories of our wet paint and smudged dandelion seeds would spread casually from whisper to whisper throughout the Draft. A story of rebels, and revolution, and hope.

The story that jumps from one mouth to the next, though, is angry and twisted and not of our design. It's a story with gnarly roots that thunder through the ground rather than dandelion seeds dancing in the breeze.

They are saying we are dangerous. We are Darlings. We threaten the One True Story, and we must be stopped.

This, I didn't expect.

I didn't expect a woman to spit at my feet as she eyed the spray can in my hand. I didn't expect two drunk men to shout atrocities at Sylvia. I didn't expect a man to push Rami into a wall, or a group of teenagers to laugh as they pulled Anita's hair. I didn't expect to be leered at, or sworn at, or made to feel smaller than I am.

But still, each time we encounter such violence, I plant something. A seed. Four words. Four words that provoke more jeers and laughter and disbelief. Four words I will use if Jay gets caught. Four words Sylvia tells me are a waste of breath. She says they won't work, we're not at the Circus at the Edge of the World anymore. But I have to try.

As our van swerves from side to side while a Blotter pursues us, though, I have to fight the darkness building in the pit of my stomach. I have to reassure myself it doesn't matter what these people think of us. We're doing the right thing. We're fighting the Creators. We're drawing some of the Blotters away from Jay.

And everything is going to be okay.

But it does matter, doesn't it? Because stories are true when we believe them. And these people do not believe in stories of hope or revolution; they believe in the Creators. Sylvia and Jay were right. Even if I told these people the story my father left for me, they would not believe it.

I expected it to be harder to plant stories the closer we got to the Final City, but I didn't expect it to be this hard. These people *hate* us. Even though we are trying to help them.

Sylvia, Rami, and Anita sit around me, silent, as Tom fiddles with the radio in the front. We're hoping to hear something that will let us know Jay and Raven are out.

There is nothing though. Just the same broadcast we heard earlier on a loop. As time goes by and the words burrow deeper into my skull, panic starts to twist inside me. It's as powerful as a tornado. Every muscle in my body clenches with the effort of keeping it inside.

'They'd broadcast it, sweetie,' says Sylvia.

'What?'

Her lips are tensed and her dark eyes hard. 'If they'd killed him, they'd want people to know. It would be on the broadcast.'

'Yes,' I say.

A CIRCUS OF INK

But it does not feel right. Something is wrong.

The Blotters have been two steps behind us all night—never gaining on us, never hurting us. When they first arrived at the scene of one of our paintings, they didn't look surprised.

It's almost as if they knew we'd be here. It's almost as if while we are trying to keep *them* busy until midnight, they are keeping us busy too.

Jay and Sylvia both thought this was a trap. They said it was written that we would die at midnight. I'm starting to think that might be true.

My stomach cramps. I can't lose Jay.

I should have gone with him. I shouldn't have left him to do this alone. His power is not in words. If someone stops him, he'll say the wrong thing. And then he and Raven will die.

'We've lost them.' Mary's voice cuts over the tinny sound of the radio. 'We have an hour until midnight. Want to do another one? Make sure they're still chasing us?'

For the first time in a long time, I'm uncertain. It's paralyzing. I don't know what the right thing to do is. I rest my head back against the cool metal side of the van.

'We would know, sweetie,' says Sylvia, firmer. 'They'd broadcast it.'

I let out a long breath. And then, just because I need to feel as if I'm doing something—*anything*—to help, I nod. 'Yes. Okay. One more.'

I don't say what I'm planning to do once we have painted the final dandelion seed. But when I meet Sylvia's eye, she frowns. She knows what I'm thinking. She knows how dangerous it will be. She will try to stop me.

She will fail.

No one will stop me.

If Jay cannot save Raven, I will save them both myself.

They will not die.
Stories are true when we believe them.

My fingers tremble slightly as I put the cap back on the can of paint. I look at the neon pink dandelion seed I have created on the off-white skyscraper wall. This is our riskiest one yet, visible from the main road. A group of people jeers at us as they pass on their way to Raven's execution. The smell of fresh paint mingles with the salty scent of the ocean.

I'm turning back to the van when Mary leans out of the door. Something cold and hard sinks to the pit of my stomach when I catch the look on her face. I shake my head.

'I'm so sorry,' she says.

I drop the paint can, and it clatters on the pavement. 'Is he dead?'

'Not yet. They're executing him with the others.'

'How long do we have?'

'Fifteen minutes.'

I force the hot, malleable panic to harden. I meet Sylvia's gaze. Then she crosses the space between us and pushes me into the wall.

'Elle, no.'

I narrow my eyes. 'You have one chance to let me go.'

'Listen, sweetie—'

I headbutt her, and she reels back, staggering against her cane. Her eyes tear up, and blood streams from her nose. I skirt past Anita, but Rami grabs my arm.

'Let's talk about this. Please—'

I shove him into the wall and run. Because what is there to talk about?

A CIRCUS OF INK

I already know what conversation they want to have. They will say this is reckless. They will say I cannot save them. They will say I'm only adding another life to the death count. They will say I'm risking too much. They will say I'm being irrational.

But if he dies, the hole he'll leave will swallow me. If he dies, something hollow will scrape away at my insides until nothing is left.

Right now, I can think of nothing more rational than what I'm doing.

What is the point in fighting if I don't fight for this? For them? For him?

Maybe Sylvia was right all along. Maybe I can't fight the Creators. Maybe men like them will always have power. Maybe I will never get people to believe in revolution and ink and stories that rage like fire.

But I can save Jay. I can save Raven.

I told him I would come for him.

The concrete jungle blurs into grey around me.

I will come for him.

When I reach the killing block, people have flooded the square. There are hundreds of them, ebbing and flowing around the raised stage where a stake has been erected. Their movements are as violent as the ocean beyond, where the waves crash against the cliff.

My pulse races, and there's a sharp pain in my side as I push into the tide of people and grab a woman's arm. 'What time is it?'

'Five minutes to go,' she says with a grin.

I repeat the four words I told people in the Draft. She frowns and then notices a splotch of pink paint on the collar of my leather jacket. Her face twists, and she yells something, but I'm already gone, her words swallowed by the noise and movement blurring around me. I grab more people as I move through the writhing masses, planting the seed with them too, determined to be the hurricane that spreads the story.

And I feel like a hurricane—violent and out of control. Panic twists and rises through my body. I need them to believe me, but they don't. So I try to feel a connection to the Ink we think runs beneath the earth, except I feel nothing but rage and fear and the ripples of sick hunger coming from the mob as they wait to be fed.

A wave of excitement crashes through them as a Teller walks onto the stage, his face concealed by the blood-red hood of his robes.

'*Once, there was nothing. Then, there was the Beginning.*' His low voice is unnaturally amplified, and it booms across the square. '*The Creators created the world out of Ink and words. The Creators were pleased with what they created. The Creators are good.*'

I clamber onto the stone podium of the statue of Michael, and I shout my story. A few people turn and jeer.

'*The first man sinned once,*' says the Teller. '*He was curious. And he was lost. For without a path to walk, he wandered away from the One True Story. The Creators are not without mercy. They looked unto him and gave him a great gift. They used the Sacred Stylus to write his story and bind him to the End. He rejoiced, for it was good.*'

Cheers ripple through the night. I scream my words over them and the sound of the waves crashing. A few people look at me with disgust. Some look to the stage with confusion. Others narrow their eyes on the frothing sea behind the killing block.

'*For all that Begins must End. Those who do not follow the path to the great End written by the Creators must be Cut for the good of the One True Story.*'

The Teller spreads his arms, and flaming torches light up around the stage. The crowd jeers wildly as a group of five people are marched onto the stage by two Blotters, their hands bound with rope. I do not recognise them. They must be part of a regular Cut.

Then Raven is brought out behind them and tied to the stake with the others. People scream and hurl things at her, but her dark eyes only look up at the sky as if she alone can see the absent stars.

A wave of nausea crashes over me. Where is Jay?

I jump down from the podium and push my way through to the stage. I grab people as I pass, spreading my story. They barely listen, too excited by the murder about to take place.

'The Creators made the Blotters to reinforce the story that leads to the End,' says the Teller. *'The Ink that created all runs in their veins. Blotters are holy men who must be revered by all.'*

Someone puts their hand on my shoulder. I turn, fist clenched, and find myself facing Sylvia. There's dried blood beneath her nose, and she's breathing hard.

'Where are the others?' I demand.

'I sent them away.'

'But once, there was a man who impersonated a Blotter,' says the Teller. *'Instead of following the One True Story, he was tempted by the weeds that were left by the First Twist. He followed their gnarly roots in search of a different End. He thought he could deceive the Creators.'*

Boos fill the air, and Sylvia's eyes fix on something over my shoulder. I spin around.

Jay is being led onto the stage with his hands tied behind his back, surrounded by five Blotters who each sport various injuries. He's looking around, jaw set, searching for something as he's bound to the pyre beside Raven.

'But no one can deceive the Creators,' booms the Teller.

Jay's eyes latch onto mine. Pain flashes behind them. *'Run,'* he mouths.

I shake my head. *'No.'*

'And like the weeds left by the First Twist, those who defy the Creators must be uprooted to save the One True Story,' says the Teller.

Sylvia spins me around. 'I take it you have a plan, sweetie?'

'Yes. We need to get onto that stage. Otherwise, my plan will kill us.'

'And if your plan doesn't work?'

'Then the fire will kill us.'

Her eyes shine, and something tightens in my throat as she lightly touches my arm, because I can see the belief behind them. 'Okay,' she says.

'Those who corrupt the One True Story must burn!' The Teller's roar echoes all around the square as Sylvia and I clamber onto the stage.

I turn to the crowd. *'Once, there was a world. And the world was grey,'* I shout. *'In this world, there was a girl, and stories raged through her veins like fire.'*

The Teller turns his head, and I feel his dark eyes glowering beneath his hood.

'She created an impossible door, she created a hurricane, and she travelled to the Circus at the Edge of the World with a Blotter who was supposed to kill her.'

The crowd jeer at me as two Blotters cross the stage towards us. Above all the noise, I hear Jay's anguished roar.

'You do not believe me,' I yell, *'but if you do not believe in me, you will fear me.'*

I'm lurched back and bound to the wooden post beside Raven. She twists towards me.

'Elle, mate . . .' Her words are choked.

'For I know what you do *believe,'* I shout.

The stake vibrates against my back as Jay tries to free himself of his binds.

'You believe we are dangerous because we are Darlings.'

I feel eyes on me from above. It's the Blotter from the motel sitting on the arm of the statue of Michael. He's watching me with interest.

'And we are *dangerous. And here is something else you should believe.'*

A Blotter punches me in the face, and I taste blood. It drips onto the stage at my feet. The Teller nods, and another Blotter grabs one of the torches around the stage and holds the flame to the firewood piled by our feet. It catches, and smoke twists up into the salty air.

'You have heard whispers of it all night.' My words are louder now, stronger.

Through the shimmering hot air, a ripple of uncertainty makes its way through the crowd. The Teller is saying something.

I blink hard. *'We planted an explosive in the ocean.'* Sweat pours down my face, and one of the people bound to the stake starts to scream.

The shouts change from hungry to panicked. People push against one another.

'Elle . . .' says Jay, his voice quiet beneath the roar of the flames.

I wish I were closer to him. I want to be with him at the end.

Raven grabs my hand, and Sylvia whispers something. It takes me a moment to realise she is whispering my words. Raven whispers them too. The words spread around the stake as quickly as the fire until all of the Darlings are repeating them.

Jay hears them and stops struggling. He turns his body so he can look at me. Though panic is rising through the mob, and people are screaming, and the flames are starting to lick us, everything slows down as we lock gazes.

His face is flushed and his skin covered in a sheen of sweat. His eyes glisten, and behind them, I see pure, unwavering belief.

He believes I will save us.

I feel the belief in the crowd as well. They believe I will kill them.

Stories are true when we believe them.

Jay's face contorts as the flames reach his legs, and time speeds up again.

There's panic all around me. The ocean roars. The mass begin to shove against one another and point at something behind. A shadow looms, and a raw animal sound comes from Sylvia. I smell burning flesh, and fire spits at my boots. I block out the pain.

I take a deep breath, tasting smoke, and add my voice to those around me.

'A tsunami is coming.'

The world comes crashing down.

Chapter Forty-Eight
Jay

There's water in my mouth and in my lungs. My head smacks back against the stake. I can't breathe. I'm not drowning though. I'm not being dragged under a pool of black Ink while my blood boils and my skin burns. I'm not praying to the Creators for salvation.

She is my salvation.

I taste the air again. It's salty and smoky and so fucking sweet. Ahead, a giant wave crashes through the square. Its movement is unnatural, and for a second, I think it has eyes and a tail and a dark, frothing mouth that swallows everything in its path. It roars like some great ravenous beast.

But my eyes are burning, stinging with salt. When I blink and wheeze for breath, it's just the ocean again, spitting people out into the walls of the surrounding skyscrapers. The night is filled with the sounds of smashing glass and sirens and dying screams.

My heart pounds. 'Elle?' I pull my wrists apart, and the frayed, burnt rope disintegrates in my hands.

Beside me, Raven splutters, but Elle's head has lolled onto her chest. I go to her and grab her shoulders.

'Elle?' I roar.

She doesn't respond, and panic stabs me in the gut. Her hair is plastered to her skull, and her skin is pale. I push my fingers to her neck. There has to be a pulse. She can't be dead. I'd feel it.

Something spreads inside of me, as cold and turbulent as the waves emptying the streets.

Th-thump.

'Blotter!' calls Sylvia, appearing beside me. 'Is she . . .?'

'Yeah.' The muscles in my body relax, and I breathe out slowly. 'Yeah. She's alive.'

I free her from her binds then scoop her up into my arms. Raven throws up seawater beside me. She wipes her mouth with the back of her hand and then turns to Sylvia.

'You shouldn't have come here. What the fuck were you thinking?'

'Yes, well, believe it or not, it wasn't my idea.' Sylvia's eyes sweep over the five other Darlings who got caught up in all this. They're alive, but one of the women is badly burnt and being supported by an older man. 'As soon as the wave goes back to where it came from, we're out of here.'

We stand in a line at the edge of the stage. We're bedraggled and burnt and bruised. But we're alive.

If you get caught, I'll come for you. You know that, right?

Elle's breath is weak against my neck, and I hold her close. I brush my lips against her forehead. She tastes like salt and fire.

'Crazy little Twist.'

Slowly, the wave retreats into the ocean in a movement as unnatural as when it was bidden. In its wake, it leaves nothing but wet concrete, smashed glass, and broken bodies.

Sylvia limps towards the steps. 'This way.'

I glance over my shoulder. The Blotter who caught me is sitting on the arm of the statue. A smile spreads across his face. With his fingers and thumb, he mimes a gun and points it at me and Elle.

I'm going to kill that bastard.

But right now, Elle is more important.

I pull her head closer to my chest, and I head after the Darlings.

Elle sleeps.

Her chest moves softly up and down, and her lips are tinted blue. One of her eyes is bruised and swollen, and her wet hair is splayed out on the cream pillow. A patch of damp spreads like ink beneath her head.

I refuse to move from the chair beside the bed. Every hour she doesn't stir, my muscles get a little harder. Every hour she sleeps, another weight is added to my chest until it's so fucking heavy I think my ribs will crack.

We're like this for twenty-five hours before she finally opens her eyes. *'Jay?'*

I can breathe again. I grip the mattress. '*Fuck.* You scared the shit out of me, little Twist.'

She touches my cheek. *'Likewise.'*

'You were fucking amazing out there. What you did—'

'It wasn't enough.' Her face falls. 'It's never enough.'

'What do you—?' I look over my shoulder when I hear a noise. Sylvia is standing in the doorway.

'She wakes and her first thought is of the Blotter . . .' she says.

'Oh. You're here,' I say.

Her left leg is stiff as she walks over. She looks me up and down. I've not washed or changed since the tsunami, and her nose turns up. 'You look like shit, Blotter. Smell like it too. Go get changed. Tom is—'

'Fuck off.' If she thinks I'm leaving Elle, she's insane.

'Suit yourself.' She perches on the edge of the bed and turns her attention to Elle. 'How you feeling? You gave us quite a scare, sweetie.'

'Fine.' She swallows. 'Thirsty.'

I grab the beaker of water from the bedside table. She props herself up on the pillows to drink half of it. Some of the water misses her mouth and dribbles down her chin.

'He's right, you know,' says Sylvia. 'What you did was incredible. Clever too. Using the Creators' story against them.'

'What?' I say.

Sylvia tuts. Elle grabs my hand before I can snap at her. I curl my fingers around hers, the weight of her grip causing something warm to spread inside of me.

'I couldn't get them to believe in me, or in our stories of hope or change or revolution,' she says. 'But they believe we are monsters. The Creators made sure of that. It's the story they have been spreading about Darlings for all their lives. So when I said the Tsunami was caused by an explosion we'd planned . . .' She shakes her head. 'They believed it without question.'

'Like I said, clever,' says Sylvia. 'Although maybe not hugely helpful to our cause in the long run. Taking out an entire square of people does add to the whole 'Darlings are dangerous' narrative.'

Elle lets go of my hand and slumps back down on her pillows. 'What cause? You were right. Both of you.' She turns onto her side, away from us both. 'I'm done.'

Elle is exhausted. She spends most of the next few days in bed. She sleeps. And she stirs. And through the day, she stares blankly at the peeling wallpaper. She doesn't wonder. She doesn't tell stories about factories of stars, or clockmakers, or dandelion seeds. Her conversations are fragmented and broken.

'I killed all those people.'

'So?'

'It's not good, Jay. I feel bad.'

'What the fuck else were you supposed to do?'

I lie beside her, but I don't know what to do. I don't know what to say. I don't know how to make this right.

'I thought the world could be fixed. But how can you fix a world that doesn't know it's broken?'

'I don't know, little Twist.'

'I'm tired. I'm so tired.'

And on the nights, I feel her pain as she sinks her teeth into my bottom lip and digs her fingernails into the skin of my back. I hear it in the raw cry that escapes her throat when she comes, and I see it in her eyes as the world comes flooding back.

'Why did my father leave me that story? What is the point if it can't change anything?'

'That's not what you said before, little Twist.'

'I was wrong.'

And eventually, not knowing any of the fucking answers, I take to wandering aimlessly around the library.

It's boring, wandering around dusty old books I can't read, but I talk to the others. Mary tells me this place used to be the Citadel. Tom gives me a load of his old clothes and tells me the broadcasts are saying we all died in the explosion we caused. I help Anita and Rami to fix the engine on the van. I even have a clipped conversation with Sylvia.

'Why didn't you tell me to leave?' I ask her.

'Because it's a long time since I've seen her get close to anyone,' she says. 'And as much as I hate to admit it, I think you're good for her, Blotter.'

'It doesn't seem like it right now.'

'No. It doesn't. But that's not because of you. I think we all have a moment in our lives when the realisation the world is shitter than we thought hits us. It hardens us one way or another. This is one of those moments for Elle. She'll get through it. You'll see.'

Later, when I get fed up of the musty air, I go above ground to the weird courtyard that sits outside one of the bunker-like entrances to the library. It must have been a part of the Citadel before it was hidden underground. I sit on one of the stone benches and look up at the starless sky. The air smells like the sea, and I hear the waves crashing against the rocks below.

'Beer, Blotter?' Raven passes me a bottle and sits beside me.

'Cheers,' I say, taking it.

We sit in silence for a while, and it doesn't feel forced or uncomfortable.

'How's she doing?' she asks.

I shake my head slowly, staring at the grey pavement slabs between my boots. 'I don't know what to do.'

We both turn as someone approaches. Mary is on the other side of the courtyard.

'Raven, can you come help me out with something in the library?'

'Yeah. Sure. Be there in a sec.'

Mary smiles, and her eyes glint as they hold Raven's for a second too long. Then she heads back down into the library. Raven watches her intently before turning back around.

'Were you just staring at her arse?' I say.

'What? No!'

'Yeah, you were.'

'Oh, piss off, Blotter.' There's a smile tugging at the corner of her lip, though, as she gets up and brushes down her dark jeans.

I raise my eyebrows as she walks away. 'Have fun . . .'

She laughs. 'Prick.'

I fiddle with the glass bottle until the darkness shifts to grey. I want to do something, anything, to help. But what can I do?

After a while, I get up, and I walk.

I walk away from the library. I walk down the long streets in the Draft as dawn approaches. I don't know what I'm doing or where I'm going. Maybe I'm looking for a Blotter to beat the shit out of. Maybe I want to see the aftermath of Elle's tsunami. Maybe

I just want to get rid of some of this tension that's building inside of me.

I turn a corner, and I freeze.

My heart jolts.

Then I turn and run back down the streets.

I tear through the library and burst into the bedroom. The door swings against the wall.

Elle's eyes widen. 'Jay? What's wrong?'

I shake my head. Then I cross the room and take her hands in mine.

'You're sad,' I say, 'because you don't think anyone will believe your story. You don't think you can spread your dandelion seeds. Right, little Twist?'

'Yes.'

I pull her across the room. 'Come on.'

I lead her through the library, up the stairs, and then through the streets. When we reach my destination, she freezes, and her breath catches in her throat.

'What was that thing your father used to say, little Twist?' I ask.

'*Stories will always grow.*' A tear slips down her cheek, and a smile spreads across her face.

I smile too. Then I brush my lips against hers, slipping one hand into her hair and one onto the small of her back. I pull her into my body. She kisses me back, and her laughter vibrates against my skin. I laugh too.

She pulls back. 'They believe.'

'It's only small, little Twist. Let's not get carried away.'

She beams, and her eyes are bright. 'It's enough. For now.'

'Yeah. It's enough,' I say as I kiss her forehead.

I slip my arm around her back, and together, we look at it.

The burst of yellow in the field of grey concrete.

The dandelion in the crack in the pavement.

Acknowledgements

Thank you to everyone who read A Circus of Ink in its early stages. I had a similar mindset to Jay when I was drafting this book - I felt like there was a small dandelion seed of potential in it, but I was stressed, anxious, and I almost gave up on it a few times! Thank you to those who believed in this story when I was struggling to.

Thank you to Bryony Leah for all your hard work on the copy edits. This is the second book we've worked on together, and as with the first, it was a joy to work with you.

Thank you to Franzi Haase at CoverDungeon for your work on the cover. I love it.

Thank you to Jamie for listening to my constant chatter about Twists, hurricanes, and dandelions over the years.

And lastly, thank you to you. Thank you for taking a chance on this book and coming on this journey with Elle and Jay. I hope to see you in book two for the conclusion of their journey.

About the Author

Lauren Palphreyman is an author based in London. She writes books full of romance and magic. She writes serially online, and her stories have garnered over 70 million views. Her other books, Cupid's Match and Devils Inc., are out now. A Circus of Ink is her third published novel.

Connect with Lauren by following her on Instagram (@LaurenPalphreyman), Twitter (@LEPalphreyman), or Facebook (@LEPalphreyman). Or visit her website: www.LaurenPalphreyman.com.

Also by Lauren Palphreyman

Ink Duology:

A Circus of Ink

Devils Inc. Series:

Devils Inc.

Cupid's Match:

Cupid's Match

Follow Lauren Palphreyman on social media to find out more:

Instagram: @LaurenPalphreyman
Twitter | Facebook: @LEPalphreyman

Website: www.LaurenPalphreyman.com

Devils Inc.

Snarky Angels. Bad boy Omens. Dangerous Demons. And a deal with the Devil..

The past twenty-four hours have been pretty weird for pre-law student Rachel Mortimer.

She accidentally sold her soul to the Devil. An Angel showed up in her bedroom. And an irritatingly hot Bad Omen has been following her around campus.

Now she has to intern at Devils Inc. – Lucifer's LA based soul trading company. And demons are trying to kill her. The undead want her legal advice. And she's starting to catch feelings for someone she shouldn't.

Oh, and someone has triggered the Apocalypse.

So she should probably stop that. .

Find out more:
www.LaurenPalphreyman.com

Cupid's Match

He's mythologically hot, a little bit wicked, almost 100% immortal. And he'll hit you right in the heart.

Seventeen-year-old Lila Black is sick of the Cupids Matchmaking Service spamming her. But her world is turned inside out when she learns not only that cupids exist, but that she's been matched with the infamous god of love, Cupid.

The only catch? She can't actually fall for Cupid; if she does, all of mythical hell will break loose, and it won't be pretty . . .

As arrows fly and feelings become stronger, can Cupid and Lila resist each other's magnetic pull? And will Lila find herself part of a deadly supernatural war that could cost her life, and her heart?

Find out more:
www.LaurenPalphreyman.com